SLEEP
AND HIS
BROTHER

BOOKS BY PETER DICKINSON

SLEEP AND HIS BROTHER

Peter Dickinson

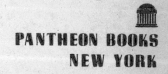

PANTHEON BOOKS
NEW YORK

1

The sack, however prettily beribbonned, tends to destroy a man's confidence; and there had never been much of that in the first place.

Pibble halted on the wide and weedy gravel to mime amusement while he studied the hideous façade and nerved himself to face the children. Childless himself, he liked the young in theory but found that he became gawky and gruff in their company—a manner which was sure to be worse with the kids at the Foundation. From one of Mary's rambling parentheses he had learned that it was part of their treatment to open the door and greet strangers; besides, with the Foundation so poor, it saved the wages of a doorman.

The Foundation had the decorators in. Painters nuzzled at windows like bees at a lavender bush; on one of the corner spires workmen spanked copper sheeting into place; the other spire was finished and now its rich metal waited for the subduing verdigris; meanwhile an elderly man was poised at its pinnacle tinkering with a fresh-gilt weathercock; a fuzz of scaffolding blurred the right-hand corner of the building, but even the sections with which the workmen had finished were not exactly clean-lined, so lavish had the architect been with terra-cotta swags and ornaments. It was curious to think of ultramodern, no-nonsense Reuben Kelly toiling away behind those curlicues. Better not tell the lady that one knows him —it'll only cause further complications in an already tedious and embarrassing mission. With a tiny groan Pibble drove himself across the flattened remains of bindweed and trefoil to the porch.

Drab November made it so dark under the arch that he had to peer for a bell or knocker; but before he had located either the hinges moaned and the door swung slowly open as if this had been the opening sequence of *Aunt of Dracula*. Inside, instead of the predictable Gothic gloom and chill, the air was almost sultry and the colors jazzy but impersonal. Below a huge sweep of carved wooden stairs a solitary figure slept on a modern settee. Wooden pillars sprang from the op art carpet to the wedding cake plasterwork of the ceiling. The total effect was as if some minor hall at the Victoria and Albert had been commandeered and redecorated to be an airlines terminal. Even the sleeper had the look of someone who has fallen asleep not because he needs the rest but because the world has become too boring to stay awake in; so he sleeps here, now, regardless.

Pibble hesitated across the threshold.

"Hello," said a voice from behind the door, a child's voice, very slow but steady. The door began to moan shut and Pibble moved out of its way.

"Copper come. Lost 'is 'at."

That was a different voice, but it had the same strange lightweight drawl.

"Lovely," said the first voice. Now Pibble could see that it belonged to the nearer of the two children who were pushing the door shut. They made it seem an effort—not an effort to move the door but to move their own limbs. Mary had said they'd be fat and sleepy, and they were; mentally and physically handicapped, and that was obvious, too; so all the way up from the bus stop Pibble had been preparing himself to greet some slow, revolting dumplings with piggy eyes above lardy cheeks, and to react with adult friendliness and feigned ease.

"Hello, you two," he said, muffing the rehearsed tone and producing instead the note of surprise and pleasure with which one greets a real friend at a boring cocktail party.

Two circular faces smiled and blinked in the bright lighting: a boy and a girl, he dark, she carroty, both about twelve years old. Their skin was heavy and pale, but not tallowy; both seemed to be wearing several sweaters. Pibble felt an instinct to pat them, as, thirty years before, when the porch would have held a litter of garden twine and mole traps and broken croquet mallets, the visitor to this hall would have patted the large and lazy hound that came to sniff his trouser cuffs. Pibble held out his hand.

The boy's hand rose slowly, like some barely buoyant object wavering up through water. Pibble felt his face stiffen at finding how cold that touch was. The girl, though she seemed to have her eyes shut, must have noticed the change, for she smiled sleepily at him.

"Cold 'and, warm 'eart," she said.

"George," said the boy, drawling the syllable out to enormous length. His eyes were large and soft, and had a ring of darker green round the edge of the light green iris—the cathypnic ring, the first symptom. With his usual twinge of ashamed surprise Pibble realized what a lot of stuff Mary had told him during her undramatic monologues about the Foundation. You had to sort it out, of course, and doubt such items as the poverty of an organization which could afford new copper for its spires; her mind was like the collection of some eighteenth-century dilettante who bought anything that caught his fancy and put it, sorted by whim and labeled by wish, into his private museum.

"Hello, George," he said. "I'm Jimmy Pibble."

The three of them stood there, smiling at each other in a trance of friendliness. Mothers spotted the cathypnic ring when their children were a few months old—such good babies, slept all night and put on pounds each month; oh, yes, a bit tiresome finishing their food but you can't have everything, and such pretty eyes. Usually by the time they were three the mother had asked a doctor about the fatness, or the tiny appetite, or the habit of going to sleep in odd corners; or she'd go to a clinic about something else and the nurse would spot the curiously low temperature. Doctors would prescribe this or that for a while, without result, and finally leaf through a compendium of human ills and come to cathypny. Often they were pleased, for it is a rare disease and not strongly marked in small children. Only when a cathypnic is eight or so can a layman really see how different he is from his contemporaries—hopeless at school, of course, fat as a hamster, and sleeping twenty hours a day. Then he goes to the Foundation. The family hate to let him go, always, no matter how many normal children are squalling round the dank basement flat; but without special treatment he now has only a year to live, and cathypnics like to be together. Hence the McNair Foundation, with its endless gluttony for funds; hence Mary's recent concern, for funds are raised by coffee mornings and bazaars and flag days; hence Pibble's useless and intrusive visit.

Something by the wall clicked, and the faint whir which Pibble had been unconsciously aware of faltered and steadied. Over the children's shoulders he saw that a large tape recorder had been churning away on a table by the wall, and had now switched itself off.

"Can you take me to Mrs. Dixon-Jones?" he said. "She's expecting me."

"The exercise will do you good," said the boy to the girl.

"The exercise will do you good," said the girl to the boy.

Neither moved from his happy placidity.

"Why don't you both come?" said Pibble. "Or must you stay by the door?"

There was no real motive in his words, any more than there was point in his visit, but he felt a mild desire to prolong his time with this pleasing pair. Their company was relaxing, so much so that he acted with tranced slowness when the boy shut his eyes (or rather failed to open them after a blink) and tumbled quietly toward the ghastly carpet. It looked cheap, but felt so expensively thick that the child could hardly have hurt himself even if Pibble hadn't managed to catch him round the shoulders and lower him the last foot. He was startlingly heavy; through sweaters, shirt, and vest seeped the strange chill of his body. Pibble had sometimes in his old job kept company with corpses, waiting for the pathology boys to turn up and meanwhile guessing by touch how long it was since this one had started the slide down from 98.6°. The child here should have been dead two hours ago.

"Is he all right?" said Pibble.

"Tain't fair. Tain't time," said the girl.

She, too, began to collapse toward the floor, but with open eyes. When she was kneeling she put her mouth beside the boy's ear and blew into it. His eyes blinked open.

"You can't see no one coming," she drawled.

"No."

"Both go."

"Where?"

"Man wants Posey."

"I'm comfy."

He looked it—like a hibernating creature on whom the diggers have broken in, bringing with them the hideous winter daylight.

"The exercise will do you good," said the girl.

"The exercise will do you good."

"Both go."

Pibble reached out a hand. Dreamily the boy took it. The corpse touch was still uncanny and the boy hardly helped himself at all as Pibble hauled him to his feet. The girl stayed kneeling, waiting for similar help; she weighed just as much. When all three were standing, the children slipped their hands together and started off at a vague dawdle across the hall. It really was a huge room. Pibble felt that his own house would have gone into it twice over; the grove of pillars rose two stories to its ceiling, and a balustraded gallery ran round it fifteen feet above the floor. To this the pompous stairs curved up, winding round a semicircular bulge in the far wall. Everything that had not been recently redecorated was heavy and ugly, but the wood from which it had been carved was beautiful, close-grained and knotless. Pibble fingered a pillar while the children drifted to a halt before the sleeper on the sofa. This was an older boy, gross and pale, with black curly hair. The smaller children watched him in silence, as though his sleep were an absorbing spectacle. Beside him another tape recorder devoured the silence.

"Fishin'," said the girl at last.

"Yellow uns," said the boy.

"Lovely," said the girl.

"What's the water like?" said Pibble. He was used to being woken by Mary's nightly mutterings and trying to make sensible answers to her dream speeches, so the question was natural to him.

6

"Dirty," said both children together, neither speaking before the other.

"Where's Posey?" he said.

They moved off again, almost at random, it seemed; but some vague current of intention sucked them into an arch in the left-hand wall and here they paused again. Pibble gazed over the children's shoulders down the startling corridor. If the hall had been bright, this place would have been dazzling; a series of arches divided it into bays, and every bay, every arch, was painted to clash as fiercely as possible with its neighbor and then lit like a film set. You could see that the series of colors was deliberate but not intended to please; the worst taste in the world couldn't have *chosen* that effect for aesthetic purposes. The children shuffled a few steps forward, then halted again as a man in a white dustcoat wheeled a cart out of a side corridor, stopped by a tape recorder, switched it off, replaced the tape with a new one, switched on, and spoke briefly at the machine.

"Which is Mrs. Dixon-Jones's room?" said Pibble.

"Posey?" said the girl vaguely.

"Yes. She's the secretary."

The children swayed, but stayed where they were, like seaweed in a rock pool. The man looked up at the sound of voices, left his cart and came down the corridor toward them.

"You lost, you three?" he said, smiling happily. He had a wispy little beard which would have suited a Chinese sage if it had been gray and not ginger. He looked about twenty. The smile was not for Pibble but for the children.

"I've got an appointment with Mrs. Dixon-Jones," said Pibble. "I was on time when I got to the door but I'm late now."

"I'll show you," said the man with the beard. He took each child in turn gently by the shoulders, turned them round, and gave them a little shove.

"Back to the hall, dormice," he said.

The children wavered off and the men watched them until they were out of sight, Pibble experiencing a strange wash of regret at the idea that he might not see them again. He shook himself out of this cozy, facile emotion by saying, as they turned toward the cart, "It's a remarkable choice of colors."

"Bit too much," said the man with the beard. "We've always gone in for bright colors—wake the dormice up a bit was the theory—but Doctor Kelly had this idea about maximum visual stimulus: see what happened if we got the colors as bright as possible. It seems to hypnotize some of 'em. Change from the old days, eh?"

They halted by the cart and Pibble gazed down an enormously long corridor at right angles to the one he was in; there was a window behind him and another at the farthest end; it must have been a dismal tunnel in Victorian days.

"Ivan," called a woman's voice.

"Here," said the man with the beard.

"If you find a Mr. Pibble wandering round, send him to me. He should have been here by now."

The voice was as genteel as a set of electric door chimes, but a shade less melodious.

"I *am* here," said Pibble, letting a lot more resentment into his voice than he'd intended. Instinct and experience told him that Mary's impromptu enemies were usually in the right, and he didn't enjoy the sighing loyalty demanded of him. He nodded farewell to the man with the beard and walked on to the door from which Mrs. Dixon-Jones's voice had emanated. Both long corridors here ran to an end window after crossing, cutting off a single room in the very corner of the building. The door said SECRETARY. Above the word a brass souvenir, vaguely Minoan in character, was Scotch-taped.

Mary, though she admired as well as hated her, had never told him that Mrs. Dixon-Jones was worth looking at; thirty years ago she must have been the gay despair of the young men at the tennis clubs, but even then she would have had good bones for her mother to boast of, and these had allowed her an easy metamorphosis from being distinctly pretty to being decidedly handsome. She contrived to hold her head as though she were taking a hard fence, riding side-saddle, and her smile combined maximum graciousness with minimum friendliness.

"Please sit down, Mr. Pibble," she said, "and tell me what I can do for you."

Dismally Pibble sat. It was a mistake to have come at all. The hell with her.

"You can tell me what I can do for *you*," he said. "I believe you made this appointment with my wife."

"Ah, yes," she sighed. "Dear Mary."

"That's the one," said Pibble. "You met at some do. She didn't tell me the details, but you must have talked about some problem which was worrying you which had a bearing on the law, and she suggested I might help. I've just retired from the police, you know."

Mrs. Dixon-Jones nodded, a priest in the social confessional. Policemen are low. They court housemaids, if not scullery maids, round basement areas. The maids have vanished, but in a certain caste of mind the myth persists.

"I was an in-betweenish kind of copper," explained Pibble. "If it had been the army, I'd have been some sort of staff officer—a major or perhaps a colonel."

Damn the woman. There was no earthly need for such defensive maunderings.

"How clever of you to talk my language," said Mrs. Dixon-Jones. "We were all riflemen, but I took it into my head to marry into the Welsh Guards."

The words were chatty, but the tone pushed Pibble's supposed commission out into the limbo of the Ordnance Corps.

"Well?" he said, scrabbling for the upper ground.

She picked up a ball-point pen and began to tap it slowly against a cigarette lighter made from a two-inch silver terrestrial globe. He let her tap, and hoped that she was thinking how to let them both off the hook. Before the wars this room had probably been the master's study. The bookshelves were still here, frilled with carvings of quills in inkpots and crowned with medallions of muses; since then someone had institutionalized the walls, garage green to shoulder level and cheese yellow above; sepia photographs of soldiers hung crooked from random nails; the new wave of decorators with their Day-Glo fantasies had been kept at bay; khaki filing cabinets and an antique switchboard hulked out from the walls, and on them dusty pyramids of paper counted the years in deepening shades of yellow; presumably the curving wall in the corner between the windows hid the spiral staircase up to the master's bedroom and ultimately to the newly weathercocked spire; some Cretan knickknacks on the mantelpiece, below a board of neatly labeled keys. . . .

"I really do appreciate your coming, Mr. Pibble," said Mrs. Dixon-Jones, not bothering to conceal the let's-get-this-over-with note. "But I am afraid there has been a little misunderstanding. I thought so at the time, but it was difficult to . . . Well, I'd better tell you just what happened. I expect you know that the McNair is a charity with very strong local connections. I won't tell you what percentage of our income comes from the good people within ten miles of where we sit, but I assure you that we couldn't survive without it. So we've made a rule that one of our senior officials should always try to put in an appearance at any large gathering or committee of the people who help us raise funds—just to show how much we value the work they do for us. Now, Mrs. Dalby . . ."

A slight cocking of the proud-held head asked Pibble if he knew that busy beldame. He nodded.

". . . Mrs. Dalby held a coffee morning the week before last, and I managed to find time to show my face there. Lady Sospice was there—she's our patron, you know; old Lord Sospice endowed the Foundation and gave us this house. She's very old but she likes to know what's going on. I was talking to her about the activities of a group of busybodies who are interfering with our work, and I used the word 'criminal,' quite fairly, I think, though I wasn't talking in *your* sense. But dear Mary happened to overhear me, and suddenly she swung round and said that if anything criminal was afoot you were the man to ask, and I'm afraid that Lady Sospice, who can be very deaf and obstinate, took her at her word and insisted that I was to call you in and that we should make an appointment there and then. Well, though she hasn't got any official standing it saves trouble in the long run if I keep on the right side of her . . . If Mary hadn't been a newcomer she'd have *understood*, but she had her diary out, so . . . I considered writing to you or telephoning to cancel the meeting, but if I'd told the truth it would have been a very *difficult* letter—I hate lying—so I'm afraid I decided that now you're retired you wouldn't mind wasting the time coming here, where I could explain it all in private and apologize for bringing you on a fool's errand. I do hope you understand."

"Oh, yes," said Pibble. He understood very clearly the only facet of the affair that mattered to him these days. In the hierarchy of that coffee morning Lady Sospice would have been top, Mrs. Dixon-Jones about third or fourth, and "dear Mary" well down in the double figures. Lady Sospice was known to be a tedious old tease. When Mary had charged unwanted into a chat among the upper echelons, the patron had amused herself by demoting Mrs. Dixon-Jones to the indignity of haggling over diaries with Mary, who, hungry for gossip and vaguely trying to conjure up some kind of retirement therapy for her poor sacked husband, had refused to be put off. So Pibble had wasted a good windless morning, ideal for spraying the roses with an early winter wash; and he would have to waste several evenings trying to iron the creases out of Mary's calm. That was all that affected him now, so why should he worry if it wasn't all that affected Mrs. Dixon-Jones?

"That's all right," he said, beginning to shuffle out of his chair.

"I thought you'd probably understand," said Mrs. Dixon-Jones. She tapped at the tiny world again.

"Don't move," said Pibble. "I can find my own way out."

"Good-bye." Her sharp smile pinned him through the thorax, another specimen in her collection of insects.

"Give my love to Mary," she added.

"Of course." For Mary's sake he almost broke his submission. For instance, he could have remarked, casually, on . . . He probably would have, too, in the days when he still had a job, and colleagues, and some self-esteem.

As he reached out his hand for it, the door handle turned slowly. Slowly the door crept into the room; knowing what the movement meant, Pibble stood to one side and waited.

An enormously fat boy, a lad who could have modeled for Master Bones the Butcher's Son, seeped into sight. By his tight dark curls Pibble knew that this was the one who had been lying asleep on the sofa, dreaming (perhaps) of gold fish in dirty water.

"Why, Tony!" said Mrs. Dixon-Jones in a voice suddenly floppy. She reached down a large ledger from the top of the shabby old telephone switchboard behind her, flipped it open, ran a quick finger down a column, and said, "You didn't have your supper last night, Tony. Or your breakfast this morning."

"Biscuit," said Tony.

His voice had the same light, unbroken timbre as the door-keepers', though he must have been three years older. Mrs. Dixon-Jones took a box of assorted chocolate biscuits from a drawer and held it out; while Tony's hand dithered over the tray she smiled at him with happy patience, quite unforced, a whole spectrum away from the acid genialities of Mrs. Dalby's coffee mornings. At last the boy selected a crescent-shaped biscuit and took a reluctant nibble at one of its horns.

"Up," he said.

"You want to go upstairs, Tony?" said Mrs. Dixon-Jones.

"Up," he affirmed.

"Oh, Tony, not yet! You're not ready!"

"Tired."

"Now, Tony, Jennifer is six months older than you, and she's stayed with us. You can sleep on the sofa as long as you like. I won't ask you to do any duties if you don't feel like it."

Tony turned slowly away, and Pibble saw Mrs. Dixon-Jones relax from her sudden, inexplicable distress. The boy was almost past him when he turned again.

"Man," he said.

"Yes. Mr. Pibble," said Mrs. Dixon-Jones.

"Help you," said Tony, speaking so slowly that he had time to take a breath between the two words. Smiling, he shambled out. Mrs. Dixon-Jones nipped across the room and shut the door before Pibble could leave behind him.

"Please sit down," she said.

He did so, and watched her return to her desk and push its bric-a-brac into a new pattern. Then she lit a tiny cork-tipped cigarette, watched the match burn for a while before blowing it out and laying it neatly on the rim of the ashtray, and at length gave a tinny, uncomfortable laugh.

"Oh, dear," she said. "I'm afraid you'll think us very silly and superstitious. One gets into the habit of paying attention to what they say—they say so *little*, you see, and when they do comment on anything outside their immediate needs it seems like a, well, sort of *sign*. I wouldn't bother if I were clear in my own mind, but they don't seem to bother either then. It's when you're in a dither, if you see what I mean. . . ."

Pibble felt awkward for her. She spoke with such difficulty, so many sighs between clauses. Perhaps she really did hate lying, and also hated having to parade to a stranger the truth about a strong and secret irrational motive.

"They said quite a lot when they let me in," he said. "They seemed more on-the-spot than I'd expected."

"On-the-spot?"

"Well, shrewd."

"Oh, that's *quite* different. What did they say?"

"The girl said, 'Cold hands, warm heart' when I shook hands with the boy—I suppose my face showed how surprised I was—and they argued twice about who should bring me to find you."

" 'The exercise will do you good,' " said Mrs. Dixon-Jones.

"Yes."

"Those are both things they're always saying. Our children, Mr. Pibble, come from rather *underprivileged* homes. Doctor Kelly has worked out an interesting theory about that. He thinks that the disease may be hereditary, with a mild and an acute form, and the acute form only occurs very rarely, so that no one has yet spotted that it's hereditary, but the families with the mild form tend to be rather slow and stupid anyway, and so to be, well, not actually *deprived*, but warehousemen and lorry drivers and so on. People like that, you know . . ."

A benign glance assured Pibble that she wasn't for the moment including him among people like that.

" . . . people like that always say the same thing when the same situation occurs. Proverbs and clichés and so on. All our children have heard their mothers laughing off the coldness of their touch or coaxing them not to lie around sleeping all day—again and again. You see?"

She was genuinely likable when she talked about the children, likable but dismal. Pibble wondered what was so horrible about Tony's going upstairs.

"You have to keep remembering that they aren't at all clever," said Mrs. Dixon-Jones. "We can't measure their IQ because all the tests send them to sleep, but Doctor Kelly says they'd be about sixty-five, and now Doctor Silver thinks even lower. He's keeping a record of every word they say, and *among them* they seem to have a vocabulary of less than three hundred words."

"But it wasn't all clichés and proverbs," said Pibble.

"Oh."

"They said something about my being a policeman when I came in. Had you told anyone that?"

"Of course not." In three syllables her voice had lost its warmth.

"And when we passed the sofa they said Tony was fishing for yellow fish in dirty water. At least—"

He was interrupted by the loud tap of her pen on the globe. She had pulled her features into their bony command, and now honed the cutting edge onto her accent.

"It has been nice to meet you, Mr. Pibble, but we mustn't sit here gossiping, must we? I'm sure we both have things to do."

Obedient to the crack of the whip, Pibble stood on his hind legs.

"Well . . ." he began to say.

She looked at him. Mouth and nostril and chin were implacable, but her eyes despaired. He saw how soft she really was, a shell-less crab scuttling in and out of the social carapace left by a dead creation. He smiled at her eyes and sat down.

"You can't leave it there, can you?" he said. "I'd be much more likely to talk, and I can see it would be hell for you if it got into the papers. You'd be smothered with cranks from all over the world."

She said nothing, but carefully stubbed out her cigarette, tipped the contents of the ashtray into her wastepaper basket, and started to wipe the ashtray clean with a tissue.

"I won't even tell Mary," he said. "Then there's this other thing—too much money all of a sudden."

"I wasn't talking to Lady Sospice about that."

"No. But I think that's what you felt I might be able to help you about. I expect you were talking to Lady Sospice about Mr. Costain and our Preservation Society—the busybodies you mentioned just now. I've read something in the local paper about their being interested in the house. But if Mary had actually heard what you were saying there wouldn't have been any misunderstanding, and I'm quite sure that you wouldn't have let yourself be cornered into fixing an interview with me if there hadn't been something you felt you might want to talk to an ex-policeman about. It's usually money. Then you changed your mind, but you still aren't really sure."

"For a charity, Mr. Pibble, there's no such thing as too much money."

"But a sudden surplus is difficult to digest. I think I'm right in saying that until recently you were always short of funds. Your own job seems to include both money raising and keeping track of the children's diet. A richer organization—"

"We've advertised for a matron."

"But you haven't had one for some time."

"Only two months."

"Another thing: I imagine that a year ago the whole building was decorated like this room, but now you can afford to paint and repaint the passage outside for experimental purposes. And I doubt if the hall carpet cost less than a thousand quid, or if the Preservation Society sanctioned *that* design, let alone paid for it. And all those tape recorders . . ."

Mrs. Dixon-Jones had stopped tapping the globe and was biting the end of her pen with a look of innocent bewilderment, like a schoolgirl in an examination trying to remember at least one fact about the Venerable Bede.

"I don't know why you should think that any of this concerns you," she said, with a sudden pulse of patrician spirit.

"It doesn't," said Pibble, "unless you ask me to concern myself. But I think it's possible that you are uneasy about some aspect of this money, where it's coming from or where it's going to, but that you aren't sure of your facts or don't want to risk upsetting the children. . . ."

"At least I don't have to worry about *that*."

"I'd have thought—"

"It's very difficult to upset them about *anything*."

"Well, that's a comfort."

"Less than you might think. Oh, Mr. Pibble, I don't know what to say. Will you just take it that since you came something has happened which makes it impossible to ask *you* to help me?"

"OK. Let's leave it at that. We've made contact now, so you can always send for me if you change your mind. Give a note to Reuben Kelly, or ring the Black Boot in Kipling Street and leave a message for me to get in touch with you. Kelly and I usually have a drink there before lunch, but I won't talk to him about this, or Mary, so there's no danger of it getting back onto the coffee-morning circuit. I needn't tell you that if you have any solid evidence of something criminal you have a duty to get in touch with the police, though you'd be wise to consult a solicitor first. I imagine the McNair has a solicitor."

"Of course—" began Mrs. Dixon-Jones. The door lock clicked. Her features frosted. A big voice was speaking from the corridor before a face showed.

"Posey, my sweetie, are you hiding a policeman from me?"

"Come in, Ram," sang Mrs. Dixon-Jones.

The man had gleaming olive skin, gray hair, gray beard topped by the downturned moustache of the mod intellectual. White dustcoat worn with such a swagger that it looked like his national dress. A large, thickset, beaming man—a truly noble presence. The room seemed to diminish but to become more exotic as he came through the door.

"A policeman?" cried Mrs. Dixon-Jones. "Are you a policeman, Mr. Pibble?"

She managed the note of surprised badinage very well, for a woman who hated lying.

"I used to be," said Pibble, "but I retired two months ago."

"Glorious news!" said the newcomer. "You lost your hat! Hallelujah! My name is Rameses Silver, and I am joint head of research in this setup. Kelly researches the bodies and I research the souls. Now let me tell you, Mr. Pribble, that you, all unknowing, are part of a breakthrough in knowledge which is going to shake the entire medicobiological establishment to its cracked foundations."

"It'll make a change from fruit flies," said Pibble.

"His name is Pibble," said Mrs. Dixon-Jones. "No *r*. I wish you wouldn't do that."

"Great! Great!" said Dr. Silver. "My apologies, Mr. Pibble. Now listen. When you came this morning, was it the first time you had been to the McNair?"

"Yes."

"Have you had any previous contact with any cathypnic children or any of the staff here?"

"No."

"What type of vehicle did you arrive in?"

"I walked from the bus stop."

"Fine. Now—"

"Perhaps policemen have a distinctive walk," said Mrs. Dixon-Jones.

"Good point, Posey! You're learning fast. They could have heard him, seen him."

"The door's very thick," said Mrs. Dixon-Jones, "and the windows are some distance from where they stand. I've never seen any of them looking out of it when they're on door duty. They usually sit back to back on the floor."

"First point good," said Dr. Silver. "Make a note for Doll to have the door tested for audiopenetrability, Posey. Second point doubtful. Subjective. Not susceptible of proof, sweetie. Let's go on from there. You knocked, Mr. Pibble? You rang? There's no sound on the tape."

"The door opened before I could do either."

"Good, good. Who opened it?"

"Two of the children. A boy called George and a girl with red hair."

"Fancy," said Mrs. Dixon-Jones. "Honestly, the names some parents saddle their children with."

"Correct!" chanted Dr. Silver. "George Harrowby and Fancy Phillips. How long did they look at you before they said their first words?"

"I don't think they can have seen me at all. One of them said, 'Hello,' and the other one said, 'Copper lost his hat,' while the door was still between me and them. Then they shut it and we introduced ourselves and they had an argument about who should bring me here, and then George appeared to faint, and—"

"Sure, sure," said Dr. Silver. "Pardon me, but that's not on the tape, so it's not evidence."

He settled himself on the corner of Mrs. Dixon-Jones's desk with his back to Pibble and made rapid notes on a scribbling pad. When he had finished he sighed and stared at the paper, scratching as he did so at the back of his neck under the shorn grizzle.

"Have you heard the other tape?" Pibble said. "They talked about Tony when he was sleeping on the sofa."

"Flimflam," said Dr. Silver. "We get a load of that sort of material, but Tony can't or won't remember what he was dreaming about, so there's no check."

"But two of them talked about it at the same time."

"Not good enough," said Dr. Silver, shaking his stately head. "It may have impressed *you*, being there, but that's subjective. *My* target is a professional scientist, sitting at his desk and reading about an experiment in a scientific journal. This chappie would *prefer* to believe that any experiment in the field of parapsychology must be either a failure or a fraud. Then he reads my paper and he's convinced."

"Put the children in separate rooms," suggested Pibble, "with the sleeper in the middle one, and—"

Dr. Silver's big actorly laugh stopped him.

"Great! Great! That's the first experiment I set up, naturally. It's the classic approach. Except that it doesn't work. You show any interest in the kids' abilities—or you don't even show it, but it's there—and they blank off. We call it feedback, because it's great to have a technical-sounding name for phenomena you don't understand, get it? But maybe we're right, copper. Maybe the mental stimulus of the researcher's interest is enough to jam the brain waves. . . ."

"Groups of children," suggested Pibble. "No researchers, only tape recorders to listen to what they say about the sleeper."

"Good try again. We got some results that way, but not significant. Put two or three cathypnics together, and one of them will curl up and sleep while the others listen to *his* dreams. Too, their dreams seem to be mostly abstract, the way abstract art is abstract. And even when they dream representational, a mighty lot happens in ten seconds' dreaming for kids with that size vocabulary to comment on. It looks easy, but it's not. Four months I've been sitting on my arse trying to figure out a way to beat the intelligence of a gang of mental defectives—"

"They're not!" said Mrs. Dixon-Jones very sharply indeed.

"Sure, Posey, sure," said Dr. Silver with an affable lack of agreement. "They're as nice a bunch of kids as you're likely to meet, but for research material into parapsychic phenomena give me revolting college students any day. But hallelujah, we've a breakthrough this morning. Two breakthroughs. Notebook, Posey. Get on to Wallace Heaton and have them send a man down. I want a cine-camera permanently trained on the inside of the door, linked with one covering the drive, so that they can both be triggered by a photoelectric cell at the gates. I want the film to carry a time indicator in each case, ditto tape recorder G, so I've proof of the simultaneity of the record. No, scrap recorder G, and we'll have a mike at the door and sound track on the film. Get it?"

Mrs. Dixon-Jones had been writing in a quick, neat, sloping hand on a duplicate pad. Now she added her initials, tore off the top copy and thrust it onto a vertical spike, and handed the duplicate to Dr. Silver.

"Remind Doll to tell me the exact figures when you've got them," she said. "This is going to cost the earth, Ram."

"Mr. T. can stand it. That part's easy. *Now* we've got to dream up a method of attracting a series of random callers to that door, in such a way that we can prove that not even you or I knew who was coming next. To think I've been sitting here four months without spotting what a unique research tool my own front door was! End of breakthrough one. Breakthrough two: meet Mr. Pibble!"

"Me!" The dozing soldier in the sentry box between Pibble's ears snapped to attention, late and guilty. He'd hardly been listening to the rattle of orders. Most of his mind had been puzzling about Dr. Silver's language. The man's accent was a very neutral, run-of-the-mill English, without lilt or distortion; not the Lebanese-American one might have expected. But he used a manic assortment of words and phrases, don and half hip and gangster and journalese and babu—what sort of scientist talks, literally, about "brain waves" one sentence after addressing an ex-detective superintendent as "copper"?

"Yes, you, Mr. Pibble. What paranormal experiences have you had, sir?"

"None that I know of."

"Ah, cock! No hunches in your job? No intuitions? How long were you a bluebottle?"

"Thirty-four years. I wouldn't call that sort of thing a paranormal experience, though. Of course I've sometimes felt a pull about a case without tangible evidence to back my instincts up; but I was probably wrong half the time, and the other half I'd noticed things subconsciously which would have been evidence if I'd noticed them consciously. I never liked hunches; if they work once, you start to look for them after that, and then the wildest fancy becomes an article of faith. That type of policeman doesn't last long. What's up, beyond my having figured by accident in the episode at the door?"

Dr. Silver picked up the little globe from the desk and held it between finger and thumb, like a conjuror about to perform some legerdemain with an egg. His fingers were very short and stubby.

"See," he said softly, "my right hand sends a signal."

He tossed the toy spinning toward the ceiling.

"And my left hand receives it!" he cried. The globe fell with a slap into the olive palm. The shock of its fall must have released the catch, for the lid shot up, loosing the spark that set the small wick flaming.

"Bravo!" called Mrs. Dixon-Jones. "I can't even get it to light."

Dr. Silver stared at the flame in a smiling trance. Pibble could see the light of it glisten off his spectacles: they were as eccentric an affectation as his language, for the glass was quite flat.

"Do it again, Ram," said Mrs. Dixon-Jones.

"Have you figured the odds, Posey?" said Dr. Silver in an accent of awe. "This surely is my day, when things go right for me. So let's get on. My hand cannot catch this little jigger, Mr. Pibble, unless my other hand has thrown it. Same with a signal. You need a transmitter, one; and a receiver, two. Now we believe our kids here to be highly sensitive receivers. They also transmit, but we can't control their transmissions. They won't receive freely from adults—"

"They always know when I'm tired or sad or angry," said Mrs. Dixon-Jones.

"So do I, Posey. So do I. But when have you seen them work a trick like this—a copper who's lost his hat? When?"

"I don't think I have."

"And you've been here how long?"

"Seventeen years."

"Hallelujah! Mr. Pibble, there's a rational chance that you're the transmitter we've been looking for."

"Well, of course I'd be glad to help, but . . ." Pibble let his doubt hang in the air. He foresaw desert days of sitting behind cheat-proof screens, under the eyes of independent witnesses of the highest probity, while he tried to transmit a mental image of a teddy bear to a child with an IQ of sixty-five. Dr. Silver slapped him jauntily on the shoulder.

"Hell, man," he boomed. "Mr. T. will make it worth your while. On, on! What mood were you in when you approached the door?"

"No particular mood. What do you mean?"

"Excited, man! Stimulated! Happy! Angry! Depressed!"

"None of those, really. My wife had asked me to come and talk to Mrs. Dixon-Jones about an idea that had come up at one of these fund-raising affairs. I suppose I was a little reluctant to meet the children, because I expected them to be much less, well, fetching than they are. Otherwise I was rather low-keyed—almost apathetic. I wanted to spray my roses."

"Stupendous!" sighed Dr. Silver in three long syllables of ecstasy. "Apathy! Boredom! They're the key. How often have I said so, Posey?"

"Often enough for me to know what you mean by apathy and boredom. For heaven's sake take the man away and get his little adventure down on paper. If you're going to put him on the payroll, let me have a note—I refuse to be hounded by auditors and tax hounds in twelve months' time, when I've forgotten all about him. Good-bye, Mr. Pibble. You'll give my love to dear Mary, won't you?"

"Of course," said Pibble, wincing at this sudden salvo after the armistice appeared to have been signed. Dr. Silver blew her a kiss, and she frowned at him—a not-in-front-of-the-servants frown. The big man gathered his notes together, and Pibble waited for him, dazed. He felt as if he were embarking on a mysterious safari, and not being allowed to take with him even the bare necessities of reason. Or were once more at the start of that unbanishable recurring dream in which he received the Police Medal from the Queen Mother with his shirttails twitching around bare thighs. That nightmare shyness was echoed by the reality, for the convulsive gusts of Dr.

Silver's enthusiasm seemed to insist that other men ought to strip off their safe, tweedy responses and prance naked. No wonder his signals did not penetrate to the cathypnics, if apathy was the key.

Dr. Silver led the way out, but paused in the doorway and looked down. Beyond him, crouched by the far wainscot, a man in a tweed cape was picking with his index nail at the sapphire paint. Cape and posture made him look like Sherlock Holmes poised over a clue, but before Pibble could make sense of him he exploded to his feet. Just as the toad, squat by the ear of Eve, exploded into the Demon King at the touch of Ithuriel's spear, so started up, in his own shape, Mr. Vivian Costain, firebrand president of the South London Preservation Society. Pibble had seen him on a lecture platform, and once or twice on television; no one could mistake the pink cheeks and the eyes permanently pop with aesthetic rapture or with public indignation and the meticulously wild wisps of silvery hair. In the flesh, and undaised, he was a dumpy little man, but he exploded to a considerable height because his hands shot, clenched, toward the ceiling. Then they came down and gripped Dr. Silver by the lapels of his dust-coat.

"Philistine!" hooted Mr. Costain.

Dr. Silver's olive fingers twitched the feverish grip away as if he had been picking fluff off the cloth.

"Any complaints must be made through the secretary," he said. "Posey! A visitor for you!"

But Mrs. Dixon-Jones had already pushed past Pibble into the corridor. Her head was held at its horsewoman's angle, but her voice teetered on the edge of squawking.

"May I ask what you think you're doing?" she said. "And who you think you are?"

Costain, adept at squabbles, public or private, instantly became calm and introduced himself in a businesslike voice.

Mrs. Dixon-Jones flushed, then went fainting white.

"What makes you think you can come barging in here without even the courtesy to make an appointment?" she said.

"Barging?" said Mr. Costain mildly. "Let me explain. I was asked down by the local Preservation Society to see how the external repairs were getting on. A great improvement, don't you think? You may not realize it, but they are affiliated to my society—in fact I negotiated with the Ministry for them over the public share of the repair costs. Naturally I thought it only polite to make myself known to you. I believe that there have been a number of differences of opinion between you and the local people, and I thought I might be able to smooth things out."

For answer Mrs. Dixon-Jones pointed at the wall. Her attitude was that of the Queen of Hearts ordering a beheading. Mr. Costain's fingernail had bared a stamp-sized patch of seaweed green amid the virulent sapphire.

"But it's *tremendously* exciting," said Mr. Costain boyishly. "Lady Sospice, you may know, has handed a lot of her papers to the local society, and among them the secretary found a receipt from the De Morgan factory for a sixty-foot run of tiles in a pattern entirely unique. Naturally when I came in I looked about me. Despite what you have done to it, this remains a gloriously typical example of High Domestic Grandiose."

The lecturer's hoot was back in his voice. Perhaps Mrs. Dixon-Jones considered herself an even more glorious example of the genre, for she sniffed derisively.

"*Gloriously* typical," insisted Mr. Costain. "Be that as it may, I arrived outside your room and heard voices, so I decided to wait a few minutes before making myself known. And down here, under this appalling gub, I spotted a checker pattern of corrugations. I could do nothing but investigate.

It'll all have to come off, you know. I will see that a schedule of suitable contemporary color schemes is prepared for you."

"I won't stand for it!" said Mrs. Dixon-Jones. "I simply won't stand for it!"

"I'm afraid you will have no choice, dear lady."

"Get out! Get out at once!"

"Please, Posey," said Dr. Silver. While hoot and scream had reverberated under the arches, he had watched the two of them through his joke glasses as if they had been part of an experiment. Now he pitched his voice at a level of calm authority that seemed to still even the echoes.

"Mr. Costard," he said. "We are here to run a home for an unfortunate group of children called cathypnics. Our responsibility is to them, and indirectly to the Ministry of Health. I say 'indirectly' because we are an independent charity, though most of the children here are covered to some extent by a grant from their local authorities; even so this leaves us with a lot of money still to find. This local society you speak of contrived to have a preservation order placed on this building, which we have accepted with a good grace. It is true that the Ministry of Works provided a substantial sum for repairs, but we had to find almost an equal sum, because (as I am sure you know) the money raised by the local society was derisory. Fortunately, we had a windfall. Now we allowed all this to happen because we wish to be good citizens and to be left in peace to get on with our proper work, which is the care of the children. It is of medical importance that cathypnic children should be surrounded by bright, simple colors. The choice of these colors is a question of science, not of aesthetics or art history. We shall certainly not allow ourselves to be dictated to over a matter like this."

"My dear sir," said Mr. Costain. "I do not believe, as I said, that you will have the option. You are sitting on an absolutely outstanding example of a type of architecture and decor

27

which is becoming increasingly rare. You are also occupying several acres of open space in an area which is badly in need of elbow room. Public opinion is certain to go against you if the dispute is allowed to become public, and the funds you need for your work will consequently decline. Whereas—"

"Who let you in?" interrupted Dr. Silver, very gently but with a weight and timing that stopped Mr. Costain dead. He had seemed so sure of the upper ground that his finger had begun to wag under the olive nose and the old Bloomsbury emphasis to modulate his hoot, so that he had said, for instance, "absol*ooo*tly outs*teehnd*ing." Now he blinked and changed gear.

"Two of the inmates," he said.

"Ah. Interested as you must have been in the architecture, Mr. Costard, you may have failed to notice one of the curious side effects of the disease. Cathypnic children have an almost instant appeal. The staff here call them 'dormice,' but visitors usually think of hamsters on first meeting them. Imagine their impact in a television documentary. Guess which side public opinion would then be on."

"No!" cried Mrs. Dixon-Jones.

"I agree," said Dr. Silver. "In the past, even when desperately short of money, we have refrained from using this appeal, for the children's own sake. But if we are forced, we will fight with what weapons we have, and we will win. Let me remind you that the Ministry of Health is not as eager to take on financial obligations as the Ministry of Works seems to be."

Mr. Costain, though clearly unused either to being put so efficiently in the wrong or to being outblackmailed, yielded with surprising grace and charm.

"My dear sir," he said, "the argument seems to have—I believe the word is 'escalated'—quite unnecessarily. Surely

28

we can achieve a compromise which will protect the interests of the children and at the same time . . ."

He completed the sentence by waving a vague hand at the blasphemous gub. Dr. Silver nodded.

"Of course," he said. "And for the time being the compromise will be as follows. We will make no objection to having the house inspected by one knowledgeable expert, provided he makes a proper appointment with the secretary. He will be accompanied by one of our officials and must follow that official's instructions. He can prepare a list of matters of architectural interest and make suggestions for repair or renovation which we will then be prepared to discuss. We will take no responsibility for any expense involved in his visits. Anybody, of whatever standing, who comes without an appointment will be treated as a trespasser and physically ejected. So will any amateur enthusiasts from your societies who try to take advantage of this arrangement."

There was a long pause, as though his hearers were expecting the soothing, world-ordering voice to flow on forever. Pibble found himself thinking what a merciful episode this was, a sop of gossip to feed to Mary so that he need not tell her about his time with Mrs. Dixon-Jones; then the dumpy enthusiast jerked himself awake and seemed to realize what a tough bargain had been agreed for him. He made a desperate gesture, like an innocent man about to start a speech from the scaffold, changed the movement into a hopping about-turn, and strutted off under the offending arches. Dr. Silver smiled as he watched him go and rubbed lazily at the back of his neck.

"But what'll I do? What'll I do?" cried Mrs. Dixon-Jones.

"Poor Posey," said Dr. Silver. "You'll have to see the little bastard sometimes."

His voice was neutral, abstract—no longer the ordered and

grammatical dominance of the judge, not yet the dislocated energy of the scientist. Pibble, who had cautiously assumed that the man was at least half charlatan—likely enough in that line of research, and nothing to stop the other half from producing real results—was now immensely impressed. Charlatan or not, he had weight, moral reserves—"bottom," they used to call it. For the last few months Pibble had felt like a trivial and discarded object, an empty orange crate perhaps, chuntering back and forth in meaningless eddies as the tide sloshed in and out of the river, each tide imperceptibly sucking him a little nearer the final oblivion of the sea. Now he had bumped into something solid—rooted like a pierhead. He wanted to stay.

Mrs. Dixon-Jones, her face still batter-colored with used fury, was starting to say something when a new figure appeared under the lilac arch where they'd last seen Mr. Costain. A cathypnic, by his silhouette, but younger than George or Fancy.

"Why, it's Tim," said Mrs. Dixon-Jones.

Her eyes softened, her thin lips broadened, and the jut of her nose grew miraculously less severe. A mild tinge, the ghost of a blush, colored her cheeks. The boy drifted toward them very slowly, blinking. His bulk and the wavering, drifting motion made him seem to be somehow more kin to the world of fish than anything warm-blooded, a deep-beamed carp sliding along behind the plate glass of an aquarium. Pibble and Dr. Silver followed Mrs. Dixon-Jones along the passage and stopped when she knelt in the boy's path.

"Tim," she cooed, "have your bowels worked today, darling?"

The child noticed her for the first time and smiled the remote smile of the cathypnics.

"Your bowels?" repeated Mrs. Dixon-Jones.

"Forgot," said the boy.

With mysterious ease, like a slow-motion film of a rugger genius jinking round a tackler, he evaded her embrace and drifted on. She rose sighing.

"It's marvelous how different they all are," she said. "Tim likes to be just a weeny bit secretive."

"So do I," said Pibble.

Dr. Silver chuckled.

"Bully for you," he said. "You and your normal metabolism. Our kids, we have to fight to make their metabolism work even at half cock. See you later, Posey."

Mrs. Dixon-Jones smiled really quite warmly at Pibble and went back to her office.

"She seems to have a lot on her plate," said Pibble as they walked into the hall.

"Right," said Dr. Silver, stopping in midstride to switch off the tape by the now empty sofa, silence listening to silence. "You reckon we could afford some staff for her, like we can afford these jiggers?" He tapped the machine with his toe. "Good point, but Posey won't have it. She wants to do every damned thing for them herself, from tying their shoes to typing their death certificates. It's her way of loving them. And who knows? Cut off that love, and maybe they'd feel it, lose one of the strings that tie them to their waking life, snuff out sooner. Where'll we put this camera?"

2

While Dr. Silver fretted across the garish carpet, checking distances and angles, Pibble stood halfway up the stairs and studied the tops of the pillars. Many of them appeared to support the ceiling in places where it needed no such help; every capital was different, so that the place looked like a pillarmaker's showroom—you could imagine silent Victorian families peering worriedly up while Father pointed with his umbrella, and eventually settling for six of the gargoyle pattern.

Silver peered out of a window, then pranced across and spoke to the doorkeepers—new ones, sitting back to back on the carpet, as Mrs. Dixon-Jones had said. Both heads swung sideways to blink at Pibble; one set of lips moved; he could see the sleepy smiles and feel the tepid wash of sentiment which the cathypnics engendered—they would indeed be formidable on TV.

What was he to do? Copper come. Lost his hat. Not much to build a career on. No doubt he did still retain elements of the approved police gait, solemn, confident, official. No doubt the cathypnics' upbringing had made them sensitive to the appearance of their natural enemy—as broiler chickens which have never seen daylight will cower if a hawk-shaped object is held above them. But the policemen they'd have seen would have been in uniform, of which the most striking element is the helmet. How would a child with a vocabulary of three hundred words explain that a policeman was at the door but he was not wearing his uniform? Copper come. Lost his hat. They must have seen him.

But the money would be useful, thought Pibble as Dr. Silver took a final scratch at his nape and crossed the hall toward the stairs, pausing to reactivate the tape recorder he had switched off. He wondered who Mr. T. was, and whether Mary mightn't get her Cretan holiday again after all.

"You got a big family, Mr. Pibble?" said Silver, coming up the stairs two at a time.

"No. Just a wife. Why?"

"I asked the dormice about you, and one of 'em said quote lot of kids unquote. Mush. No use, even if you were father of twenty. Too many kids in the building anyway."

"Oh," said Pibble, and then, "I see."

No point in mentioning the father with the umbrella—it was unprovable and would make him seem too eager. Anyway, Dr. Silver's was the better explanation.

"By the way," he said as they started up the second flight of stairs, "the children who let me in said that no one else was coming, but Mr. Costain turned up. I'm quite sure that that's what they meant."

Dr. Silver, with his eager pace, was already ahead of him and seemed not to have heard. But when he reached the landing, or gallery, which ran round three sides of the hall, he halted and took up the stance of the president of a banana republic receiving birthday plaudits on the palace balcony.

"There's just one comfort about this damned job," he said.

"The kids don't understand the trick they do, either. *If* they do it. Let's keep an open mind on that one. But except for Rue Kelly, the folk who've worked here long—and most of 'em stick around once they've come—are quite sure they do *something.* The kids, too, natch. Then you've got to remember that cathypnics are dumb, dumber than the dumbest doll in Dublin. They see their trick work once, twice, so they reckon it always will. And you're making the same mistake. Parapsychic phenomena aren't made that way. Listen. Say I set up an experiment with my assistant turning over a pack of twenty-five cards—we mostly use special packs, five sets of five symbols shuffled together—while a sensitive sits out of sight and hearing and tries to guess which card has been turned. Normal expectation of correct guesses is just under four for each run of the pack. Odds against eight correct guesses are high enough to be significant. Get frequently into double figures and the odds are astronomical. As-tro-nomical. You just don't bother with hundred percent correct. It happens. Oh, yes, it happens—but then even I start looking for the way the experiment was rigged. I reckon you could say, Mr. Pibble, that George and Fancy, who let you in, are statistically naïve—and yourself only a mite less."

"Then what on earth can you hope to achieve?"

"Good question. 'Ram Silver,' I say, three o'clock in the mornings, 'what on earth can you hope to achieve?' Answer: at the lowest level I hope to prove to the meanest-minded skeptic that parapsychic phenomena exist. That's coming soon, here or somewhere else. Matter of fact, it's already *been* proved, several times, best by J. B. Rhine at Duke, but always using statistics. You produce consistent experiments with odds of a million to one turning up for you, and people don't want to think about it. Even professional scientists.

"Second, I hope to discover how parapsychic phenomena

work. That's further off. It'll take a real breakthrough. But that's what Mr. T.'s paying me for. Once we know *how*, we'll be getting our hundred percents whenever we want them. We're like the Wright brothers, or maybe someone even further back—one of those guys who jumped off towers dolled up like a bat. We spend years, we spend fortunes, putting our machine together and it makes a noise and it stinks and then it trundles across the grass like a lead bird. And then, maybe, it gives a little hop. In that hop, in those eight yards when you can see daylight under the skids, lie supersonic airliners and the dominion of the skies. Only we don't know how yet. But perhaps you are that kind of hop, Mr. Pibble. Come and look at my lab."

He led the way along a passage immediately above the one to Mrs. Dixon-Jones's room, turned right at the crossing, and at last opened a door some distance down the even longer passage.

The room whirred and clicked. It muttered to itself its bright inanities, the lingo of machines.

"Like to listen?" said Dr. Silver. He fiddled with a tape recorder and a slow, light voice spoke from it.

"Tain't fair," it said.

Pibble looked at the machine and saw the tape whirling at rewind speed. All at once it slowed.

"Turned out nice," it drawled.

"Lovely."

The tape spun faster again.

"That's cunning," said Pibble. "I wondered how you came to be listening to my entry so soon after. How's it done?"

"Easy," said Dr. Silver. "Double pickup. The first discriminates between silence and noise and slows the tape down for the second head to rerecord onto a master tape. We've got twenty machines here, all running sixteen hours a day, but the sounds on them can usually be got onto one tape which my girl transcribes every day."

"Green," drawled the tape.

"Lovely," it answered itself.

"Hiya, dormice," it called. "You can't go sleep there. You'll be run over by my cart."

"The exercise will do you good," it whined.

It whirled again, and slowed.

" 'ot," it complained.

"No, darling, it isn't," it cooed. "It's just right. But I'll take one of your sweaters off if you're quite sure."

"I'm frightened."

"There's nothing to be afraid of, darling. You come with Posey. You aren't hot, really you aren't. I can feel."

"Cold 'and, warm 'eart."

The next whirl was very short.

"Now for heaven's sake, Posey," said the machine in the clipped, aggressive accent Pibble knew so well.

"But I can't just leave it like that."

"Of course you can. Whether you're right or wrong it comes to the same—"

Dr. Silver pressed a button and the machine renounced vocables for its former clicks and whirs.

"I keep telling 'em," he said angrily. "But will they stop filling my tapes with mush? Will they hell! That applies to you, too, Mr. Pibble. If you want to talk to anyone except one of the dormice, you make damned sure either that you're out of range of the mikes or that you switch off. And switch on when you've done."

"I'll try to remember. Mrs. Dixon-Jones told me that cathypnics are very difficult to upset, but just now one of them said he was frightened. Or was it a girl?"

"Marilyn Goddard," said Dr. Silver absently. "She dreams

nightmares. She's aberrant. Mother was a clinging, sloppy, man-hungry moron—unmarried, of course. The guy she took up with when Marilyn was two was the one who did the Paperham jobs. He settled in with them, though you wouldn't have reckoned he was the type. There for three years, till he was copped."

"Crippen!" said Pibble. His scalp had twitched involuntarily at the name of Paperham, as though horror for the dead women could be communicated directly to nerve and flesh without having to pass the censorship of thought.

"Do the other children say 'Lovely' to her?" he asked.

"Yeah, but at a lower ratio than they say it to each other. I forget the figures. I've got them on file. 'Lovely' doesn't mean a thing—it's an all-purpose reaction. Our dormice are damned efficiently insulated from the cold world. Now let's get this experience of yours down on tape. Come into my den."

It would be hard, Pibble thought, to design anything less like a den. The avocado tree looked as though it had been loaned from a stand at the Ideal Home Exhibition, and the rest of the furniture—filing cabinets, half-acre desk, shin-level tables, black-leather-and-steel chairs—failed to declare any characteristic of the man who had chosen them beyond extravagance. Even the one touch of art—a bronze and bulbous paperweight, vaguely post-Brancusi—had the look of one of a large issue of multiples. Pibble found himself sweating with absurd nerves as the doctor leaned forward and made passes at him with the microphone. His voice emerged strained and textureless, as though he were lying, but Silver seemed not to mind; he twitched the microphone back to his own chin to ask the exact question needed to unravel a wooliness in Pibble's tale. He insisted on recording every drab and tiny detail, often repetitiously but steadily clarifying the absurd incident until, by the time he clicked the recorder off, it contained a total account of two minutes in the life of James Willoughby Pibble, unique, unconfusable with anything else that had happened, or might have happened, to him, or anyone else, anywhere. He'd have made a good if tiresome lawyer, Pibble thought. But then he'd have made a good priest, a good mayor, a good surgeon. He possessed a kind of moral omnicompetence which persisted through his rapidly changing roles—and perhaps that was the reason for this neutral room: more character-defining furniture would have been grit in the smooth gear changes. Now it was the executive of a world-tentacled combine who spoke into a flashy intercom gadget on the desk.

"Doll," he snapped.

"Yes, Doctor Silver."

"I've got a tape here for you. I want it on paper, fast."

"I'll come in."

As the door opened, Pibble stood up. This was a happy surprise.

"You won't remember me, I expect," he said.

Her yellow-brown eyes looked at him, puzzled.

"You know our honorable Doll?" said Dr. Silver. He sounded as though he disapproved of the acquaintanceship.

"We met in the Black Boot about a month ago," said Pibble.

"Of course!" said the girl. "You're Rue's policeman friend."

"Ex-," said Pibble.

A curious silence engulfed the room, as though each were waiting for one of the others to make a betraying move. Wild Rue Kelly was the only subject they had in common, and Pibble was unsure of the girl's relationship with him. He could hear the rasp of those olive fingers raking at the stubble.

"Well," said the girl at last, "I'd better—"

The telephone rang, and she picked it up.

"Doctor Silver's secretary."

She listened, then put her hand over the mouthpiece.

"Mister Thanatos wants to talk to you. I didn't know he was back."

"Nor did I," said Dr. Silver.

"There's a piece about him in the *Guardian* this morning," said Pibble. "He's come to give evidence about this South Bank hotel site."

So *that's* who Mr. T. was. No wonder . . .

"Fine, fine," said Dr. Silver. "I've got a lot of news for him. Forget the tape, Doll. Just take Mr. Pibble and show him round."

His hand was twitching for the telephone. Pibble followed the girl out, enjoying once again the strangely seductive way in which she held herself; her figure looked as if, from hemline to neckline of her plain orange dress, it was swathed in a single ultra-fine bandage, which held her taut, contained her, prevented her from flopping with luscious abandon into the nearest arms. Her manner and walk were prim and neat, but somehow implied the opposite.

"I thought you worked for Reuben," said Pibble as he walked back toward the hall with her.

"I worked *with* him, for nothing, but he traded me to Ram, the bastard."

"In exchange for what?"

"I don't know, but I get a salary now."

"Are you taking me to see him?"

"Any excuse is better than none."

Her wide mouth smiled with the shared secret. One day she would have jowls, but now her soft, flattish face seemed simple and scrumptious, like Elysian marshmallow.

"It's funny to think of Rue working in a place like this," said Pibble with a gesture as they passed the grove of pillars. "You know, it took me several weeks to discover he was a doctor. Before that I thought he sold things."

"He's got very strict rules against talking about doctoring to laymen. Or laywomen. What sort of things did you think he sold?"

"Fast cars, probably."

She laughed. She seemed to have the secret of perpetual animation. Moses had struck the rock and high spirits welled out unstinted.

"He never told me you were an honorable, either," he said. "Are you, in fact?"

"Last of the line," she said smugly. "Rue says I'm England's most dishonorable hon. My grandfather bought the barony from Maundy Gregory, and my father died of drink when I was twelve, and that was the lot of us, not counting Granny."

"Lady Sospice?" guessed Pibble, extrapolating from the scandal of the drunkard son.

"She's nicer than she looks."

"I'm sure she is. I haven't met her, but my wife has once or twice."

"Oh, she hates women. So do I."

Pibble laughed.

"Oh, yes," she said. "When I get old I'm going to buy a house on Capri or somewhere and fill it with gigolos. Granny can't, poor old cat, because she was brought up wrong to enjoy that sort of thing."

"But I expect this Preservation Society has some dashing young architects in it."

"No such luck. I think they're a lot of ignorant stuffpots who don't like things for what they are but because they want to keep the world just as it always was. Granny brought them in to tease poor Posey, but now they've run amok. She hates Posey more than anyone. This was *our* house, you see, and now Posey runs it. If you like I'll show you the room I would have been born in if we'd still been living here."

She stopped at the far end of the gallery and gestured to the right.

"Rather a remote sort of fame," said Pibble.

"Nonsense. I can get much remoter than that. The room above Posey's is called King Charles's Room because it once contained a bed in which King Charles was said to have slept in a different house. But I'll take you to Rue. He uses what we called the Picture Saloon, but it never had any pictures in it because Alma-Tadema refused to give Great-Granddad a reduction for quantity. Isn't it funny to think of all this once smelling of potpourri and furniture polish and eau de cologne?"

It smelled of hospitals now. She had stopped to finish her sentence outside a big pair of doors, mightily carved with swags of fruit, which stood where there should have been a long passage running to the back of the building if the plan had been totally symmetrical. The doors had been painted cream, and somebody had nailed a piece of packing case to one of the panels and stenciled it with the words KELLY'S KINGDOM. Mr. Costain would have cause to hoot if he came up here, Pibble thought.

One of the doors opened and a uniformed nurse glided out, weeping quietly. Doll made a face and bit her lip, then led the way in.

"I've brought a friend to see you, Rue," she said.

Of course it had been built as a picture gallery, once you knew, but it would have needed several regiments of odalisques and vestal virgins to fill the vacant walls. It was a vast room, stretching the full width of this wing and nearly half its length, and here, too, nails had been driven callously into the paneling; from each dangled graphs and records, below which stood a white iron bedstead. There must have been over twenty beds in all, but a few were empty. Rue Kelly was bending over one of the patients. He had lifted the child's eyelid and was peering into the pupil through an ophthalmoscope. At length he stood up, rubbing his long chin. His green eyes glanced rapidly at Pibble, then flickered round the room before coming back to him.

"Be with you in a minute," he said genially, speaking in a normal voice as though there were no danger of waking the sleepers. He bent to the other eyelid.

The outer windows were half obscured by scaffolding and hoists, though a great swath of London rooftops could be glimpsed below the planks; so Pibble went and peered out over the courtyard. From here he could see how simple the design of the house was, beneath all its frills and flounces. A rectangle, two stories high, surrounded a cobbled courtyard; an arch led out at the back, flanked by round-topped coach house doors—so the ground-floor rooms must maintain their pompous height the whole way round. Yes, the passage on the other side had run to the back with no sign of stairs; presumably it continued from there over the coach house and the arch and joined up with the back of Kelly's Kingdom.

Pibble grinned to himself at the idea of how wickedly Rue must have enjoyed bashing those nails through the coarse timber and into the beautiful wood of the door behind the notice. Rue was the most violent antiaesthete he had ever met, clever and voluble, happiest in extreme positions. The garish corridor below, scientifically useful and aesthetically awful, was a perfect Rue production, a physical equivalent of his pub argument that Oscar Wilde should not have been jailed for his morals, but should have been shot for his philosophy.

For a moment, gazing blankly out of the window, Pibble

could see the ugly interior of the Black Boot, hear the jostle at the bar, smell the steam from the vast shepherd's pie behind the snack bar. He'd found the place a couple of years ago, when the pub he'd used before became involved in a brewer's "rationalization" and started to dispense a bitter he despised. He'd had a job then, so had gone there only on a few evenings or sometimes on weekends, and had merely noticed the thin-faced, green-eyed young man who was occasionally present; but his being sacked had changed that, bringing him there at weekday lunchtimes to prevent Mary's hydra-headed guilt feelings from forcing her to cook him yet another square meal. All of a sudden he and Rue Kelly were cronies.

Not friends. That implied a wider knowledge. Not acquaintances, an altogether weaker relationship. Cronies. Pibble, in his new, disoriented life, was uncomfortably aware of how intense his reliance on Rue Kelly had become. Before, work and the abrasion of colleagues had kept him tuned, sharp, *alive;* now the rust and dust of retirement were settling on him. His garden kept his muscles in trim and he'd always been lucky with his digestion, but he needed the two-man debating club in the Black Boot much as a prisoner doing solitary needs his daily trudge round the yard.

Wondering, not for the first time, what the other member of the club got out of *his* company, he turned back to the ward in time to see Kelly straighten and stand humming. The sleeper's eyelid fell like treacle. Kelly ticked the chart on the wall, checked a tube which ran into the child's nostril, and spun round grinning.

"Pint of blood, mister?" he said.

"There jokes the eternal student," said Pibble.

"Who's died, Rue?" said the girl.

"No one."

"Angela was crying."

"Was she? I told her Mickey Nicholas had six days."

"You can't be sure."

"Yes I can. Another brick is added to the house of knowledge. Rue Kelly sees the future! Let him foretell your fate!"

He clapped the ophthalmoscope to his eye, squinted at them across the room, and began a singsong chant.

"I see through the clouds. I see the mists part. I see you, my pretty one. There is a man with you. I cannot see his face. But I can see what he is doing. He is cutting you up and putting you in a trunk. Now he is taking the trunk to the left luggage office. Aha! Now I see his face. He is old, he is ugly, he has just been fired from the police force—"

"Oh, shut up, Rue," said the girl. "Can you really? That's marvelous."

"What are you trying to do?" said Pibble.

"Find out what makes them stop ticking."

"When will this one wake up?"

"Never."

Pibble felt a chill, like the touch of the children, run through his veins; he must have paled.

"Nasty thought, isn't it?" said Kelly cheerfully. "And now I'll answer your next question, seeing that you aren't going to ask it as it's not in very good taste. We don't let 'em die, straight away, as soon as they fall into their everlasting doze, because it's not ethical. I belong to a very ethical profession, mister, and it just so happens that this hands me a unique collection of research material. They beat rats and rabbits into a cocked hat. They've got no feelings, no future, no individuality, so I can use 'em as I think fit—with the utmost respect, of course, the *utmost* respect."

The last phrases were spoken in parody of some medical spokesman mouthing his obscene euphemisms.

"As a matter of fact," said Pibble, "I was going to ask if you knew what they were dreaming about."

Kelly snorted with amusement, then stilled. His eyes flickered and remained angry, though he laughed again.

"Ram's been getting at you," he said. "You mustn't believe any of that cock."

"Oh, Rue," said the girl. "You *know* there's something in it. All the staff think so."

"Darlint," said Kelly, "if you'd be listening to me ould friend Father O'Freud, there's some knowledge of wish fulfillment you'd be having."

"Begorra," said the girl.

"Begorra indade!" cried Kelly, doing a short wild jig in the aisle between the silent beds. "The raisin, I mean reason, why my admirable colleagues think the kids are telepathic is that without some asset like that they'd be spending their lives trying to cultivate an allotment of moving vegetables. They *want* the little bastards to be extraordinary, and therefore worthwhile."

"But then we'd all choose different extraordinary things about them," said the girl.

"Would you hell? You've got one ready-made myth, so any further superstitions accrete to that. Belief in the unreasonable is always collective—look at medical history."

"When I arrived," said Pibble, "two of the children opened the door. Before they saw me one of them said, 'Copper come. Lost his hat.'"

"You never wear a hat," said Kelly.

"I was thinking about the psychological effects of being sacked—or I just had been."

"Very sophisticated metaphors you think in, by cathypnic standards."

"It's very close, isn't it?" said the girl.

"What is?"

"The copper and the hat."

Kelly snorted again.

"My cousin from County Clare," he said, "dealt himself all thirteen spades once. They threw him in the Liffey for cheating, but we in the family knew he hadn't the wits."

Pibble laughed and Kelly joined him, but the girl remained serious.

"Doctor Silver did bring two of the dormice in here," she said. "He wanted to find out if they were all dreaming one communal dream."

"What happened?" said Pibble.

"The kids said 'Lovely' and tried to go to sleep too. I hustled them out."

"How beautiful is sleep," said the girl. "Sleep and his brother death."

Kelly snarled at her like a wildcat.

"Haven't I told you that if you quoted once more from bloody English literature I'd never buy you another drink?"

Her hand flew to her mouth and the peachy softness of her face began to crumple as she bit at her knuckles.

"What *really* happened," said Kelly, "was that Ram Silver queered my pitch with Posey Dixon-Jones. You met her, Jimmy?"

"This is what the children call 'upstairs,' is it?" said Pibble. "I imagine she doesn't like the waking ones to know that it's here."

"They all *know*," insisted the girl, risking a glance at Kelly to see how he took this continued defiance.

"Course they do," said Kelly. "It's a big house, but not that big. They're stupid, but not that stupid. Anyway Posey's mad. What did you make of her, Jimmy?"

"She seemed tough but sensible. I suppose she might have sudden emotional patches—like air pockets. You're flying along and without warning the bottom falls out of the sky."

He explained about the meeting with Mr. Costain.

"Psychotic," said Kelly. "Her own drives make the rules,

and the hell with the rest of us. Of course she's never thought that she has any drives—that type never does. There's a reason for everything. I hope the bloody little pansy doesn't drive her too far. She might do anything, absolutely anything. She wouldn't worry about the consequences. She'd blow the whole place up, with us in it, rather than let him move one brick without her permission. Love has passed her by, poor old bitch, and—"

"May I enter your territory, dear colleague?" boomed Dr. Silver from the door.

Kelly smiled, sharp but charming.

"One for your notebooks, Ram," he said. "I've been praying all morning you'd come, and you came. Telekinesis or telepathy? I've got something to show you."

"You have? In fact I was looking for the good Mr. Pibble. Mr. T. has expressed a wish to see him."

"Oho!" said Kelly. "Be a pal, Jimmy, and ask him when I'm going to get my scintillation counter."

"Do no such thing," said Dr. Silver. "Mr. T. needs very precise handling."

"Only Ram knows how to pray to the rain god," said Kelly.

"Perfectly expressed," said Dr. Silver, beaming. "Show me this something, Rue. Your somethings are becoming most interesting."

Like coequal hierarchs of a schismatic church, the two doctors paced down the aisle and turned up a side chapel between two beds; here they bowed their heads over a graph.

Athanasius Thanatos! said part of his mind. Crippen!

The rest of his mind told it, prissily but vainly, to shut up. A man is only a man, it said, even if his name sends shivers down the spines of gossip columnists. Think, it said, of that hotel at—where was it? Mary would remember—not that the Pibbles could afford to stay there, but they'd seen the thing, seen how its drab slab diminished the Aegean sky and its reflection polluted the blue bay. And now the man was maneuvering to build something just as ugly, but five times bigger, on the South Bank.

Athanasius Thanatos! Him!

And what about the Thanatos Disposable Hotel, only a few weeks back so loudly deplored in every responsible paper? A pure despoiler's idea, a quick, cheap prefab shipped in to wherever he could find sun and a beach and a cheap local booze, just to catch the ever-quickening eddies of the tourist mania. He'd boasted to *Time* magazine that any government who asked for a tourist resort one autumn could see it pullulating the next spring. And when the tourist tide receded, all the rooms and equipment could be shipped elsewhere, leaving only the scar tissue of dead cement where the hotel had stood, pocked with a few drain holes. He had publicly rejoiced in the fact that few of the ardent preservationists were likely to be citizens of the countries that actually needed the currency.

And Pibble's long apathy was stirred at the prospect of meeting the man. To allay his shame he glanced at Doll and saw that she was at the teetering point of recovering her composure, and wouldn't welcome chitchat now. So he looked back to the doctors. Both of them were playacting— that is to say, Pibble was aware that their poses would have been different if there'd been no one to watch them. It probably meant nothing; Silver, however impressive, was something of a poseur; and Pibble had seen Rue use almost the same expanded gestures in the Black Boot, during the long campaign to persuade Oenone behind the bar that he really was a spy, just as Pibble really was a policeman. Oenone was never quite convinced, never quite disbelieving, and both Rue and Pibble got steady pleasure out of her wavering faith. Now Rue was teasing Dr. Silver in much the same way. An olive finger shot out and pointed at the chart. Rue gesticulated blandly.

And all around the motionless sleepers dreamed their way down the long slope to the dark. It was an easy ride for them, freewheeling; not the tumble over the cliff, not a slither down agonizing scree; down they glided, dreaming as they went. What dream? Lovely, the waking children had said—but they said that about everything, not counting Marilyn Goddard, whose stepfather had done the Paperham jobs. Odd that Silver should extend his multiple persona to using thieves' cant about so sick and sensational a horror. Pibble shivered. Retirement was softening him, or the atmosphere of the room was unmanning—twenty-something ex-dormice, not long ago capable of summoning up in strangers a freshet of unwonted affection, now lying inert, fed through tubes, evacuating into diapers. Mrs. Dixon-Jones would never bring her ledger up here to harry them about the movement of their bowels. The room was more dismaying than a mortuary, because it was not formaldehyde but some still functioning processes of life that prevented the young flesh from rotting away to reveal the not yet fully hardened bone. How old? Fourteen, fifteen? And already they had retired—or been sacked, if you were a theist. He shivered again.

"Are you all right?" whispered the girl.

Pibble jerked his head toward the door and followed her quietly out.

"It's horrid until you get used to it," she said. "Then you find it sort of restful. Rue put that notice up to stop us from coming and hanging about between the beds."

"How long has he been here?"

"Not long. About three years."

"And Doctor Silver's been here four months, and so's the money."

"That's right."

"So Rue stuck it out for . . . It must have seemed quite long to him. I mean, it's not the sort of setup you expect to appeal to anyone with Rue's brains and drive."

"There aren't a lot of jobs where you can do fundamental research absolutely on your own. Rue says 'colleague' is a dirty word."

"He seems to get along all right with Doctor Silver."

"He was bloody to him at first. Have you been to Whipsnade?"

"No."

"You go in winter. Choose a dismal day and walk up the path from the main gate. There's a pine wood on your right, tall red trunks, quite empty. It looks as though the animals in it must have been taken away for the winter, so you walk on. Then something snags at the corner of your attention, like a bramble catching your skirt, and you look again and it's eyes. Green eyes. Hundreds of them between the trunks. And then you see the notice which says the wood is called Wolf Wood."

"I see what you mean about the eyes. But the wolves have colleagues, don't they?"

"Rue is a lone wolf. Lone, alone. Wolf, like a wolf in Wolf Wood."

"Um. How fundamental is fundamental research?"

"I don't know. Hasn't he told you?"

"No."

"It's just he hates talking to laymen about what he does. But he admires you an awful lot. He brought me to that pub specially to meet you, you know."

"I'm glad I didn't at the time."

"I think what he's doing must be pretty important. I mean you're right—he wouldn't have stuck it here if it wasn't. And before Ram came, when he thought he was going to have to associate a professor at Saint Ursula's with his work, he . . ."

They had begun to whisper outside the door like school-girls agreeing on a lie before facing a teacher with their unfinished project. When the ornate leaf swung open they jerked into aloofness—if Rue didn't like talking about his research, still less would he fancy his girl and his bar crony guessing about it out of earshot. But now he was smiling as he followed Dr. Silver out into the passage, the cheerful smile of the angler home with a full creel. He flung a long arm round Doll's shoulder.

"It's forgivin' ye I am, darlint," he said.

"Begorra," she answered dully.

"Begorra indade!" he cried. "And me being the doctor, it's a cure I have found for your craving to be quoting always. When you go this night to your lone and narrow bed, take with ye a bookeen of the poets that are bad, and never snuff your candle till you have in your heart a hundred lines of balderdash, such as you'd be shamed to let fly from your darling lips."

"Great!" cried Dr. Silver. "The Abbey Theatre! I have bestrode those boards."

"Bestridden,"—corrected Kelly in a sour tone. Even in the Black Boot he didn't like other people elaborating on *his* jokes. Dr. Silver seemed to feel the rebuke, enough to lose his fizz and turn to his secretary.

"Now, Doll," he said. "Let's have that tape transcribed before Mr. T.'s car comes for Mr. Pibble."

"Christ, Jimmy," said Kelly. "What have you done to earn yourself the red carpet treatment?"

"Mr. Pibble represents a breakthrough in biological knowledge unparalleled in this century. Mr. T. is decidedly impressed."

Pibble was surprised to hear how much more respectable his adventure had become, statistically speaking, since the magic phone call. Kelly stopped watching the plump rump of his girl as she walked away.

"All I ask," he said, "is don't persuade the old monkey he's immortal until I've got my scintillation counter and had time to do a couple of biopsies. See you in the pub, mister."

He still sounded as sour as raw rhubarb. Pibble watched with regret as Kelly spun away and shut himself back into his kingdom. It had been a disappointing meeting, curiously strained, but that often happens when two people who know each other well but only in a leisure context meet in what is for one of them a work context. In fact, for a moment when Rue had come out of the ward, he had suddenly reverted to the easygoing Black Boot Kelly, teasing his girl about Eng. lit. And then Dr. Silver had spoiled it, and both doctors had overreacted in a curious way. Never mind. It was unlikely to have any bearing on the Problems of Posey.

"That's a very sound young man," said Silver in his statesman's voice. "Very brilliant and very sound. We are lucky to have him. Now let us walk in the garden and I will try to give you an inkling of what Mr. T. is like and why he is important to us. If we go down the back stairs we may get out unseen and be able to converse in peace. The car will not be here for forty minutes."

He opened a door in the big convex around which the stairs curved, and Pibble found they were on another landing, with a wooden spiral staircase leading down. For the first time he really felt the true nature of the house, the aspirations and assumptions of the people who built it. The change from carved and inlaid panels to cheap stain, from exotic timber to plain deal, was startling. He could sense the ghosts of stunted tweenies who had lugged, up this cruel curve, the coals for the gentlemen's bedrooms.

"If Rue meant anything by his joke about immortality," he said, "I imagine that Mr. Thanatos is supporting your research in the hope that you will find proof that there is life after death."

Dr. Silver stopped with his foot on the top stair.

"I had not realized that you knew my colleague so well," he said. "Did he suggest to Posey that you should come?"

"No. Mrs. Dixon-Jones didn't know I knew him. We just drink together at the Black Boot quite often, and set the universe to rights. He never talks about his work here, or yours, either."

"Ha! I was surprised earlier by how quickly you appreciated the nature of my work. And now you are right about this, too."

He started down the stairs, still talking.

"I have told the good Mr. T. that his is a most unscientific attitude, which I cannot condone, but unfortunately he has been reading books. Many serious researchers who have done good work in my field have also attempted to make this leap. They think they are Einsteins, and on the few grains of evidence that they have collected they try to construct a General Theory of Immortality. . . . Ho! This is too bad!"

He stopped and stared in mock dismay at the final flight of stairs. The workmen had evidently been using the scullery at the bottom as their paint store, and the last few steps as extra shelf space. Tottering columns of paint cans rose from a heap of rags and spirit bottles. There was even a twenty-gallon barrel of turpentine blocking half the door. Once again Pibble was struck by the high quality of materials which Mr. Thanatos and the Ministry of Works were paying for together.

"So we cannot sneak out after all," said Dr. Silver. "No matter."

As they started to climb, Pibble bonked the wall of the stairs with his hand and heard it ring hollow.

"That's ingenious," he said. "One stairwell does for two sets of stairs."

"That architect was some boy," said Dr. Silver. "You saw the lodges by the outer gates? They have their cesspits in the foundations, to save the expense of digging two holes. Would little Mr. Costain want to preserve that, d'you think?"

"Not if he had to live in one of them," said Pibble, amused to find that Dr. Silver had deliberately called his antagonist Costard during the dispute in the passage. Pribble, too. Ah, yes—a touch of the absentminded scientist to lend authenticity to the aura of genius. Silver didn't need it, but it was an engaging vanity. A solid man is all the better for a few ornate flourishes, just as even this monstrous building was to some extent rescued by its efflorescence of decor, whereas the Thanatos hotel on the island had been offensive as much for its starkness as for its bulk. The contrast amused Pibble all the way down the magniloquent stairway.

Mrs. Dixon-Jones came fretfully toward them across the hall. "Marilyn's disappeared," she said. "She's not in any of the usual places. I've asked Simon at the door, and he just said, 'Out.' If she goes to sleep outside, she'll catch pneumonia."

"OK, take it easy, we'll have a scout round. Don't buzz me unless it's important. Mr. T.'s car will be coming in forty minutes; buzz me then."

"Is *he* coming down here?" said Mrs. Dixon-Jones icily.

"Not a hope. He wants to see Mr. Pibble."

"Because he's a policeman?"

"Not any longer," said Pibble.

"But he has a great future in telepathy," said Dr. Silver. "A great future."

"I'm sure he has," said Mrs. Dixon-Jones, thawing into artificial warmth. "Thomas, where's Marilyn?"

"Dunno," drawled a drifting child.

"They could easily find her if they wanted to," complained Mrs. Dixon-Jones. "I'm afraid they don't really get on with her. She had an unfortunate childhood, and it disturbs them."

Unfortunate! thought Pibble. The sly, dark, handsome face of the Paperham murderer drifted into his mind, black eyebrows meeting over the bridge of the nose. Sam something. Sam . . . The child had stopped. Slowly he turned, like flotsam rotating below wharves.

"Inna wood," he said. Into the almost toneless voice had crept a hue of distaste. He began to turn away.

"You do that?" said Dr. Silver, glancing at Pibble from under his thrusting white brows.

"I don't know. I was thinking about the Paperham case."

"Oh, you mustn't do that," snapped Mrs. Dixon-Jones. "It doesn't do any good to anyone."

"But it might this time," said Dr. Silver. "We'll walk up to the wood and practice our scoutcraft."

"And I'll try to think pleasant thoughts," said Pibble.

"Please do," said Mrs. Dixon-Jones. "They have so little time, you know."

She turned and strutted back toward her office, head high.

"That's a very good woman indeed," sighed Dr. Silver. "They're the worst sort."

It was impossible to tell which parts of this statement were ironic, if any. A different point struck Pibble as they reached the door.

"Nobody seems to have inquired whether *I* want to see Mr. Thanatos," he said with deliberate stuffiness. Dr. Silver guffawed.

"Everybody wants to see Mr. Thanatos," he said. "It is one of the axioms of life. Look in your heart and you will know it is true."

"I'm afraid so," said Pibble.

3

Outside the house Pibble shivered again, but this time with ordinary cold. He wished he'd brought his overcoat; the apparent mildness of the morning, compared to the last icy fortnight, had turned out to be mere darkness, dismal after the kindly warmth of the house. He wondered what it cost to keep that huge space heated for its lizard-blooded inmates. The frightened child had even complained that it was too hot—or perhaps the heat was part of the nightmare. That dreary basement in Paperham, familiar four years ago from hundreds of gritty photographs, had been just the milieu for a paraffin stove to spill and flare. Had Sam . . . Sam —never mind now—put the blaze out and saved the children's lives, presenting an ironic balance sheet to moral auditors?

Dr. Silver, silent, led him slantwise across the weedy gravel, away from the drive, into the dozen tangled acres which the obstinacy of the Sospice blood had preserved from being smothered by rank upon rank of brick, bow-windowed, slate-roofed villas. Would Mr. Thanatos' mad, selfish charity extend to leveling the tussocks of the lawn, and set the rakes going again where this year's leaf fall lay fox-colored on the blackish slime of last year's? The garden was a long oval, following the ridge of the hill and covering the top quarter of its western slope. Dr. Silver stopped on a terrace constructed to take advantage of what must once have been a rural vista. In front of him from suckers the rose bed had grown to a savage barrier of briers, and behind him a row of Irish yews stood all uncorseted.

Dr. Silver looked at his watch, sighed, and took a black cigar from the breast pocket of his dustcoat. "You smoke?"

"No, thanks."

As he trimmed and prodded the poisonous-looking thing, he began to talk, so quietly that Pibble felt like a contact who has met his spy in the deserted park of a foreign capital.

"I want to tell you about Thanassi," he said. "We call him Mr. T. here, so that outsiders don't cotton on. Doll slipped up when she took that call this morning. It was Posey's notion—she fixed it with Thanassi before I flew in. In fact she told him she wouldn't have me here if there was going to be any publicity about him and the McNair. You mightn't think it from what you read, but he's pretty damned good at keeping his affairs quiet if he feels like it. It's not all Van Goghs at Sotheby's and fancy-dress splurges on the Grand Canal. I'm going to tell you how I first met him, because that'll give you some notion what kind of guy he is.

"I was sitting by the yacht basin in Iráklion wondering where my next drach was coming from. I'd had a job at the hospital, but the cops had jumped on me because I didn't have a work permit, and the reason I didn't have a work permit was that I'd been in Katanga and all my papers had gone up in smoke, so I was using a passport which was, well, not so good, because I happen to be not very popular with my own government. I was OK with the local police, because their captain had a bitch of a wife who'd got him pretty near impotent, and then he'd nigh on killed himself experimenting with aphrodisiacs, and then he'd come to me because he reckoned that a doctor without a passport would tell him secrets which respectable doctors keep to themselves, and I coaxed him round to trying a course of psychoanalysis. I could have spun that out another couple of months, and I was getting one free meal a week from a bar where I was massaging the proprietor's father's spine, but I was broke until charter flights began. Any fool can make a living then, but this was a month too early.

"So I sat and waited for my free meal, pretty damned depressed, and watched a bunch of tourists come cackling down the quay. They stopped right opposite the bar and a Scandinavian-looking dolly, all thigh and teeth, came over and asked if she could take my photograph. Pidgin Greek, but I don't speak it much better myself. I told her I would charge a small fee, and when she understood she got angry and went back to the others. I was cursing myself, because she might have tipped me if I hadn't asked, when a thug in a chauffeur's rig came over. I thought trouble until I saw he had a silver jug and a tumbler, and then I looked at the tourists properly and recognized the big one with the red face, so I let the chauffeur pour me a big Bloody Mary, and I stood up and said, 'Zeto o thanatos,' which means 'Long live death,' and drank his health. Then he came over himself and asked me what I meant, apart from politeness, and I told him that as I was a doctor my trade was death. He took me a sight more seriously than I meant; but he went back to his party and spoke to them, and they went on down the quay while he came and sat at my table with the jug and another tumbler. We drank, and talked of this and that, including my own troubles, and after a bit the chauffeur came back with a couple of bottles of champagne and a cold roast duck. We drank all that champagne and we ate the duck in our fingers and threw the bones in the harbor. We went on talking. I liked him. I was just thinking it was a bit of a sod this happening on a day when I was due to get a free meal anyway, when he asked if I'd like to come and be his personal physician for a bit. I turned him down, which I'd not have done sober. I told him the truth, which was that I was sick of orthodox doctoring and all I wanted was to get to London and research into the telepathic powers of cathypnic children.

"Well, that meant another hour of talk while I explained about the McNair and we drank Costa's filthy coffee. About quarter to four he paid for the coffee, tipped Costa a bit over the odds, but not much, said 'So long' to me, and walked off. I watched him sail out of the harbor dressed in his swimming trunks and playing backgammon with the Swede. But for the champagne, I thought, I'd have been on that boat. I just sat there. Five o'clock my police captain patient came and fetched me in his private car and took me up to the mayor's office, where he and the mayor helped me fill in the papers for a new passport. After that we drank ouzo for a bit and I went back to the bar. Costa shooed a couple of sailors out of my table, and brought me the best food on his menu and a bottle of wine. No payment. He told me to come back to lunch next day, and said that he was so grateful for the improvement to his father's spine that now I could have two free meals a day. My passport came back from Athens inside a week, and by then I'd found that my credit was good all over Iráklion.

"Two weeks later I was woken by the chauffeur thug with my breakfast. We drove round town and paid my debts, went to the British consulate and got my visa. I'd already found a greasy young woman who didn't feel sick at the idea of going with the police captain, so I dropped in for a final crash session with my patient. A month before he'd have locked me up for what I told him about him and his wife, but I straightened him out and told him where to find the girl. Then we drove to the airport and the thug flew me to London in a twelve-seater jet. No trouble with those bastards in Immigration. Thanassi was in Canada, but the chauffeur drove me down here. The post was waiting for me, with a budget bigger than the Foundation's whole income in the last five years."

"You knew Mrs. Dixon-Jones already."

Dr. Silver gave him the same sharp stare as he had in the hall.

"Somebody must have told you about the telepathy," said Pibble, "and I don't think it's common medical gossip. She has some Minoan-looking scraps on her mantelpiece."

"I know the guy who makes them. Sure, they're fakes, but they're good fakes. Don't tell Posey."

"I suppose the point of your story is that Mr. Thanatos is unpredictable, but you know how to handle him."

"Crude terms, Mr. Pibble, crude terms. The other point is that he is very powerful."

"Why does he want to see me?"

"Aha! I fear I may have oversold you. We are his hobby, and he is not a patient man. But I was much cheered by that episode in the hall just now."

"Oughtn't we to go and look in the wood?"

"Sure," said Dr. Silver, and moved on toward where the terrace disappeared into a tunnel of trees.

"I'm not certain that I want to get involved with any of this," said Pibble, awkwardly trying to match his step to the doctor's big stride.

"Makes you uncomfortable?" said Dr. Silver sympathetically.

Pibble shrugged. It wasn't the right word, but what was?

"I, too, am not hardened to the children's fate," said Dr. Silver. "I think no one here is, which is extraordinary in a charitable organization."

"What about Rue?"

"Perhaps. And yet he is likely to do most for them in the end."

"It's not only the children," said Pibble. "At least not like that."

"Aha! You feel I am exploiting them for my own purposes?"

"Well . . ."

"I am! I am!" cried Dr. Silver, beating his breast with a generous *mea culpa* gesture and almost laughing with pleasure. "But from my wicked selfishness spring all sorts of fringe benefits. The children are more comfortable and better fed. They will live a few months longer. Rue may even cure them with his scintillation counter. Posey is very unhappy about the whole shoot. She sent for you?"

Something about the long self-revelation had warned Pibble that he would be expected to offer some revelation in exchange, so he was ready for this tiny trap.

"Not exactly," he said. "My wife asked me to come."

"Of course, of course. Fund raising, wasn't it? But that'll have to wait. This is going to be a truly rewarding adventure for you, both intellectually and financially. Doesn't it grip you, man?"

"I'd like to think about it," said Pibble. A thought struck him: had Mary known about the rush of money to the McNair, and sensed a job in the offing? No. Impossible.

"It all seems to be falling very pat," he said.

"But that's the point!" cried Dr. Silver. "The kids respond to you like no one else! How many significant incidents have you figured in already this morning?"

Bip. Bip. Bip, went an unfamiliar bird, or grasshopper.

"One and two halves," said Pibble. "But I can think of rational explanations for all of them."

"Hell!" said Dr. Silver. "I told Posey not to call me."

He pulled a gadget like a fountain pen from his breast pocket. *Bip. Bip. Bip,* it sang.

"Don't bother about me," said Pibble. "I'll go and see if I can find Marilyn in the wood. If she's there, it might jack one of the halves up to a whole."

Dr. Silver laughed and tossed his horrible cigar, half-smoked, down the slope into what had once been an orchard.

"Do that!" he said. "And here, take this damned thing, so we can call you when the car comes. It's important that you see him, vital—and you'd be a fool not to. He's a five-star attraction. So long."

He was already striding off, heavy and masterful, while Pibble settled the little receiver into his pocket. *Bip. Bip Bip,* it creaked forlornly. That was an odd episode, nothing much said directly, but Pibble felt as though he had only just withstood the blandishments of a door-to-door salesman on the threshold of his soul. The white dustcoat flickered at the far end of the terrace, as though the scene had been set for a fraudulent photograph of a ghost, then vanished. On a police pension there'd be no more holidays in the Aegean, however cheaply packaged. He turned gloomily into the tunnel under the trees. *Bip. Bip. Bip,* creaked the cricket in his pocket.

It was barely a wood. The darkness at the entrance came from overarching hollies, and elsewhere a thick undergrowth of evergreens spread below the boughs of elderly elms. A widish mossy path led up the middle toward a dim building near the garden's outer wall, but as Pibble started along it his eye was caught by a footprint in a patch of mud at the entrance to a side path. A child's footprint. No water lay in the deep heel mark, though the laurels were sodden with the night's rain. This was real detecting. He turned along the side path, more depressed than ever.

Dowsing, yes. Precognition, no. The former felt right and limited, but the latter burst the fabric of logic. Between these poles Pibble had always ranged, on grounds as much aesthetic as rational, all the rest of paranormalia—ghosts, poltergeists, Ouija boards, telepathy, shamanism, faith healing, mediums, and garbled telegraphese from the Great Beyond—but his mild interest had been wholly academic. One dawn, years ago, he had been woken in his own room, in his own bed, by a gnatlike voice piping in his ear, "My name is [indistinguishable]. I have come down to earth to tell you . . ." And Pibble's mind had shouted "Why *me?*" just as his heart had given one thump of panic which had truly woken him to his own room and bed, all slightly different from the ones of his dream waking. But even fully awake he had lain sweating with the nightmare of being *chosen*, rigid with that total stillness of muscle which must be a legacy from the generations when ur-man needed to cower from his fanged hunters.

And he was strangely frightened now, in a sane and waking fashion. He was going to be sucked in, to become an exhibit, a phenomenon, a *thing*. Men (oh, distinguished and clever men) would come to inspect him, not because he was Jimmy Pibble, minor expert in beer and murder and the treatment of ailing lawns, but because he had this irrelevant knack, this kink. As though he were to open his eyes one morning and find a circle of serious medicos bending over him to inspect the odd growth that his forehead had sprouted in the night. He'd have opened three eyes. No question of "Bad luck, Jimmy!" No "How do you feel, old man?" Only "Please close the two lower organs, Mr. Pibble. Now you observe, gentlemen . . ."

Bip . . . and then no more. Dr. Silver had reached the switchboard.

Pibble pushed on along the narrow windings, drenched each time he had to ease a laurel branch aside to let him through. A stream rattled sideways out of green gloom and under a stone bridge, very artificial-rural. It must be fed by a real spring, but felt as though there were an electric pump at the lower end, ceaselessly recirculating the same water. Along this path, once, chaperoned damsels had glided beside potential husbands; the bends and the screening evergreens would let them out of sight for one protestation, one blush, and then propriety again. Now it would be a pig of a place to search for a child who had simply crawled off the path under the black branches. The path looped back at last to a clearing round the building he'd seen from the entrance, and by the time he reached it he hadn't seen another footprint: Marilyn must have done just that.

Mr. Costain was in the clearing, hunched over a large, old-fashioned camera. Pibble coughed, and Mr. Costain flashed him a look which said, "I'm within my rights." The shutter clicked, and the photographer skipped to a new position and hunched again.

"I'm sorry," said Pibble, "but have you seen a sleeping child? Or one just wandering about?"

Mr. Costain took another picture.

"We're only just in time," he said.

"It looks in very good condition."

"Great bricklaying," said Mr. Costain. "Truly great."

A wincing and tentative patch of sunlight shone through the elm boughs. At once Mr. Costain darted in like a dragonfly, poised his lens about two feet from the brick, flashed a light meter, fiddled with the shutter, poised again, and clicked. Pibble remembered the glowing gold closeup of a pillar at Sunium with which Mary liked to start her living room odysseys.

"I suppose it's a good deal older than the house," he said.

"No no no no," fluted Mr. Costain. "Your eighteenth-century landowner might amuse himself by putting a Neo-Gothic fal-lal in his grounds, but he had the sense to *live* Palladian. Old Peter Sospice turned the idea inside out, though the house isn't exactly Gothic—in fact it isn't exactly anything, which gives it its weird charm, don't you agree? But he insisted on very rigid classical for his garden ornaments. *This* started as an exact model of the Colosseum at a scale of one in ten, but it gave his wife nightmares about tiny gladiators coming to get her"—Mr. Costain gave a freakish giggle—"so he pulled it down and stuck this up instead. I should think it's one of the ten ugliest old buildings in South London, wouldn't you? Of course they didn't have the resources for uglification that modern architects command. On the other hand, it's great bricklaying—I assure you of that. They must have had men over from Battersea to do it."

Pibble looked at the squat curve of blank brick and the flabby dome. Between the two a line of letters ran. RS MORTIS MORTEM MORTI NISI MORTE DEDI was all he could read.

"It's a mausoleum, isn't it?" he said.

"Yes. I take it you're some kind of lawyer."

"No. Why?"

"I saw you outside that harridan's office, didn't I?"

"Yes."

"I imagined they'd started hiring professional help to fight us off."

"If they have, I'm not it. I came about a personal matter, but I had some time to spare so I said I'd look for this missing child. There's a theory she might be sleeping in the wood, and I found a footprint back there."

"She's round the other side," said Mr. Costain, jerking his head toward the west of the mausoleum.

"Thanks," said Pibble, starting off.

"Come back a moment."

"They say she'll catch pneumonia."

"I wrapped her up in my cloak. She'll do for another five minutes. Just tell me, if you know, what's going on down there. Why are they all so rabid?"

"Rabid?" Pibble was unable to conceal his surprise that Mr. Costain should apply the adjective to anyone else.

"The woman is psychotic—I think that's the jargon. That Arab I talked to this morning seemed a reasonable type, but he took up a very extreme position—quite unnecessarily so. Our local preservation group are sensible and businesslike—much more so than most. But from the very beginning all the officials at the McNair fought like maniacs against any suggestions at all. The Ministry was unusually generous about the repair grant, largely thanks to my efforts—it's not at all the type of place that everybody hankers to see preserved, don't you agree? But that seemed to make them more furious still."

"When did these negotiations start?"

"Almost a year ago."

"I don't know much about it, but I think there are two things. The obvious one is that until four months ago the Foundation was desperately poor, and hated the idea of spending anything except on the children. Then, Dr. Silver told you, they had a windfall in the shape of a very rich man who became interested in cathypnics. The other thing is vaguer, but you must have come across setups where worthy people have been struggling along against difficulties for so long that they've become used to their own discomforts and react fiercely against having them changed. And you've got to remember that the children really do have a strong emotional appeal which doesn't wear off. To outsiders the staff's attitude to them might look, well, rabidly overprotective."

"But why *here?*" exclaimed Mr. Costain, pointing westward between the tree trunks. "D'you realize that there isn't a decent open space within two miles in any direction. I sometimes imagine a hand coming out of the clouds holding a vast aerosol and simply spraying on these grisly hutches and garish, soulless high streets. This could be a center, a smaller version of Kenwood, a public park and garden with a gallery of Victoriana in it. It's badly needed. And surely the children would be much better off out in a clean little modern prison somewhere in the country. I cannot see how the welfare of forty or fifty morons can outweigh the needs of tens of thousands of normal citizens."

Pibble felt it was not an equation he'd care to cancel out.

"Who does the place actually belong to?" he said.

"Trustees. They seem to be local bigwigs and lawyers from London."

"Are they rabid, too?"

"They were hell at first. The harridan had them completely under her thumb. And then, just before it all built up to a really big row, they suddenly caved in."

"They hate the idea of publicity," said Pibble. "For the children's sake, that is. And I think they're right about it— I mean it may be overprotective but I don't think it's irrational."

Mr. Costain concertinaed the lens of his camera back into the body and shut the lid with a snap.

"I'll go and do the grotto while this light lasts," he said. "I'll come back for my cloak if you like. I couldn't wake her, so you may need a stretcher party."

He sounded suddenly very gruff and abrupt, as though his care for the child might be construed as the irrational over-protectiveness that the staff were guilty of. Pibble decided he was simply shy—shy of the danger of being caught in a direct emotional appeal, unmitigated by aesthetic theory or the scholarship of London bricklaying.

"I'll see if I can wake her," said Pibble.

On the westward side of the mausoleum a monstrous porch sprouted; its luxuriant stonework, of a blotchy yellow-ish hue, made it look like a heavy fungus growing from the curve of a rotten tree trunk. Slumped in its shelter, wrapped in mottled tweed, a girl slept. She looked no different from any of the others.

When Pibble knelt on the flagstones and blew softly in her ear she stirred and mumbled; he blew harder and she opened her eyes, irises a pale cloudy green with the cathypnic ring very marked, the color of laurel leaves.

"Tain't fair," she said in the usual slow whine.

"The man lent you his coat," said Pibble. "Now he wants it back."

"Ta," said Marilyn.

Pibble eased the cloak off her and handed it to Mr. Costain, who said, "Thanks. You'll cope now?" and darted off.

"We must go back to the house, Marilyn," said Pibble.

"Stay here."

"But you'll get cold."

"Cold 'ands, warm 'eart."

Yes, she was very different from the others. She said it without smiling. Pibble, awkward and stiff with her as he was with normal children, hesitated.

"All right," he said. "We'll stay here for a little, then go down."

"Lovely," she breathed, and her eyelids began to droop. Pibble seized her by the wrists like a lover.

"Hey!" he said. "You mustn't go to sleep. That's not fair."

He dragged her into a sitting position and let her flop against the porch wall. She seemed unsurprised.

"Game," she said.

What game does one play with a nine-year-old child with the intelligence of a three-year-old? Pibble groped in his pocket, found sixpence, put his hands behind him, then held them forward with the coin tight in the left fist.

"Which hand?" he said.

A slow finger came up and touched chill against the back of his left hand.

"Pennies," she said.

Pibble blinked and showed her that she was right, but she didn't smile. She could have seen what he'd brought out of his pocket—he wasn't sure. The movement had been too trivial to remember. This time he did the same trick with his penknife, taking care to hide it all the way.

"Sharp," she said as she touched the hand that held it.

A loose button he'd been carrying around.

"Button."

The nut from the lawn mower which he was trying to match every time he passed an ironmonger.

"Hole in it."

Nothing, then—but think, Pibble, think of the burnished horse chestnut in your right palm, fresh-fallen, cold and shiny to the touch, mottled with dark ripples, white pith still filming the pale patch at the bottom where it grew from its cushioning husk.

"Conker."

He relaxed the effort of imagination.

"Not there."

He opened both hands, empty, to show her she was right and smiled at her. She was terrified.

The facial movements of cathypnics are very slight and inevitably difficult to interpret through the mask of fat, but he had been staring, thoughtlessly astounded, at the stodgy and unresponsive features and so actually perceived the change. Now he could see the whole round of her irises, so wide had she opened the drowsy lids, and that clue made him see how the curve of her cheeks had hardened and how her lips had become yet paler.

"I won't hurt you," he said gently. "It's only a game."

"Good day," she whispered.

"Yes, but it's not very warm. Let's go down to the house now. The exercise will do you good."

"Good day for Posey."

"Oh."

"Poor Posey."

"She'll be glad to see you. She doesn't know where you are. She asked me to look for you."

"Goin' upstairs."

Bip. Bip. Bip.

"They're calling me, Marilyn. We must go now. I'll help you up."

She looked slowly at his outstretched hand and rolled herself away, onto all fours, then used a barley-sugar-shaped pillar to haul herself upright. There she looked at him again, still so tense with terror that he stepped away from her, out of the porch into the pithless sun. After all, it would be no trouble to hurry down to the house and tell Mrs. Dixon-Jones where he'd left her—one responsibility less, in fact. But the girl maundered out after him. She wasn't frightened of *him*, he guessed—simply floating on a tide of fright which the guessing game had released. Why? Had Sam . . . ?

Into his mind slid a picture, a dismal interior scene, a basement, stuffy but cold and smelling of damp dirt; a pregnant blonde held a pasty babe to her breast; on the worn mock-parquet linoleum knelt a boy who piled three cotton spools into a tower, knocked them across the floor with a wooden spoon, fetched them, piled the tower again . . . and on the bed sat a dark, sly, handsome man holding out his two fists to a small girl, and her fat hand came slowly up to touch the back of one of his, and her lips moved. Sam would have found out her gift. There are few games you can play with a child like that, few objects to play with in a room like that. He was superstitious—hadn't he invented his own elaborate diabolism on a basis of pulp astrology? But what was frightening? Had he punished her when she was wrong, as she'd been wrong over the conker? Or . . . If the brat could tell him what was in his fist, she could tell him how his luck would go with the latest prim matron who'd caught his fancy, tell him when to start the hunt, which was a good day. . . .

Bip. Bip. Bip.

Today was a good day for Posey. She was "going upstairs."

Something with the chill of autumn touched his hand.

"Come on," drawled Marilyn.

Still she did not smile, and neither did he. He took her offered fist and they walked in silence down the mossy path toward the house, confident in the communion of terror.

The Rolls was long enough to hold a coffin, but it had been painted peacock blue. Tinted windows hid its innards, secretive against the flaunting coachwork, an effect like sunglasses on a teen-age idol. A chauffeur in peacock blue livery marched up the slope and saluted.

"Mr. Pibble."

"That's me."

He was blond, and had the look of a killer, but he turned deferentially, led the way back to the car, and opened a door into a vision of lush living.

"I must find someone to take charge of Marilyn," said Pibble.

"Please hurry, sir." It was an order.

"Three minutes."

Pibble dragged Marilyn to the door. He had to open it for himself this time, and inside he found the two doorkeepers sitting back to back on the floor, like bookends waiting for a library; they turned their heads away as he pulled Marilyn in. Hustling her across the hall and along the corridor was like driving a car with the brakes on, and after all he found Mrs. Dixon-Jones snapping too vigorously into a telephone to be interrupted. She managed a moment, while the fellow at the far end was making some unappeasing excuse for his inadequacies, to put her hand over the mouthpiece and say, "Go to the nursery, darling. Find Ivan." But before Marilyn had drifted, without any farewell, from the door she was snapping at her enemy again. Pibble decided he could keep the peacock storm trooper waiting one more minute, but to save time he took the electric gadget, still bipping, out of his pocket and put it on the mantelpiece. Mrs. Dixon-Jones had modulated into a coda of chill disgust, so he picked up a tear bottle and compared it mentally with Mary's. It looked several degrees more plausible. What he was going to say seemed more absurd with every wasted second. Mrs. Dixon-Jones said, "See that it doesn't happen again," and put the receiver down. He turned with the tear bottle still in his hand.

"They're all fake," she said. "But don't tell Ram—he found them for me."

Perhaps it was the exhilaration of browbeating an enemy

that now made her sound relaxed and pleased.

"There's Doctor Silver's bipper," said Pibble.

"Thank you. And thank you for finding Marilyn. Where was she?"

"Sleeping by the mausoleum. The next bit sounds like complete nonsense, and I haven't time to explain it, but she seems to think, as far as I can make out, that you are in some sort of personal danger."

"Me! Oh, that's stupid. The only person in any danger round here is that little rat Costain. You can never be sure you really understand what they're saying."

"I know. I'm not sure. I'll tell you this afternoon. Mr. Costain found her, incidentally, and wrapped her up in his cape."

"It isn't fair!" said Mrs. Dixon-Jones.

"See you later," said Pibble.

"Sorry," he said ten seconds later as he scrambled through the flunky-held door of the car; it contained chairs, not bench seats, and by the time Pibble had settled into the cradling black leather and discovered that the chair swiveled on its central column, the car was moving. His last glimpse of the sane world—already suffering the alienation effect of the sepia-colored glass—was of Mr. Costain standing open-mouthed among the rhododendrons.

"May I suggest you fasten your seat belt, sir?" said a voice from the ceiling. It was another order, so Pibble fiddled with silk straps; the buckle was platinum, decorated with a Greek theta in sapphires. Secure, he began to gaze in wonder at the minuscule luxury of the interior: white carpet, black leather, silver fittings, all costly but severe and at the same time slightly kinky. He spun his chair round, for the fun of it, and ended facing a rear corner where hung the selfsame snow scene by Sisley that he had given Mary the Christmas before

73

last, though naturally Mr. Thanatos could afford a more expensive reproduction. No, he could afford the real thing. Crippen, that would make a hole in his no-claim bonus if it were nicked!

Pibble swung back and was surprised to see how far they'd come, how fast this cassette of high life was being whisked through the dreary townlands south of the Thames. The windows must be double, so little of the flurry of other traffic reached him, but an even greater luxury was the manner in which the blond thug drove. The man was hurrying, floating his large machine through the other traffic, picking gaps which looked about right for a mini, judging the run of the lights with uncanny cunning but when he got it wrong braking and moving away with such smoothness that, had Pibble shut his eyes, he would not have been sure that the car had ever stopped. The effect was as if he were seated in a peacock blue electric iron, with which some celestial housewife was placidly smoothing out the creased traffic. Hello! Wrong turn! No, of course, they were mucking about with the Old Kent Road again, but by turning down here and left at . . . Yes, this thug was as far superior to a good police driver as a good police driver is to your average rush-hour tachypath.

The necks of flunkies are unnerving, ever more expressionless than the drilled face muscles, more noncommittal than the toneless sirring. But up and down that poised column raced the electric pulses which commanded toe and finger to cradle one insignificant ex-detective through these cut-above-slums as though he were a fresh-picked, morning-scented virgin being wafted to an emperor's bed. Yet the guy had opinions, preferences: somewhere above the shaved neck a few braincells must be linked together in a fashion which composed a picture of the passenger, elderly and dispirited, not a nonentity only by the fact of Athanasius Thanatos being momentarily interested in him, made visible, so to speak, like a rock on the moon by the shadow which the sun forces it to cast.

Not a blond bristle stirred on the pale column; no finger rose to ease the itch of his scrutiny. That, curiously, was the point at which Dr. Silver scratched himself so vigorously. Pibble fell to wondering whether it was the blondness which was offensive, an instinctive anti-Aryanism in himself. If the neck had been Silver's color—and it was not all that different, given the whole spectrum—would he have disliked it so much? Surely not. Or take the halfway house of Rue Kelly's skin, for Rue was a sour Celt, black Irish . . . And Silver had bestrode the boards of the Abbey Theatre, so he was black Irish in a different way, with his reference to the dumbest doll in Dublin. . . .

Far down the corridors of his mind the words began to reverberate and acquire a different meaning, like the distant call of ushers in the law courts which change their shape as they echo along Gothic passages but can be interpreted back into their meaning by anyone familiar with legal ritual.

Black Irish was dead, surely. But Silver wore fake glasses; spoke of the Paperham jobs, and like Pibble put one immediate meaning on the ambiguous word "copper"; in Crete he sold fake antiques to tourists; he created an image of vagueness by deliberately getting people's names wrong on first meeting them; exploited a hypnotic personality, so that strangers felt an impulse to rely on him. . . . Pibble tried to remember about the Black Irish known to the Yard, but only saw vague stirrings in the mists of his memory, like Turner's Polyphemus.

He leaned forward and rapped on the glass partition between him and the nape. The man's voice answered from the ceiling.

"If you open the panel to your left, sir, and press the second switch from the left, you will be able to speak to me."

The panel fitted like the lid of a jewel box, and under it lay a rank of switches and a rank of ivory knobs with symbols on them. Pibble clicked the second switch.

"Speak in your normal voice, sir."

"I know we're in a hurry, but I've just thought of a point which I ought to check before I meet Mr. Thanatos. Can you stop at a phonebox?"

"Would you please pull the button third from the right, sir?"

The button had a picture of a telephone on it; at Pibble's touch a hitherto invisible panel beside the switch console flopped open and a thin handset slid out and offered itself to him. There was no dial.

"Tell the girl the number you want, sir. You may experience a degree of fading between tall buildings, but if you have trouble I will stop where the reception seems adequate."

"We'll see," said Pibble. He flicked the switch up to return himself to his soundproof world, picked the handset off its cradle, spoke, waited, told the girl at the Yard the extension he wanted, waited. . . .

"Bradshaw," said the voice.

"Brad, this is Jimmy Pibble. Sorry to bother you."

"Balls, Jimmy. It's good to hear your voice. How are you doing?"

"So-so. I haven't really sorted myself out yet. Freedom's nice, but boring. I miss you all."

"Whereas office work is nasty but boring. What can I do for you?"

"Well, Mary's trapped me into giving a talk to one of her lots of ladies. It's supposed to be about role-playing the criminal mind. There's a couple of things I wanted to check on."

"Fire away."

"What became of Black Irish?"

"Died in Katanga."

"Are you sure? Sorry, I mean . . ."

"Came through Interpol. Someone saw the body. You think he's still alive?"

"I just didn't know he was dead. He was a big fellow, Irish background, wasn't he? Hawk-faced, very strong personality, specialized in roles with real class, doctors, priests, archaeologists . . ."

"Jimmy?"

"Still here. This is a funny line."

"What are you playing at?"

"Eh?"

"Now look here; you've come across some villain in the same line of business, haven't you? If you were giving a lecture, the thing you'd have started from would be the Southward Islands."

"I was coming to that," said Pibble, hoping that his gulp sounded like an effect of the erratic line. "I wanted to clear the other stuff up first. I can only remember bits of it. Give me a quick run-through."

"Korean war helped the Colonial Office to hush it up. We sent out a duke to govern the islands. Local resistance group spotted that he looked something like your fellow—Goldsmith he called himself then, or was it Irons? No, it was Nicholl. . . . Kidnapped the duke during a stopover in Rio, caught him as he went into a brothel, I believe, and Nicholl walked out half an hour later wearing his clothes. Caught the plane, came down the gangway, cock-hatted and spurred, ran the islands better than they'd been run for years. Then skipped. Someone in the liberation movement peached on him, I think. Islanders petitioned for his return, anyway."

"That's fine."

"He didn't get away with much loot—never did, I believe. He had nerve. There's a story he spent several weeks at Saint Eustace's, mostly in the operating room, even did a few ops himself. When they got on to him he skipped, and about three months later somebody noticed something familiar about the padre who was burying their failures at the cemetery next door. We had him inside twice in England, and I should think he knew what a few foreign cells looked like. That all?"

"Not quite. Can you remember whether the Paperham murderer had a good luck piece?"

"Wow, that's a nasty one for your old ladies. What do you mean?"

"Well, he had a weird homemade religion, didn't he? Diabolist, vaguely. Did he have any sort of object, or possibly some animal or person, which he consulted, like an oracle, to tell him the right time to start laying for his next victim? Something like that?"

"Can't help you much. There was something, Ned Callow told me, but Gorton was damned cagey about it and it didn't affect the case. Ned thought it was a cat. I think I remember a newspaper cutting about Gorton having a cat as his familiar, but the writer probably got it from Ned. There wasn't a cat in the basement, anyway, or in any of the other flats, as far as I can remember. OK?"

"Fine. Thanks. That's all."

"Jimmy, you'll take it quiet, won't you? I've been a long time in this hole, long enough to see a lot of good men given the push for bad reasons, some of them worse than yours, mate. I've seen them get jobs with private agencies, run into something that was our business, and try to keep it to themselves. Now listen—the people here who know you know you were hard done by. They matter; the other creeps don't. You won't prove anything to either lot if you try thief-taking on your own account."

"I wouldn't try. I'm thinking of getting a job helping a doctor with research into the intelligence of mental defectives."

"Sounds just like old times. So long."

Pibble's thanks were spoken to the dial tone. The girl's voice broke in and asked him if he wanted another number. He said no, put the handset back on the cradle, pushed the ivory button, and watched the contraption glide into its nest and the lid click shut. Brad's a good man, he thought—so the hell with him. You can cultivate a stern and fastidious morality if you sit all day in your gleaming basement surrounded by files and microfilm and computerized memory banks whose function is to provide you with answers. Naturally you treat every question as though there were an answer to it; you are never asked the sort of question which leaves you with nothing but an option between wrong answers, a choice of betrayals.

He relaxed against the sexy leather and raked at his shin with the slow, unconscious strokes which so infuriated Mary. Role Playing and the Criminal Mind! Crippen, if he'd really been preparing a lecture on it, he couldn't have chosen a better specimen. Goldsmith, Irons, Nicholl, and now Silver. Presumably he'd called himself Steele at some point, or even Copper. Michael O'Lybdenum? T'ung Sten, the Chinese acupuncturist? Sheikh Al Umi n'Um? Pibble wondered how he had once passed himself off as an English duke and was now so convincingly Levantine. It cannot be done for more than a day with makeup and stains always show—still the aristocracy has seen some swarthy members in its day. He was convinced it was the same man, not only because of the name; he felt proud to have met him—if your idol has feet of clay, it is some compensation that they have been modeled by a master hand.

There was that Californian who had spent ten years working his way though half the hospitals of the state on forged credentials, diagnosing and healing and operating, never for more than a few months' salary at a time. It is a sort of madness, an obsession with authority, a yen to be your own father figure; the need to make money in types such as Silver is very secondary. Pibble wondered whether something had happened in Katanga to shake his nerve and reduce him to the role of olive-skinned antique shark on the unprepossessing quay at Iráklion. Though even there he had the role of Great Lover to play, and perhaps the color was an asset, a thrill for spiky widows relaxing in the notorious Mediterranean air. You couldn't imagine Mrs. Dixon-Jones babbling secrets about her charges to every chance-met pot seller; and she had drawn Pibble's attention to the link between her Cretan knickknacks and the head of paranormal research with a curious air of pride and pleasure. Still, when Silver turned up at the McNair, trailing clouds of money . . . His story about meeting Mr. Thanatos was probably true; no point in lying when Pibble would be able to check in a couple of hours; so he must have used his nugget of knowledge with skill and nerve—though presumably a professional con man makes it his business to know the foibles as well as the movements of every millionaire in the Med.

So poor Posey. The money was useful, the man who brought it a fraud. Lover or no, she must have cottoned on to that. And being a very good woman indeed—the worst sort—she had refused to shut her eyes to the fraud. To judge by the scrap of tape that had so irritated Silver, she'd only recently screwed herself up to action and asked Rue Kelly what she should do. Alas, Rue was not the type to shoulder responsibilities other than his own; in fact one of the pleasing things about him was his ability to keep his life compartmented, so that you never felt, laughing in the Black Boot, that he was about to borrow money off you or sour the easy time with tales of domestic intransigence.

Then she'd snatched at a man of straw, old Pibble. Alas again, George Harrowby and Fancy Phillips had guessed his trade as he came through the door, and their whining intuitions were on the tape which went straight up to Silver. The moment she learned that, she tried to send him packing. But then Silver had barged in and hired him. Poor Posey.

No. Actually the morning had run very well for her all of a sudden. She had got her affairs to a sort of balance. She had not needed to betray her lover to get a genuine crime fighter onto the staff—and a conveniently spineless one, she must have reckoned. The money would continue to come in, but Silver would have to watch his step.

Pibble suddenly grinned at the notion of Rue Kelly working with a fake colleague. That's what the scene in the ward had been about. Pibble had stood in for Oenone, while Rue tried to persuade him that Silver was a real medico. And the curious little episode outside the ward door—Rue had tried to shut Silver up as he started to boast about his prowess on the boards, and Silver had taken the warning, and added a little unnecessary encomium on Rue's "soundness." So it was conceivable that there was something between them. Could Rue's expensive equipment—scintillation counters and such—be going to arrive in empty crates? It didn't seem a likely move for an ambitious man, who had stuck the McNair for two and a half years for the sake of his research. No. More likely Rue wanted to prolong the joke of a secret revenge on his properly qualified colleagues, by working with a fake one, just as good as them. That was a relief.

Anyway, what should Posey's man of straw do? Did duty call? If it did, the note was muffled and off key. Who was going to suffer if Silver remained unexposed—except Athanasius Thanatos, that monstrous freebooter? The image of the hotel across the bay leaped to Pibble's mind; and after all, suppose Silver was now going straight—and he did seem fizzingly enthralled in his loopy research—there'd be a case for slander supposing Pibble got him sacked. And would the lush tide of money continue to reach the children? Pibble had never believed that any of us ever acts from a single motive —the smallest fidget rises from a choice between several drives. Now a welter of reasons decided him to keep quiet— quiet for today, anyway. He'd be in a mess if Silver suddenly decamped with the petty cash, because Brad was sure to hear of it, but for the moment . . .

The warm, pure blob of air in which he had been sitting chilled suddenly, and reeked of old fish; the car had stopped imperceptibly and the chauffeur was holding the door for him.

"I was instructed to bring you to the private entrance, sir."

"Are we late?"

"No, sir."

"I enjoyed the way you drove."

"Thank you, sir."

4

The reek welled from four decrepit dustbins, and the chill smote off a dirty brick wall and hummocky cobbles. Pibble stepped out into an alley between warehouses; red hoists jutted into the skyline; he could smell the river. It looked a good place for a knifing, with the dustbins handy to dump the resulting rubbish in, but the chauffeur was already unlocking a side door into one of the warehouses. He held it open and Pibble walked through, into an industrial lift. The chauffeur pressed the single button and retreated, the gate hissed, the warehouse door blanked out the daylight and left only a dim bare bulb, the hoist whined. When it stopped the gate hissed open and somebody unlocked the further door from the outside—this door was polished steel. Beyond it lay a plush vestibule with a Degas on the wall and an equally rare and perfect artifact holding the door—a bland, stooped, youngish man wearing an Old Etonian tie.

"Superintendent Pibble?" he said, smiling and holding out his hand.

The smile was charming, the hand fine-boned as a woman's.

"I don't use the rank any more," said Pibble.

"I'm Antony Catling. Thanassi's in here."

He opened a door into a large, light room; light because one wall was a window and there lay the river and the stolid barges and Saint Paul's and an anthology of Wren steeples. Pibble was astonished by how many stories the lift had whisked him up. Between him and the window stood an extremely beautiful girl wearing a purple trouser suit; Pibble smiled nervously at her and she stared back at him with the princely disdain of a wax model. She was a wax model, so Pibble switched the remains of his smile to the large, red-faced, crew-cut man who was now tossing the *New Statesman* to the floor and levering himself up from a lying position on the sofa.

"This is Mr. Pibble," said Catling.

The man stopped moving. His gray eyes, very bloodshot, stared at Pibble for a few seconds, then he sprang to his feet like a schoolboy.

"Fine," he said. "Now we can have a drink. What's your first name, feller?"

Mr. Thanatos had a metallic New York accent. His voice sounded like a disc jockey's filtered through the cheapest possible transistor, except that his enthusiasm seemed more genuine.

"James," said Pibble.

"I'll call you Jim. You call me Thanassi. You'll have to call Tony Tony because if you try anything else you'll get in a tangle. He's a viscount."

"Thanassi likes to show off his possessions," said Lord Catling cheerfully.

"Champagne, Jim? Bloody Mary? Filthy ouzo? Scotch?"

"Champagne, please," said Pibble, plumping late for what was least unlike his idea of a prelunch snifter. Evidently he didn't manage to keep the doubt out of his voice.

"Milk shake if you prefer it," said Mr. Thanatos earnestly.

"No, really. Champagne would be fine."

"Quite right. If you're going to booze with a millionaire you ask for bubbly. D'you know many millionaires, Jim?"

"Only one old man who'd given it all away."

"Decided that the club was getting crowded, I bet. You eaten, Jim?"

"No, but—"

"What can we rustle up, Tony?"

"I've ordered hamburgers."

"That'll do."

Mr. Thanatos turned and began to rattle at bottles on a silver tray under the only picture in the room, a vast Canaletto of roughly the same view that lay outside the window. It was a curious room; the things in it looked battered but newish, as though they had had their sheen knocked off them in a few weeks by the millionaire's clumsy energy. Only the disdainful model was perfect; Pibble wondered whether his host owned, in her, the only fully clothed Allen Jones statue in the world. The *New Statesman* had come unstapled under his glare. Mr. Thanatos seemed to have been reading the same article that Pibble had seen on the weekend, about how the disputed South Bank site ought to be converted by the government into a world center for student protest, and not allowed to swell the profits of this notorious crony of the Athens colonels.

Mr. Thanatos swung round holding an oddly shaped bottle from whose neck gold gouts fell foaming to the carpet. Catling produced two tall glasses and when they were full handed one to Pibble. Mr. Thanatos returned to his rattling and sploshing, and emerged at last with a pint-sized Bloody Mary.

"Sit down, Jim. Here's to life. Sit here."

Mr. Thanatos fell into the sofa like a demolished factory chimney and banged the cushion beside him to stake a claim for Pibble's buttocks. The red goo in his mug slopped slightly onto the fabulous carpet, but he paid no attention—judging by other bloody flecks it had happened before. Pibble took a beer drinker's swig at his glass; it was not at all like the stuff you get at weddings. He sat, feeling as though he had been lowered into an upholstered bear pit.

"Pretty foul deal you got over your job, Jim," said Mr. Thanatos.

"I'd have been retiring in a year or two, anyway. How did you know?"

"Tony was at school with a guy. That's what I pay him for."

"I don't think they were necessarily wrong," said Pibble. "I seemed to be becoming sort of accident prone."

"Sure. But there are ways of giving a guy the push, and there are other ways. You don't feel sore at my checking, Jim? Ram Silver gave you a pretty hard sell this morning."

"Of course not. Sacked policemen don't exactly inspire confidence."

"Depends where you are. Some countries they're the only guys you can trust. What's your attitude to life after death, Jim?"

He gave the phrase capitals—Life After Death—and his Brooklyn vowels shifted a few degrees toward Billy Graham-land.

"I'm afraid I haven't thought about it seriously enough to have an *attitude*. Usually I don't believe in it, I suppose, and when I do it's not exactly a fervent belief."

Mr. Thanatos nodded and looked sad.

"Tony's the same," he said. "It's something to do with

your bloody weather. But Ram's onto something pretty exciting down there, wouldn't you say?"

A faint bell sounded, and Catling, who had been standing looking out at Saint Paul's, went and opened a small door in the wall and brought out a plate whose meaty reek filled the room.

"I've only known about it since this morning," said Pibble.

"Spread a lot of mustard on it," said Mr. Thanatos, watching Pibble's movements very closely as if to make sure that Pibble prepared his hamburger in such a way that no droplet of pleasure should be wasted. The big rolls were warm from baking, the meat in them a steaming, oniony swadge. Pibble smeared on the mustard, took a good bite at his roll, chewed, and washed it down with the princely fizz. It was schoolboy food, a truant picnic, buns and lemonade rendered fabulous by the touch of Midas. Eating it made him feel strangely cheerful and gave him time to think.

"I'm quite certain, myself, that some of the children are telepathic in certain circumstances," he said.

"Tell me."

Pibble explained between mouthfuls about his meeting with Marilyn Goddard by the mausoleum in the wood.

"Hold it," said Mr. Thanatos when he'd got to the first of the hidden articles, the sixpence.

"Give me some wine now, Tony," he said. "And fill Jim's glass. We'll try it again, Jim. I'll be this girl, you can be you. Do just what you did with her. I'll guess what you're holding and Tony can try to spot if there's any way I could be cheating. She was sitting on the ground, right?"

Mr. Thanatos threw himself with a thud to the carpet and Pibble squatted before him to produce in turn the knife, the mower nut, and the invisible conker. As each try ended he told them what Marilyn had said. Mr. Thanatos leaned against the sofa and glared at Pibble's fists in a fury of concentration, breathing so hard that he snorted at the end of each breath. Catling lounged above them, aloof but apparently just as intent, as if the charade had been some game on which he had wagered his whole estate. When it was over Mr. Thanatos erupted back to the sofa, emptied his glass, and bit a huge crescent out of a fresh hamburger.

"Two out of three," he said through his chewings. "Crap. Bloody near evens, and that's only guessing which hand. I should have known you'd carry a penknife, Jim—you're the type—but that would have been experience and reasoning, which aren't what we're looking for. The other two were as near impossible as makes no difference. What did you spot, Tony?"

"Damn all. I think if I'd been behind him I might have seen what he took out of his jacket pocket—that was the nut—but not from the front."

"And this kid got all four of them, Jim? Hand correct, object correct?"

"Well, not quite," said Pibble. "They've got a very small vocabulary, and I expect 'Hole in it' is as near as she could have got to the mower nut, but I'd have thought that she'd know the word for 'knife' and she said 'sharp.' "

"Crap. That's the word she'd know. It does for knives, scissors, anything that might cut you. Have another bun. Finished that bottle, Tony? How did this kid react?"

He sprang from the sofa, picked another bottle out of the ice bucket, ripped the foil and wire off it and hoicked the cork out, as though he were too thirsty to let the pressure blow it out for him. But once the wine was frothing out he stood there and let it fall to the carpet while he listened to what Pibble had to say.

"You can't tell what they feel until you know them very

well, which I don't. I got the impression that it really was just a game—a way of staying awake until she felt like going back to the house."

Mr. Thanatos nodded, filled his glass, and sat down again.

"That's pretty interesting," he said admiringly. "Yes, that's pretty interesting. What do you say, Tony?"

"It sounds like a remarkable experiment. I wonder whether Jim could repeat it."

"What did Ram Silver make of it, Jim?" said Mr. Thanatos.

"I didn't get a chance to tell him before I was brought up here. You'll remember I may be lying, won't you? Or at least exaggerating."

"Tell me."

"Well, the McNair Foundation was very poor and ramshackle, but suddenly there's a lot of money available. The money depends on your favor, and that depends on the continued significance of Doctor Silver's work. He's offered me a post, so it must be in my interest to produce apparently remarkable results with the cathypnics."

"I don't know why I ever come to England," said Mr. Thanatos. "It rains all the time, softies and lefties take turns to ruin me, and the streets are full of hypocrites. Listen to me, Jim. I don't know who my family was, so I can't have a family tree or a scutcheon like Tony wears on his underpants. But I can have a motto. It says 'Everybody is lying.' "

"Not just Cretans?" said Catling.

"Everybody."

"Have another hamburger, Jim," said Catling. "Thanassi's going to tell you about life, and that takes time. Don't hold back—he'll eat eight—there's more coming up. Where's your glass?"

"Adana," said Mr. Thanatos.

Pibble felt blank, and no doubt looked it.

"No, no one's ever heard of it," said Mr. Thanatos. "It's a town in Turkey."

"Just north of the top right-hand corner of the Med," explained Catling. "Not far from Tarsus, where Paul came from."

"That's the place," said Mr. Thanatos, "but it might have been any other hick town, anywhere, except that in 1909 they had a bit of a riot there. The local Turks decided that the local Armenians were letting the tone of the place down, so they knocked them about a bit. Thirty thousand Armenians got the chop in that riot, Jim. Thirty thousand. You wouldn't say I looked like an Armenian, would you?"

"No," said Pibble, bewildered.

"Nor would I. Sometimes I think I may be Georgian—there'd have been some of them down there, and a lot of Greeks, and some Jews and Bulgarians and other trash. When you go on the town like those Turks did, you don't stop to ask exactly what sort of foreigner the guy you meet is—if he's not a Turk you give him the chop. Sometimes I think I might be German. Germany was building up influence in Turkey, so there'd have been a fair sprinkling of Huns even in a hole like Adana, but they'd all have run to the consulate and if anyone was missing there'd have been one hell of a fuss. I've looked through all the documents, and the Herrenvolk made no complaints about any of their friends being sliced up and thrown into a mass grave. You needn't look at me like that. I wasn't sliced, but I was thrown. A little old Greek priest snuck out in the dark to pray by one of the big holes they'd dug and hadn't filled in yet in case they found a few more oddments lying around; and he heard something moving in the pit. At first he thought it was just the bodies slithering against each other as they settled, but it went on and the moon came out and he saw something moving, so he climbed down and walked over the corpses and found a child, two or three years old, crawling about down there. He was pretty struck with the incident, so he called me Athanasius Thanatos, but he didn't tell me why until he was dying of pneumonia in a sod of a cattle boat trying to get across from Smyrna in 1922, full of hysterical Greeks. Course, *he* didn't think it mattered who the hell I was—I was going to serve God and wear a stupid black hat and smell of incense, and for all civil purposes I was Greek. But I'm not. Since those two days on that cattle boat I belonged to no nation. I was sore about it at first, but in the end it's got me where it has. Do you know why this Common Market crap you've fallen for won't work, Jim?"

"Tell me," said Pibble. He had drunk a lot of champagne and his glass seemed full again. Catling had passed him a fresh plate of hamburgers. He felt happy, as though Mr. Thanatos' dervish energy was enough to change the air of the room and give all who breathed it new hopes, new strengths, new fires.

"Right," said Mr. Thanatos. "You try and do business with an Italian. You'll lie British and he'll lie Italian and you'll finish your deal with both of you feeling that the other one's a dirty customer. That's why countries have to go to the crazy expense of hiring ambassadors—they all lie diplomatic. But if I have to do business with a wop, I lie wop and we get along fine. I can even lie alongside prickly sods like you, Jim. OK, so I *know* you're lying, because everybody's lying. But you aren't lying about what this kid said and did—you're lying about something else; I know that, too. Get it?"

"Thanassi rides his hobbyhorses harder than any man I know," said Catling.

"And the pale one hardest of all," said Mr. Thanatos. Pibble thought it was a good joke, but that he had made it before. It is a considerable measure of luxury to have a viscount as your straight man. But Catling had somehow altered the flow, so that Pibble no longer felt compelled to tell his host about the Paperham murderer—an irrelevance which he had deliberately left out.

"OK, I'm lying," he said. "And it's no business of mine who you trust. Tell me why you think that the telepathy of the children at the McNair can throw any light on life after death."

"You done any prospecting, Jim?"

"No. But I do believe in dowsing, as it happens."

"Water divining," translated Catling.

"I go prospecting when I can," said Mr. Thanatos. "It's a thrill. I like it best in bits which other people haven't thought of. You trek and you trek and you come to a stretch of desert which looks like any other stretch of desert and the guy you've hired to do your guessing for you says, 'Here, maybe,' and your team sets up the instruments and you let off a few bombs—I do that bit—and you take the readings to another guy back in the city and he says it looks promising and takes his fee. So then you go and haggle with governments and try and find some suckers to pay for the drilling, and it's two, three, four years before you can say for sure whether the stuff really is down there. I've lost more money over oil than I've made—tell him so, Tony."

"I'd have thought you'd just about broken even," said Catling.

"Not even enough. Now, Jim, death is a desert. Same all over, nothing growing anywhere, nasty. But under it there's a secret, an answer. I can't go tunneling down there—no one can—so I've got to judge by what I can see on the surface, right? Those kids of Ram's look sort of promising to me, so I hire a guy to test for results: that's Ram. He tells me he's getting interesting results from a new seismograph: that's you. And I'm the sucker who's going to pay for the drilling, because this matters one hell of a lot to me. I had sixteen years of my life stolen, and I mean to get them back."

Pibble thought of the swathed shapes of children lying in Kelly's ward. Hamburgers are good food for negotiating over, because you have a chance not to say anything while you chew; then you say something different, provided the champagne lets you.

"Do you think the medical side of the disease is important?" he said.

"That Irishman?" said Mr. Thanatos. "What's he like? What's he up to?"

"I knew him before, as a matter of fact. He's clever and works hard, and he seems to be learning quite a bit about the physical aspect of the disease."

"That's a pretty serious aspect," said Mr. Thanatos. "I don't want an afterlife if it's not physical. When Ram and this Irishman have worked out everything about cathypny, they'll know how the kids see into each other's minds, and then we'll get hold of somebody who isn't a moron and induce the same effect in him, and then we can go places."

Crippen, thought Pibble, he means it.

"You'll have to look for a very dedicated volunteer," he said. "The children's abilities are probably the result of some deficiency, or a combination of deficiencies. They're deficient in almost everything that makes life worth living. Have you met them?"

"No, and I don't want to. I like things to be perfect, and people to be perfect. Of their kind. I choose girls who are perfectly beautiful, even if they are perfect bitches—I prefer them that way. I like Tony because he's a perfect specimen of his class. I'm not sure if I like *you* yet, Jim, and I know I wouldn't like a lot of kids with metabolic deficiencies. I don't

93

like *any* kids—they can't be perfect till they've finished growing. I never was a kid."

"If you look at it the other way," said Catling, "you still are one. Shall I open another bottle?"

"Do that," said Mr. Thanatos.

"Not for me," said Pibble. Mr. Thanatos drank much faster than he did, but had given the Englishmen the start of his Bloody Mary, so they'd all three drunk about two-thirds of a bottle. Not that it was the type of champagne that makes you think after your second glass that it's time for a different taste—and the second lot of hamburgers had been much spicier, perhaps deliberately mixed to keep the thirst pricking. Catling turned, bottle poised, and Pibble put his hand over his glass.

"Crap," said Mr. Thanatos. "I haven't done talking to you. Too, you have a moral duty to drink as much of this stuff as you can pump into your gut. You'll never drink it again, but if you swill away like a soldier now until it's coming out of your ears, you'll get to know the taste of it like a catechism. You won't forget it. Twenty years from now you'll be able to say, 'Once I drank Thanassi Thanatos' champagne and it tasted *so!*' "

He pointed the last syllable with a quivering hand cupped under Pibble's nose, as though he were offering him this immortal taste as a physical gift. Then the hand snatched Pibble's away from the glass and Catling filled it up.

"It's worth remembering," said Pibble. "Did you know that there aren't any perfect beers left? I can remember what Bass tasted like before the war, in pubs where the landlord knew how to nurse it."

The thought made him suddenly melancholy, darkening the tone of his voice.

"Jim," said Mr. Thanatos, "I believe I'm beginning to like

you. Let's have some more hamburgers."

"Coming up now," said Catling.

"What's on your mind, Jim? You think somebody down there is trying to take my money off me? Ram Silver? Your Irishman?"

"Nothing as clear as that," said Pibble. "Doctor Silver's an extraordinary man. How did you come across him?"

Mr. Thanatos laughed.

"It was the damnedest thing," he said. "Iráklion. I wouldn't go near the place normally, but we were trying out my new boat and my girl bullied me into going over to Crete and putting in to the Venetian Harbor so that she could rook me for some Minoan junk. I reckon she knew some of the junk sellers and was getting a rakeoff, but the day you start fretting about that kind of graft is the day you find you can't get along with anyone except a bunch of other millionaires, and I hate their guts. I'm rogue rich, Jim—I belong to the club, but they'd all be happy to see me slung down the steps. Anyway, we bought these fakes and we all went back to the harbor; but just as we came out of the Khánia Gate Karen spotted this very spectacular Arab type sitting at a table in front of a taverna, and ran over to photograph him. He said she'd have to pay. She was sore—she's used to *being* paid. I like to see 'em sore, so I sent my man over with a drink for the guy. He stood up, poured a libation like a priest in a temple, and said, '*Zeto o thanatos.*' You know what that means?"

" 'Long live death,' " said Pibble. "You said 'Here's to life' just now."

"Correct. Now, Jim, I was having a hell of a time. My girl was a drip, my lovely new boat was a sow, and Mrs. Gandhi was trying to nationalize me. Those kinds of things don't matter, but they seem to at the time and you forget the things that do. And then this Arab wipes them away in three words. So I sat down at his table and talked to him all afternoon. I reckon he wanted me to take him aboard as my doctor—they're all on the make, Arabs—but I'm never ill. He was in some kind of fix with the police, he told me, and he'd made it worse by using a fake Egyptian passport, and you could smell he hadn't a drach in his pockets, so I made a deal with him. If he came over to the McNair, I'd fix the police and the passport. You don't fancy that kind of deal, Jim?"

"It's no business of mine. I doubt if you could do it in England."

Mr. Thanatos threw his hamburger to the floor, where it broke into several pieces that scuttered across the carpet. Catling sighed and pressed a bell push, but no servant came. Instead a low cupboard opened under the Canaletto and a shiny green gadget stalked into the room, muttering along on eight metal legs and groping blindly with a vacuum snout. Beneath its belly a couple of brushes rotated. It fussed along by the wainscot to the corner, sucking and brushing, then up by the window. It seemed to know where the obstacles were.

"Lift your legs up when it gets to you, Jim," said Catling. "Have you finished with your paper, Thanassi?"

"I hate the English," whispered Mr. Thanatos.

"Don't chuck him out," said Catling. "Remember he's given you a chance to show off your toy."

"There's that," admitted Mr. Thanatos. "All right, Jim, so you think you are all average, normal, and all the rest of us are some kind of freaks. Of course I'd have a bit of trouble fixing police and passports here, but you bear in mind that there are things I can do here which I'd never even dare to try on those clods in Athens, even though I was building them twenty hotels on stinking barren lumps of rock."

"I suppose Doctor Silver told you about the cathypnics."

"Yeah. That's another thing about being rich—people like to show you that they've got something you haven't got, something you can't buy; all the poor bastards have got is secrets, so they tell you them, and then you've got them, too."

"You must have thought it a curious corner for a qualified doctor to fetch up in."

Mr. Thanatos put his glass on the floor with uncharacteristic care and leaned forward to stare, gray-eyed, at Pibble. Close to you could see that he was older than he looked, old enough to have been picked out of a mass grave in Adana in 1909. The surface of his skin was innumerable tiny wrinkles, and the pinkness not the flush of health but a crazed lacework of strained veins and blood vessels.

"I get it," he said. "You *are* trying to warn me. Against my friend Ram Silver. You've talked about lying, you've asked about how I met him, and now you've talked about his qualifications. You know something I don't, like I said earlier."

"I've been a policeman all my life," said Pibble. "I haven't any evidence that anybody is trying to cheat you in any way, but in my experience rich men don't get cheated in the area of their main business—they're on the lookout all the time there. It's the odd enthusiasms—what you call the hobbyhorses—that seem to have the pitfalls in them. You've arranged a very odd setup at the McNair, with a lot more money floating around than you'd lose over a bit of casual grafting in Twenty-sixth August Street."

"Twenty-fifth," said Mr. Thanatos. "Tell him, Tony."

The antics of the green gadget had given Pibble an excuse to look away from Mr. Thanatos. It had, during its second circuit of the room, found the biggest bit of hamburger a foot out from the wall and had tried to suck it through the nozzle. Failing, it stopped and the nozzle thrust itself inward like the

97

trunk of a feeding elephant and pushed the bread into the brush·s, which scrubbed ineffectually at it until a couple of paddles extruded themselves, scooped inward along the carpet, and hoisted the object into the hidden maw. The gadget purred, jerked, and trundled on. It made surprisingly less noise than the ordinary domestic vacuum cleaner.

"We *think* it's all aboveboard," said Catling aloofly. "I take it you've met Mrs. Dixon-Jones."

Pibble nodded.

"A rum egg, wouldn't you say? But uncomfortably honest. We did a crash investigation of her as soon as Thanassi told me what he wanted. Nobody had a kind word to say for her, except that she'd do anything for these children and that she'd cut off her right hand rather than a steal a halfpenny. So all the money goes through her, and . . ."

He stopped, eyebrows slightly raised, because Pibble had laughed aloud.

"Glad you approve, Jim," said Mr. Thanatos. "What d'you think, Tony?"

"He probably knows something," said Catling. "But if he does he won't tell us."

"Open another bottle," said Mr. Thanatos.

"Not for me," said Pibble quickly.

"Not for me, then," said Mr. Thanatos. "Ram's got pretty good qualifications—they could afford decent doctors in Katanga—but it wouldn't bother me if he were as phony as a Hong Kong pearl. What's the use of passing a raft of examinations on the spleen when you're going to do soul research?"

"Ah," said Catling, "but Empedocles believed that the seat of the soul was in the spleen. Or was it Pythagoras?"

"Crap," said Mr. Thanatos. "All Greeks are liars and thieves. Now, Jim, you're going back to the McNair, and you'll take this job Ram's lined up for you, and you'll get through to those kids—I know you will. And on the side you'll keep an eye open and get in touch with Tony if you come across any monkey business. Right?"

Pibble stood up. His head felt as clear as well water and his stomach cozy and content, but the connection between these two organs was, for the moment, tenuous, while his limbs seemed to have developed a curious autonomy.

"I'll talk to Doctor Silver," he said. "And if I can be useful I'm prepared to help. I'm certain that *if* we get any results they'll be far more readily accepted if I'm not paid. I won't spy for you. If I learn anything which concerns you but which is being kept from you I'll try to see that you are told about it. And if by any wild chance I come across anything which looks like police business I'll have to tell them."

"Hoity-toity," said Mr. Thanatos. He was grinning and looked satisfied. "Phone your wife from my car and tell her where you are and who you had lunch with. Tell her oysters, not hamburgers. I like you, Jim, but you are short on glamour. Ask Alfred to show you how to disconnect the tape recorder if you want to talk secrets."

"Tape recorder?"

"I had one put in," said Catling. "It's wired up to the telephone so that I know how many hotels Thanassi has bought and sold when he comes back from a spin. You'd better see this before you go."

He pointed behind the sofa, and Pibble turned. The green gadget, trundling round its ever narrowing rectangle, had come at last to the spilled pages of the *New Statesman*. First it nozzled at them, then it stuffed them between its legs toward the brushes, then the paddles came down and scooped at them without success, and then the whole machine shook itself irritably and began to buzz. Under the glistening carapace a new door opened, into which the paper rose, only to be excreted almost at once as a pyramid of fine shreds. The nozzle probed back between the legs to the base of the pyramid and sucked the shreds in, and in less than half a minute all that high-minded gossip, those solemn admonishments, those lucid analyses of cultural dandruff, were gone the way of Mr. Thanatos' hamburger.

"See you, Jim," said Mr. Thanatos.

"Good-bye," said Pibble, "and thank you for the wine."

As Catling unlocked the lift he said in a low voice, "Well done, Mr. Pibble. You managed that very well."

The door hissed shut. Pibble decided he was paid to say that to all the visitors.

Only among the dustbins did he discover how drunk he was, as the fresh air smote him, but a deft fist caught him by the elbow and wheedled him through the peacock door and into his chair with a solicitude that implied that only age and weariness had overcome the traveler. Practice makes perfect servants.

"Thanks," said Pibble. "Mr. Thanatos said that you would show me how to disconnect the tape recorder from the telephone."

Alfred slipped into the compartment, opened the switch panel, and raised a switch.

"Was my other conversation recorded?" said Pibble.

"Yes, sir. You told me it concerned Mr. Thanatos, so I have sent the tape through. I hope that was right, sir."

"Fine," said Pibble. Now he had betrayed one side and lied to the other, not a bad position for a neutral. "If we pass a chemist I'd better have some Alka-Seltzer."

Alfred, still crouching to attention, flipped himself round like a gopak dancer and fiddled with the wall below the glass partition; silver flasks slid into view, and a gnome's pharmacopoeia; Alfred fiddled and buttled, then turned with a foaming tumbler.

"This is Mr. Thanatos' own prescription, sir."

"Thanks."

Ten seconds later the car was drifting up the alley, while a commissionaire held up the lorries in Park Street to allow them out.

The drink was pink. Ice from the tiny refrigerator jostled amid the bubbles. Pibble waited till the foam was less eruptive and drank it all in three huge swallows; it was scouringly bitter and made his ears ring. When he could see he settled the tumbler into the holder which Alfred had pulled from the wall and pressed the button with the telephone on it. This time he noticed the elaborate aerial extruding itself to the left of the windshield. . . . She was out. . . . No. He was so relaxed that for the first time in years he noticed how welcoming Mary's voice could sound.

"Hello, pigeon. I'll give you a million guesses. Not just tiddly—*tight*, but it's in a good cause. I've been swilling champagne with Athanasius Thanatos—yes, him—and now I'm sitting in his Rolls on my way back to the McNair. It's all right, he told me to—he said I lacked glamour. I'll tell you when I see you, about half past six I should think. Look, pigeon, when you talked to Mrs. Dixon-Jones and Lady Sospice . . . No, nothing shady, but they've offered me a job. Yes, it would, but there are snags. I'll tell you. Of course. But what were they talking about before you, er, joined them? Not the Preservation people? You're quite sure? I met Mr. Costain this morning, by the way. Liked him. Lady S., though—was it anything to do with the new head of research? Oh, well. Do you know anything about her granddaughter, Dorothy, though everybody calls her Doll? Not even any cousins? Is there much in the kitty? Oho! Yes, I've—"

"Have you nearly finished, sir?" said the ceiling. "Mr. Thanatos would like to speak to me."

Pibble gave the man a thumbs up: if he didn't have eyes in the back of his head Thanassi should sack him.

"I must ring off now, pigeon. There's a queue of millionaires waiting for the phone. I love you, too. Bye."

The instrument sighed back into its niche and Pibble sighed with it. The romance was over. Despite the dream luxury of the car he was outside the pale again, trudging along the public tarmac and unable to see over the eight-foot, league-long wall behind which Wealth and Power lolled or sported. Even when you come to open gates between ludicrous lodges the driveway always bends behind screening trees, lest any finial of the mansion should be contaminated by an outsider's glance. Hemingway was an ass, he decided (not for the first time): there *is* something different about the very rich, an attraction—no, not an attraction, because it also says DO NOT TOUCH—but you feel that if you *did* touch the silky skin your fingertips would tingle. Did Mary receive the same prickling shock from the presence of horrible Lady Sospice? It would be difficult to ask.

Pibble decided to go and see the old girl himself—perhaps the honorable Doll would take him, supposing she was on speaking terms with her grandmother. They might live together, but it was hard to imagine so attractive a child fitting in easily with a tyrannical dotard. He remembered that Doll had said the old lady was nicer than she looked, but he knew too well the mysterious way in which people will find peripheral or meaningless virtues to praise in their most obnoxious relations. To be nicer than you looked, if you looked like Lady Sospice, was low praise indeed.

Pibble found himself thinking about Rue Kelly, and

fidgeted in his chair, only to find that his seat belt constrained him—Alfred must have fastened that with unnoticeable tact. There were two possible explanations, as far as he could see, for Rue's cooperation with Silver. Either he was expecting to muscle in on some sort of fraud, or he simply enjoyed the deception; the secret and mildly risky betrayal of his whole profession might give him an iconoclastic kick. The trouble was that Pibble so much wanted the second explanation to be true that he suspected its plausibility for that very reason. And similarly, how remarkable was Rue, really? How clever? How good a doctor? Mightn't an elderly failed policeman elevate any young man who happened to be polite to him to the rank of genius? You make allowances for cronies because they are part of you; you have grown to fit in with them as a limpet's shell grows to fit in with one particular area of rock, on which alone it is watertight when the tide goes out. The Pibbles had once owned a black-and-white mongrel, a dull dog but eccentric in its small way, which was to lie brooding in front of the coke boiler in the scullery even when the thermometer stood at eighty. When Pibble came to fill the boiler the dog would sit up and watch without interest but with its head in such a position that the swung coke scuttle bonked the back of its skull; if he tried to miss the dog he missed the boiler, too, and coke scrunched across the scullery floor. The dog never learned to get its head out of the way, so after a while Pibble developed a trick of pawing the animal aside with one foot as he swung the scuttle; months after it had been run over by the school bus, he realized that he was still making a sweeping motion with his left leg to scuff it out of the way as the scuttle began its backward swing. There could be few weirder reasons for installing an oil-fired boiler, paid for out of inadequate savings.

So was Rue really only a habit? To the outsider, who didn't

owe him what Pibble did, would he have seemed merely a rather hard young man on the make? But hard young men on the make don't trap themselves in dead ends like the McNair. On the other hand, he had been brutal to his soft pretty girl in front of other people, and . . .

For a while Pibble dozed. His dreams were about arresting the Paperham murderer.

5

"I hope you don't mind walking a short way, sir," said the ceiling.

Pibble woke, shivering. He was soberer, but not yet sober.

"The exercise will do me good," he said.

"Can you suggest anywhere I could hide the car for a while?" said Alfred. "You're a local, aren't you, sir?"

Pibble looked through the window and saw where he was.

"One, two, third on the left, Mortimer Street, there's an undertaker. Joy riders stole one of his hearses a month ago and it was a write-off, so he might have room."

"Mr. Thanatos would appreciate that, sir."

"I'll walk from here. Have you got something to change into?"

"Yes, thank you, sir."

A blush of surprise mantled Alfred's pallid tones. Pibble walked up the hill feeling that he'd won a small but immortal victory against flunkies. He felt happy and excited, and strode springy-footed, filling his lungs with the dank, familiar air. First he must try to explain to Mrs. Dixon-Jones about his game with Marilyn, so that she could judge the evidence for herself. Then find Rue alone, and coax him or startle him (perhaps with details about Ram Silver's past) into saying what *else* was nasty in the woodshed.

Rue knew something about Silver; he was not the type to rest till he knew all. Ask the honorable Doll for an introduction to her grandmother. Give Silver a report on his tête-à-têtes with Marilyn Goddard and Mr. Thanatos. And only *then* could he reasonably look for Marilyn herself.

He stopped suddenly and laughed aloud, so that a mother wheeling a pram down the pavement glanced sharply at him and swung out to cross the road before they met. He walked on more slowly, fascinated by the discovery that an elderly policeman had been running like a lover to the mental embrace of a nine-year-old moron—though if she slept twenty hours a day it was five to one that she'd be doing so now. But amid all the seductions of Thanassi's Bower of Bliss his subconscious had remained faithful, treasuring the weird stimulus of that meeting of minds. Well, if he could repeat the effect he had a moral duty to explore further; not to do so would be a sin against Holy Knowledge, as bad as book burning. So he couldn't tell Brad or anyone at the Yard about Silver, or they'd send a bobby up to lean on the doctor's shoulder and say, "We're watching you, mate." At which point the experienced con man picks up his traps and goes, and with him goes the chance of adding Pibble's pebble to the cairn of knowledge. And that in turn meant that he, useless, sacked, demolished old Pibble, had to play cops again, find out what Silver's lay was, prevent the moment when a custom-built electron microscope arrived in an empty crate just as a new numbered account in Zurich achieved a gratifying credit balance.

Thanassi knew about Silver now. He'd listened to the tape and ordered Alfred to stay in the area and watch over his interests, which would not be easy to do inconspicuously in peacock livery. Alfred for Thanassi, then, and Pibble for the rest. If Brad got to hear about it, there would be no defense; it was Pibble's bad luck that it seemed the only thing to do.

He was feeling considerably less exhilarated by the time he pushed the door of the McNair open, but cheered at the sight of the two doorkeepers sitting back to back on the carpet.

"Hello, you two," he said.

"Man," said one child, unsmiling.

"Shove off," drawled the other.

"I'm the copper who lost his hat," explained Pibble. "I want to see Posey again."

"Poor Posey," said one child.

"Man," said the other.

Perhaps they weren't even reacting to his presence at all —Marilyn had said "Poor Posey."

"Shove off," said both children together.

He crossed the hall to the glaring passage.

Mrs. Dixon-Jones did not look in the mood to play Poor Posey. Her face and lips were pale except for a bright red blotch below each cheekbone. She hardly opened her mouth to free the acid syllables.

"Come in, Mr. Pibble," she said. "I've just been talking about you."

"Oh, who to?"

"An employee of Mr. Thanatos called Catling."

"Viscount Catling."

The title was not emollient.

"He says it is Mr. Thanatos' wish that you should be taken onto the staff in an advisory capacity, to help Doctor Silver with his research, and that I am to settle your salary with you. I can understand that, though I cannot see the point of it. But he also says that you are to make any recommendations about the Foundation which you think fit."

"Oh, I say, that's a bit thick!"

"He says that you are to have full facilities to investigate my department, as well as Doctor Silver's and Doctor Kelly's, and that you are responsible to no one but Mr. Thanatos himself."

"But this is nonsense!" said Pibble.

"I'm glad to hear you think so."

"I had lunch with Mr. Thanatos and Lord Catling and we talked about the telepathic abilities of the children. I agreed to talk to Doctor Silver about helping him with his research, but that was the only practical result. Most of the time we were talking about life and death and things like that."

Mrs. Dixon-Jones was once more tapping her pen against the little silver globe, punishing the Bering Straits for Pibble's shortcomings.

"What salary do you suggest?" she said.

"I told him I didn't want to be paid, at least for the time being."

"He usually gets what he wants the way he wants it. He finds a lever."

"That's one advantage of being retired," said Pibble. "There isn't a fulcrum any longer, if you see what I mean."

(Even if you have a betraying tape, there's no longer a job for you to lever against.)

"Well, that's something," said Mrs. Dixon-Jones without relaxing. "I can put off filling in those ghastly forms for you. What do you want to know about my department, Mr. Pibble?"

"Nothing. I just—"

"You'll have to ask me," she snapped, "or Mr. Thanatos will decide that I've been obstructive and I'll be sacked. After seventeen years!"

"He can't do that—there are limits to his power. He's not God. He doesn't own the place."

"As good as," she said. "I went down on my knees to the trustees, but he had them hypnotized. They called it 'a very happy solution to the Foundation's financial difficulties.' Oh, God, I wish I'd never . . ."

Been born? Been to Crete, more likely.

"Was this what you were talking to Lady Sospice about?" he asked.

She nodded.

"He must be putting up a very large sum of money," he said.

"He's mad, but it's not as much as you'd think. We were nearly broke, but we got along. Ram's toys are expensive, and Rue's even more so, but apart from that it didn't need a lot to put us on our feet."

"This place must eat money," said Pibble. "Couldn't you have sold it and gone to live somewhere easier to run?"

She shook her head, still stately but less enraged.

"It isn't worth much, because no one would get building permission here. And we'd have to get a bill through Parliament to vary the Trust, because one of the conditions is that we live here."

"Who are the trustees?"

"The mayor, the bank, and one of the Sospice family lawyers."

"Not Lady Sospice?"

"She's the patron, which means she has no powers except to make life hell for me."

"We all seem to do that. I really came to explain about my talk with Marilyn Goddard this morning."

"Yes," she said. Despite the sharp impatience of the monosyllable, Pibble began at the beginning. She snorted when he described Mr. Costain's camerawork, but with less fire than she would have that morning—perhaps Thanassi's tampering with the hierarchy had given her a new foe. Pibble began to describe the guessing game. . . .

"You're not making this up?" she said.

"No, as a matter of fact, not. But I quite see why I might be."

"Go on."

"How much do you remember about the Paperham murders?"

"I wish you wouldn't."

"It matters."

"I got one of the books out of the library, but I couldn't read it. They should have hanged him."

"I don't know," said Pibble, uneasy because he really didn't.

"Go on, anyway."

"When she saw I hadn't a chestnut she was terrified."

"You can't read their faces."

"You could this time."

"She's often frightened. She's different from the others."

"I know. I know why."

He told her about "Good day for Posey," and what he thought it meant, and Marilyn's sudden friendliness, and Brad's half-confirmation of his guess. When he'd finished piecing it together it didn't sound like a rigid logical structure, but she took a different line of attack.

"They can't see into the future. They think they can, but I'm sure they can't."

"Yes, but—"

"And the man's locked up, so it's nonsense."

"It doesn't have to be that man. The victims at Paperham were all very respectable women, well-to-do, smart by Paperham standards. They had quite a lot in common with you, and if somebody round here were thinking of harming you —making plans, as it were—Marilyn might have been aware of the impulse and felt it was the same as her stepfather's."

"No doubt I have a lot of enemies," said Mrs. Dixon-Jones, and looked it. "You said that little rat Costain was there—*he* might be thinking about strangling me, but it's ridiculous to suggest he'd actually *do* anything."

Pibble shook his head. If Marilyn had picked up a murderous echo of her past from Mr. Costain, he would need to have been thinking about his human quarry with excitement, pleasure, a sort of lust. So far only great brickwork and the Domestic Grandiose seemed to have moved him to passions of that stature.

"I probably shouldn't have worried you with this," he said.

"Never mind. You'd better tell Ram about your game."

"Yes. What do you want me to say about the second half?"

"I'd rather you left it out."

"OK. It doesn't prove anything."

"Not yet," said Mrs. Dixon-Jones. Suddenly she laughed with a strange and bitter glee.

"I'd like to see him try," she said. "You'll find Ram in his office. Do you want me to do a memo for him and Rue Kelly about your being allowed to snoop into their affairs?"

"I'll leave it to you," said Pibble, and left.

The tape recorder in the corridor was listening to silence with a diligence that so irritated him that he shouted "Boo!" into the microphone for the pleasure of watching the machine's green eye wince with the shock of sound. But the children by the door, though they had moved round face to face and were now playing a slow, strange finger-touching game, ignored him as he crossed the hall, even though he thought with every cranny of his mind about the richness and pinkness of raspberry ice cream.

Depressed and ashamed of himself, he mooched up the monstrous stairs. He had been behaving like a tiresome old hen, the sort that you hear in the bay windows of public libraries rattling away to some unwilling stranger about her premonitions of family debacles. The intensity of the guessing game by the mausoleum was already fading, becoming more like a dream or a daytime fantasy of self-importance; and his own guesses about the meaning of the child's words —which had seemed so sure, so confirmed by her sudden trust—he could now see would bear a hundred other explanations. And Mrs. Dixon-Jones, in sour contrast, had behaved extremely well. You'd have expected her to be jealous that this tedious newcomer should have been able to make contact like that with one of the children, while she, who had known and adored them—generations of them, living their moth-short lives—had never been allowed to. She could easily have shown she disbelieved him, but her heroic animosities were above bothering with Pibbles.

A boy was asleep in a doorway on the landing. Pibble knelt and with some difficulty found his pulse, slow but quite firm.

"That's Peter," said Ivan's voice above his head. "Don't worry—he's OK."

"They manage to look very, er, inert," said Pibble.

"You get used to it. We don't lose many, honest. We've had a lot of practice looking after them—keep them warm, you know, and that. We've only lost one in my time, apart from cathypny itself—a kid in Doctor Kelly's ward got meningitis month before last. Can't do much about that."

Pibble straightened up and walked with Ivan toward Dr. Silver's domain.

"Do you like working here?" he said.

"Sure. I sometimes think that it's going to feel a bit funny when I marry and have kids of my own, normal kids, not dormice. They'll never be quite the same thing, somehow. See you."

He went into the room with the purring recorders in it, and Pibble took the next door.

Dr. Silver was also asleep, lying in his black, expensive chair with his mouth slightly open and his arms dangling. He slept with great authority, as if giving a demonstration of the techniques of slumber. Pibble was almost able to persuade himself that he could remember seeing that noble head among the thousands of photographs of trivial villains which year after year had passed across his desk. He tiptoed across the lush carpet to the door from which the secretary had emerged that morning.

"Mr. T. treat you properly?" said the rich voice as his hand started to turn the handle.

"I was trying not to wake you up."

"Time I woke. That guy Doll quoted was half right. Sleep is beautiful. In short doses. Death goes on a bit long for my tastes. How did you make out?"

"Oh, he gave me champagne and hamburgers, and he said he liked me. He wants me to take the job we were talking about, but I decided I'd rather do it for free and see how it goes. I imagine that paid performers are more suspect than volunteers, in your kind of work."

"It's better than it used to be, that way. Did you tell him about losing your hat?"

"Yes. And there was a much more extraordinary thing which happened when I found Marilyn Goddard this morning. I'd have told you then, but there wasn't time."

He sat and for the third time he related his adventure. Repetition made the phrases more precise, but the events somehow less real. If he said it often enough, he felt, it would become fiction. But Dr. Silver was virgin soil.

"Hallelujah!" he shouted, springing from his chair. "If we can repeat that under laboratory conditions!"

"I think we should be a bit careful," said Pibble. "About Marilyn, I mean. I think that her stepfather, the one who did the murders, may have played the same game with her."

Dr. Silver seemed not to have heard; he was banging drawers open and shut, taking out small objects and putting them on the top of his desk.

"It's hell working with these kids," he said. "They can't tell you anything, almost. D'you reckon she'd know what that is?"

He held up a paper clip as he spoke into the intercom.

"Doll, bring me the little pencil out of your diary. A match, too. Then go and find Marilyn Goddard. Get the nurse to wake her if she's asleep."

"Can you do that?" said Pibble.

"After they've had an hour they'll wake up for a bit, but try it often and all you do is hustle them into Rue's kingdom. We'll give this thing a trial run here, now, Mr. Pibble, and that'll clear my mind for setting up a series of demonstrations which I can get witnesses along to and write up into a paper. What we want is household names of known probity. Any chance we could get the Duke of Edinburgh to come? He's the type who'll try anything once. Or how about your chief commissioner? Do you know him well?"

"I'm not in a position to ask him favors just now," said Pibble, smiling at the man's admirable nerve. No—he meant it. He was lost in his fantasy of honor and respect; the experimenter who was going to shake the medical world to its cracked foundations was the reality for him, the shabby con man only a stupid dream.

Doll came in with a little pencil and a box of matches.

"Thanks, thanks," said Dr. Silver. "Got anything else little and easy, something the kids would recognize? Lipstick?"

"I'm not wearing it this winter."

"Borrow your ring, honey?"

She took it off her ring finger and tossed it onto the glossy leather of the desk.

"Ivan's gone to look for Marilyn," she said, as the telephone began to ring. She picked it up.

"Yes, he's here. I'll tell him. C-a-l-l-o-w. I've got it."

She put the receiver down.

"A message for you, Mr. Pibble, from Posey. Will you ring Superintendent Callow at Scotland Yard as soon as you can?"

Pibble stood up. Ned. Bradshaw had talked to him. Was it conceivable that he kept on his shelves an unclosed file on a con man who preferred metallic aliases? But Ned Callow was not the type to get himself landed with a dingy little task like that. His hunting ground was the rich uplands where the headlines grow, cases like—

The door opened, and there was Marilyn pale and blinking. Ivan nudged her into the room, and behind her back made a grimace and a thumbs-down sign. With a conjuror's pass Dr. Silver scooped pencil, ring, paper clip, and the other knickknacks into a manila envelope.

"Hi, Marilyn, honey," he said. "How are you feeling?"

"Frightened."

"Non-sense. We'll take care of you."

"Man."

"This is James, honey. He's a great guy. You met him in the wood."

" 'nother man."

"You dreamed him, honey. There's only James and me and Doll and Ivan. We want you to play a game, like you played with James this morning."

"Game."

"That's a girl. We'll play it again now, so that we can all see how clever you are."

"Don' wanna."

Pibble was fascinated to see that Silver was a little ill at ease with the child; skilled tracker though he might be through all the adult jungles, he was not at home with these hints of an earlier and other creation. So Pibble picked the envelope off the desk, felt in it, and took the paper clip, making sure that it was in the fold of his right fist before anybody in the room could see it. He swapped it into his other hand behind his back, then crouched in front of the girl with his fists level with her face.

"Which hand?" he said.

They icy finger rose and touched his left hand.

"What is it?"

"Dunno."

He opened his palm to show her the little racetrack of wire.

"She might mean she didn't know what you had in your hand," said Doll. "Or she might mean she couldn't describe it."

"Sh," said Dr. Silver.

Pibble took the ring this time and juggled it into his left hand again, but when he crouched and concentrated on the green stones and the almost bristly feel of their hardness in his palm, the finger rose and touched the wrong hand.

"Pretty," she said.

He showed her. If those were real emeralds the ring must be worth the better part of a thousand quid. The child looked dully at it, and when Pibble tried again with a small plastic measuring spoon she did not raise her hand.

"Don' wanna," she said.

He showed her the spoon but she turned slowly away, in a manner that made him see that under all the layers of fat every muscle and nerve was taut.

"It's all right," he said. "He can't hurt you. He can't hurt anyone. We've shut him away. You'll never see him again."

She swung back and looked at him as if he were lying.

"Bad moment," sighed Dr. Silver. "All kinds of feedback operating there. When, when, when will I learn not to rush into things? Nil result on the which-hand test, but you seem to have got through to her with the ring. That what-is-it test is going to be a sow to evaluate statistically. Thanks, Ivan; take her away and tuck her in."

Pibble watched her waver out, not with the free-floating motion of the other cathypnics, but as though something heavy and dragging, some weighted object on a chain, constrained her to follow her erratic course.

"May I use the telephone?" he said.

"Go ahead."

"This might be confidential, I suppose, though it's probably only to ask me where I left some file."

"Use Doll's. The black one, not the gray one. Through that door. You'll have to ask Posey to give you a line."

"Thanks."

Not a sign of personality marked the room, no pictures, postcards from Zermatt, potted plants, scuffed shoes, or significant litter. It was just a cubic space where a girl worked on new furniture between fresh-painted white walls.

Typically, Ned Callow kept Pibble waiting until the hardness of the receiver seemed to have altered the shape of his ear; he heard voices, door bangs, other phones ringing, scufflings of paper, and wondered what point there could be in impressing an *ex*-colleague with these melodramatic background noises. Perhaps there really was some kind of a flap on.

"Callow!" snapped the machine.

"Jimmy Pibble here. I got a message to ring you."

"Yeah. You were talking to Brad about Gorton this morning."

"About who?"

"Oh, for Christ's sake! Samuel Gorton. Paperham."

"Oh, yes, I was."

"You shot Brad some line about a lecture, but he said it sounded as if you had something up your sleeve."

"Not really. I asked Brad whether the man had some kind of living mascot."

"Yeah, he did. Does. The writer johnnies decided it was a cat, but I never cottoned to that."

"I think it might have been his stepdaughter, the one who was about five when you got him."

"Why, Jimmy?"

"Something she said to me."

"For Christ's sake! Where is she?"

"At the McNair Foundation in South London—it's a small hospital for cathypnic children, and she's one. Is he out, Ned?"

"He is. He was cleaning the bogs when the driver of a team of busybodies who were visiting the prison came in for a pee. Gorton croaked him and locked him in the cleaning cupboard; took the uniform and drove the busybodies back to London; stopped the car at the Hyde Park traffic lights and nipped into the underground. The busybodies hadn't even noticed they had a different man, so they drove themselves back to their offices and reported it there. He had half an hour's start, and probably a quid or two out of the driver's wallet. He's got a knife."

"The woman he was living with—had she visited him?"

"Not for a couple of years. She's in Australia."

"But he'd know the child was here?"

"I'll check. What's your evidence, Jimmy?"

"It wasn't evidence, it was a guess, but enough to make me ring Brad up, and find there was something in it. Grit your teeth, Ned. The children at the Foundation are mentally deficient, but most of the staff are sure that they are also telepathic. . . ."

"Oh, for Christ's sake!"

"No, listen. If the staff believe that, Gorton might have, too. It doesn't have to be true for him to believe it, and it would fit in with his obsessions, wouldn't it? It'd take too long to explain what she said, but I guessed he used her as a sort of oracle, so I rang Brad up out of curiosity."

"I'll have someone go through the notes and see if it fits in. If it does . . ."

"He might come here."

"Bloody long odds. I'll get some bods out from your local station. What's the address?"

"Ned?" said Pibble when he'd spelled it out.

"Yeah? Make it snappy."

"See if you can manage to keep the telepathy business quiet. Once this gets on the Fleet Street files they'll send reporters down here every silly season to pester the staff to make the kids perform."

"Make a change from the Loch Ness monster. I'll do what I can for you, Jimmy, but if he *does* come I can't keep anything quiet. Got any of his type there?"

"One."

"Keep an eye on the bitch. Don't tell her why. See you."

The brisk quarterdeck voice snapped off. It had always irritated Pibble, coming from a man so devious—when war series were showing on the telly it had been intolerable. Now he had sounded like a hardened veteran of desert campaigns giving orders, impatiently disguised as advice, to a puffy major in the Home Guard. Well, the major was going to disobey. Pibble sat in the insipid room, slowly becoming aware that the tinge of his dread had changed. Before, it had been an abstract emotion, momentary but intense twinges of horror at the knowledge that a species of monster had once existed, which was also a man. Now the thing had returned out of the realm of fiction, which is what the past becomes; any rustle in the rhododendron bushes might be it. Now he had definite duties to attend to. . . .

He leaped a foot from his chair as the window sash banged up, then he whirled, muscles tense. A painter poked his head in.

"Just checking your sashes, sir."

Despite the carefully desuaved accent Pibble recognized Alfred.

"Carry on," he said. "What's it doing outside?"

"As 'orrible as it can manage, without your actual rain."

Pibble walked to the window, as if to see. Alfred slammed the sashes noisily up and down.

"The Paperham murderer has escaped."

"Saw the headline in the town," muttered Alfred.

"I've been talking to the Yard. He might come here."

"Uh-huh."

The news was evidently unimportant beside the affairs of Mr. Thanatos.

"He's, er, interested in one of the children. He might have the same idea as you."

"I'll keep an eye open."

"Have you finished?" said Doll, smiling round the door. "Hello! Trouble?"

"Just checking the sashes, miss," said Alfred.

"But somebody did that yesterday."

"Got to be done more'n once, miss. It's your wood swelling and shrinking under your new paint. Nowhere for the moisture to go, see?"

"But it's all red cedar," said Doll. "My great-grandfather wouldn't have anything else. I told the man yesterday."

"Well, he didn't tell *me*," said Alfred with admirable painterly truculence, and ran back down the ladder.

"Rue wants to see you," said Doll.

"I'll go and look for him as soon as I've seen Mrs. Dixon-Jones. I've forgotten to tell her something. I'd very much like to meet your grandmother sometime, if it's possible."

"Why on earth?"

"If it's a bore, forget it, but I'd like to meet someone who knew this area when it was all countryside."

"Oh, she'd love that. She thinks the world has never been the same since Lloyd George's 1910 budget. But she'll make you pay your way by telling her about a lot of gruesome murders."

Pibble chilled.

"Most of mine were merely quaint," he said.

"I'm sure they'll do. I'll take you home for tea today."

"I don't know about today. I'm half expecting somebody to come here, and—"

"I say, you *have* made yourself at home! I'll look for you at four-thirty and you can come if you're free."

"That's fine."

Mrs. Dixon-Jones was on the telephone again. Pibble wondered whether the plastic was worn thin, like the toe of Saint Peter, with the ceaseless brushing of her ear. A small cathypnic child was asleep on her lap.

"Really, Mrs. Abrahams," she was saying, "you can be quite sure that Sandra will be very happy with us. They like to be together. No. I've got her with me at the moment. Well, we'd *rather* you came in visiting hours, but if that's awkward

. . . But I gave you the list. I saw you put it in your handbag. Never mind, I'll tell you now if you'll get a pencil and paper. No, I'll hang on. . . . This is going to take ages, Mr. Pibble. The woman can hardly read and write. . . . Yes, I'm still here, Mrs. Abrahams. Ready?"

Pibble picked an envelope out of her wastepaper basket, tore it open, and began to write his news on it. It would be a mercy not to have to talk it over, but simply land the responsibility in her lap. He sensed a stir in the room and saw that Sandra had woken and was drifting toward the door; as she went she watched him out of the edge of her eyes. Mrs. Dixon-Jones said, "Wait a moment, Mrs. Abrahams," and ran to the door.

"Ivan!" she called. "Ivan!"

The echo fluted along the corridors.

"Look, Sandra," she said, "there's Melody. Melody, come here, darling. Good girl. This is Sandra—she's new. Will you take her and find her somewhere warm to curl up?"

"Lovely," whined the two cold voices together, and the children vanished hand in hand. Mrs. Dixon-Jones scurried back to the telephone and Pibble carried on with his message, but she dealt with the mother much more brusquely now that Sandra was out of the room, and had finished before he had. He looked up to see her wrenching the cords out of the switchboard as if she had been hoicking groundsel out of a neglected bed.

"It's about that horrible man again, isn't it?" she said.

"How did you know?"

"Sandra. Well, what about him?"

Pibble told her. Her pen tapped steadily at the silver globe —no wonder its lighting was erratic; when he finished it continued its impatient pinging.

"I'm going to be rude," she said at last. "But I've been here a long time and I've seen people behaving like you before. It wasn't really their fault, but I did expect you to be more sensible than serving maids and nurses. Anyway, you're making most of this up. I don't mean lying, but deceiving yourself. It doesn't usually matter, and the people who come to work here grow out of it, but you're doing it in a way that upsets the children. Look at Sandra just now. Of course it's very exciting to come into contact with a group of children who can talk to each other's minds, and it's only natural to persuade yourself that you can do it too, but it isn't true. Very occasionally something slips through to them, like that silly business about your hat in the hall, and your game with Marilyn if you're not making that up. But you can't control it. Ram's got his own reasons for taking you seriously, and I daresay that's helped to mislead you, but as for this man coming here, you've got absolutely no evidence except three words of Marilyn's that might mean absolutely anything. All the rest's your own imagination."

"Marilyn's been very frightened today," said Pibble.

"She has on other days, too."

"She told us just now that she wasn't frightened of me, but of another man."

"Would she call her stepfather that?"

"I don't know. You may be right. You heard me tell Doctor Silver that I distrust hunches and intuitions, and I still do. After I left you this morning I rang up a friend who looks after the records at Scotland Yard, and he told me that Gorton did talk about some living creature as though it were a sort of familiar, which confirms a little bit of my guess. And the officer who's in charge of the hunt for him, who isn't a friend of mine, thinks it a serious possibility that he'll come here. You've got to remember that I was in the police force for a long time, and—"

"You were asked to resign," interrupted Mrs. Dixon-Jones, putting an emphasis on the verb that showed she knew how peremptory the asking had been. Mary must have let that out, in the course of a loyal defense.

"Yes," he said, "but for a different sort of reason. Another thing: if, simply by writing a note to you in your room, I can unintentionally produce an effect like that on Sandra, you can't say that I'm not 'getting through' to them, at least some of the time. I'm not making that up. You saw it happen."

"I expect we could all do something of the sort if we were prepared to think about horrors the whole time. Sandra had never met Marilyn."

"Oh, well. Put it this way. Gorton has escaped; he had no friends, and the rest of his family are in Australia. If she showed any signs of telepathic powers when they lived together he would certainly have been interested. After his arrest he talked about somebody or something which had supernatural knowledge. I'm not making any of that up, am I?"

"I suppose not."

"So there is at least an outside chance that he'll come here and look for Marilyn. Even if it's a hundred to one, it's worth taking a few precautions. Perhaps Ivan could keep an eye on Marilyn the whole time—you could tell him it was to see that she wasn't pestered by hopeful journalists, as she's the only relative."

"They'd have to come through me," said Mrs. Dixon-Jones stiffly.

"Of course they ought to, but I've known inexperienced local chaps have a go at cutting corners, thinking the scoop will bring them fame and fortune—but it doesn't matter, it's only an excuse. I think in fact that you'd be wise to keep all the children together and accounted for; if he can't get Marilyn, he might decide one of the others would do. The painters should lock up all their ladders. You can't do much about the scaffolding, but the local police are supposed to be sending some men out, and they can look after that. If he *does* come, he'll be coming for Marilyn, not you. He doesn't know about you."

"I should think not."

"I mean when I talked to Marilyn this morning, I thought that she had recognized a situation in which somebody was planning to hurt you, and had tied this up with her own memories of Gorton. Now I think that what she said meant that she knew Gorton had escaped and was thinking about her, and that she mentioned your name simply because you fitted in with the previous pattern of his victims."

"If it meant anything."

"Exactly."

"All right," snapped Mrs. Dixon-Jones. "I think you're mad and I know you're a nuisance, but I'll do it. Oh, my God, I'm sick of the whole place and everybody in it!"

"Can I do anything to help? For instance—"

"No! Go away! Go away!"

She turned to the switchboard and stabbed cords murderously into sockets.

As Pibble walked along the gaudy corridor the image of her furious face hung in his mind like the head in the poem, on a canvas sky depending from nothing. Love had not missed her, but it had come to her strangely, in the deathlike fondlings of the cathypnics and perhaps the occasional stately embrace of the mock-Arab upstairs. Ram Silver must once, among the tavernas and the junkshops, have conned some of her tourist pittance off her, and she did not have the look of a forgiving woman. He'd have paid her back her "loan," of course, the moment he'd arrived at the McNair, and at once begun, almost casually, to defraud her of her power and control over the children. Every instant seemed to diminish her hold, every newcomer—Silver himself, Mr. Costain, and now old Pibble. So she sat there, poor good woman, raging, tapping the litter on her desk, flinging up ephemeral ramparts round herself, the children, and her outrageous autumn lover. It was another point in the con man's favor that he was able to inspire and feed such an improbable passion.

Several cathypnics were waiting in the hall, listless and solemn, but Pibble didn't feel armored enough to endure another of their whining rebuffs, so he walked straight to the stairs, still thinking about the perils of Posey.

"Poor Posey," said the nearest child.

"She'll be all right," said Pibble. "We'll all look after her."

"Poor Posey," said another child. Their tone made the words quite emotionless, not an expression of pity but a statement of fact. The whole group drifted away from him with the casual wariness of deer in a public park. He met two more coming down the stairs—it looked as if there was going to be a mysterious gathering of the children, like the seasonal congregations of some animals which still puzzle zoologists.

Prickly with the distress of his interview, and then the curious foreboding omen which the children provided— though their actual language was scarcely more interpretable than the rustlings can have been among Dodona's magic oaks —he stopped on the gallery to look down at the slowly assembling cathypnics. Yes, the whole building was prickly, like the air over London before summer thunder. His shirt felt sticky, and not just with the greenhouse heat of the rooms. He longed for ease, contentment, relaxation, and there was only one place to go for that. As he pushed the door open into Kelly's Kingdom he wondered how much of his unease was hangover from Thanassi's champagne, suppressed by Thanassi's pink fizz but still grumbling subliminally away.

These children would not be attending the meeting in the hall. They lay exactly as he had seen them before, except that the two nurses had stripped one set of blankets back, turned the child over, and were now rubbing the fat back under a sunlamp.

"Doctor Kelly wants to see me," whispered Pibble.

"I'll take you," said the plump one. "I won't be a minute, Angie."

She wiped the pungent oil off her hands and led Pibble through the far door of the ward into a little laboratory—microscope, test tubes, something that looked like an X-ray apparatus, shelves of jars all ranked and dustless. Everything looked fanatically tidy, except where one bit of bench was half dismantled and a clutter of splinters and a few tools lay on the floor. If that was to accommodate the hoped-for scintillation counter, it meant that Rue was not yet ordering expensive toys as partner in a fraud with Ram Silver. The relief and relaxation he longed for were already settling on him as the nurse opened the door into a tiny office where Rue lolled, feet on his desk, reading the *Evening Standard*.

"Stop following the nurses around," he said. "At your age, Jimmy, your mind should be on less ephemeral delights."

"The gentleman asked to see you, Doctor," said the nurse in a parody of primness.

"Do you realize she's mine?" said Rue, rubbing his hands together. "All mine! But you can have her if you want her all that much, me old mate. Molly, you're to go home with this lecherous dotard and provide him with every comfort."

The nurse flounced virtuously away, but the effect was spoiled by Rue reaching out a long arm to nip the neat buttock.

"You dare!" she hissed. She blushed easily and frowned

convincingly, but her glance would have done credit to Brewer Street. Rue chortled as the door slammed.

"It's good to be alive in a permissive society," he said, and tossed the paper to the floor.

The picture was a poor one, with that dead look which is all the police photographer ever elicits from his sullen sitters. Pibble doubted whether any but a trained eye would recognize Gorton from it.

"Interesting bod," said Kelly. "Highly inventive in a very narrow discipline. Did you know we had one of the kids here?"

"Marilyn? I've met her."

"You're a citizen of a mealy-mouthed stupid country, Jimmy, all hypnotized with liberal drivel. A man like that should have gone for research—poke about in him, find out what makes him bonkers, keep him alive as long as any bits of him are useful, then put him down. And in twenty years' time there wouldn't be any more like that—we'd know how to spot them in the ovum and abort them. And in a hundred years' time we'd be able to tinker with their genes and pow! another model citizen rolls off the assembly lines."

"Don't give yourself nightmares."

"Bloody sight more deterrent than hanging. Bloody sight more useful than locking him up for twenty years and letting him out in time for his old-age pension. But the way things are we'll still be squatting round jabbering about ethics when the hundred years are up."

"Are you trying to tinker with genes?"

"Christ! With the kit I can buy in this job! Until Ram found us a fairy godfather I was doing my research with a thermometer and a stethoscope and trotting down to Saint Ursula's with a little bag of samples once a week. If you want to know, Jimmy, my prime research tool has been a pencil and paper."

"What can you achieve with that?"

"Write down two and two and notice that it makes four."

"Do you need a scintillation counter for that?"

"I've got to check my sums, haven't I?"

"Mr. Thanatos says your part of the research is very important."

"Ho! Does he just? What caused that flash of sanity?"

"You're researching on the physical side, and he doesn't want a life after death if it isn't physical."

"Oh, Mary and all the Holy Angels! That a young man should have to finance his research on that kind of codswallop!"

"What does your research consist of?"

"You wouldn't understand if I told you."

"Try."

Rue laughed, the embodiment of professional scorn.

"When you get your Nobel Prize," said Pibble, "you're going to keep popping up on the telly, explaining what you got it for to ten million viewers just as dim as me. You might as well get a bit of practice."

Rue sneered at him, rubbed his chin, looked at him again, eased his crotch, and held up a bony finger for the class's attention.

"I am an endocrinologist. Glands to you. The endocrine system sends out signals to the rest of the body telling it how to react, how to function, how to grow, when to stop growing, how to repair itself and fight off disease and maintain its own inner balance. The signals take the form of a chemical code. Some of them stimulate activities and some inhibit them. Your endocrine glands are dotted hither and yon round your decrepit cadaver, but the little beggars all work together by signaling to each other—more this, less that— and affecting each other's output of hormones. Hormones,

Jimmy. Remember the word, because that's what we cunning specialists call the juices which the glands shove out by way of signals. We give them a nifty name to show we understand 'em—we've got 'em taped. Only we don't and we haven't. We understand a bit here and a bit there. We've spotted fifty separate hormones, of which fifteen are major ones, but the overall picture remains a mess of guesses.

"Only, out in the wilds, all unbeknownst, there's a brilliant and handsome young Irishman working with a group of kids called cathypnics. Next year, God bless my native wit, there are going to be seventeen known major hormones, and on top of that there's going to be a glorious chart accounting for all possible hormone structures—several thousand—and explaining why so few of them actually work and finally—glory, glory—predicting the existence, structure, and function of half a dozen ones which haven't been noticed yet but must exist."

"Crippen!" said Pibble. "That sounds like ten men's work. How did you manage that?"

"Well, you may have noticed that the kids here are a bit different from other kids. You have? Great. You'll make a detective yet. They suffer from one straight hormone deficiency, which I got taped some time ago. All cathypnics have that missing; it's hereditary; it makes 'em a bit stupid, but not enough for anyone to think they've got something physically wrong with them—in fact there are quite a lot of 'em about. They're all men, by the way; the women can carry the gene, but it doesn't affect them; they simply pass it on unknowing, and then it's got a fifty-fifty chance of surfacing in each one of the next lot of lads, which is the Lord Almighty's idea of a good joke. That's what we call the heterozygous form of the disease. But if both parents carry the gene, then you can get the homozygous form, which is what the kids here have got.

In their case there's another hormone, very closely linked with the first one, which has come out kinky. It's there, all right, but it's got its message slightly wrong. Now think of this as a code. While it's going out OK along the wires you can't crack it, but as soon as it becomes a bit garbled you've got a clue to go on, and once you've got that you can work on the ungarbled bits—and from there, in this case, you can go on to cracking a whole bookful of similar codes. I, Reuben Saint John Gogarty Kelly, have done that thing. And you, my old mate, are the first person in the world to hear about it."

"That's thrilling," said Pibble. "Like Michael Ventris."

"Michael who?"

"Oh, he was a young architect who cracked the Minoan Linear B script and proved that it was early Greek, and after that a whole lot of puzzles fell into place."

Rue's act shattered at the wrong note, as a glass is said to at the right one.

"That's all balls!" he shouted. "Can't you get it into your head that I'm doing something *important?*"

"It seems a funny place for you to be doing it," said Pibble mollifyingly.

"Funny it is, I don't think. I worked at Saint Ursula's under an old dotard called Professor Kington, who was just not so blind that he didn't spot he had a bright boy on his hands. Old Cory, the GP who used to come up here twice a week to look at the kids' tongues, met him at some sort of medical bean feast and Kington had the wits to guess that it might be a hormone deficiency disease. Practically all the discoveries in the hormone field have been made by research on patients who are missing something, Jimmy."

"That's interesting."

"It's obvious. You can't track the juices which make a

healthy liver work. But if it's not working, and you can spot a difference between what's going into it and what goes into a healthy liver, you're on to something. Anyway, Kington hustled a grant for me out of his pals at Pharmacoid Limited for me to come up here and see whether there was anything interesting. Six months' soft money."

"Soft money?"

"Hard money is what your hospital pays you; or your patients; or the NHS. Soft money is pennies from heaven, some dirty big company deciding to earn a bit of tax relief by financing medical research. They paid me a salary, and paid Saint Ursula's for the cost of my using their kit—blood counts, spectroscopy, this and that. After six months I knew I was on to something, so Kington hustled me another eighteen; he didn't know his arse from his elbow, which is a weakness in a doctor, but when it came to licking the boots of industry you couldn't beat him—I'll grant him that."

"Doctor Silver seems to have the knack."

"Ram?" said Rue sharply. "He doesn't know a thing. He's your pure, otherworldly boffin. He's just been lucky with Mr. T. He'd never have got sixpence out of toughs like Pharmacoid."

Pibble was not in a position to say how pleasing he found it that Rue should try to protect his phony colleague from the prying eyes of an elderly policeman. Hitherto he'd seemed good company in the Black Boot, but not markedly altruistic in his dealings with the rest of the world.

"Kington gave me a bit more time on the machines," said Rue. "He even got the word round his staff that they were not to spit in my face when I asked them for a hand. He had a notion that we were going to pip Campbell at the Maudsley with the next big breakthrough—typical of him that he hardly knew what the Americans were up to. And you heard that 'we,' Jimmy. It was going to be Kington and Kelly's discovery, Kington's knighthood, when he'd done about as much original work on it as a knob designer does on a TV set. Still, all I could do was plug along, and then there was a takeover at Pharmacoid and Kington's cronies got the push and just when my grants came up for renewal a little toad of a man came down from the company to check on my research. I told him I was going to produce results in another year, which was about three times as fast as anyone else could have done it; but I was stupid enough to let on that the results wouldn't include Pharmacoid selling two hundred million pills a year to the suckers on the NHS. I told Toad his firm should consider itself bloody lucky to be financing a breakthrough in medical knowledge, though I didn't then know how big a breakthrough it was going to be. Toad told me that the firm had decided to retrench on its prestige advertising. End of soft money."

"But you stayed on?"

"I had a sod of a time. I did my nut, for a start, and told Kington what I thought of him for letting it happen, and after that I couldn't use the kit or staff at Saint Ursula's."

"But Pharmacoid had stopped paying for them anyway."

"Oh, I could have got by smarming to a few chaps for use of this or that on Saturday mornings. Glad I didn't have to. If I'd gone on like that—taking little samples, measuring radioactive iodine—I wouldn't have sat down to read a lot of literature I'd missed and then got out my pencil and paper and cracked my code. I've a lot to thank Mr. Toad for."

"What did you live on?"

"Posey got me three hundred a year out of the trustees. It meant getting rid of old Cory, but they only hadn't done that years before because there was no one else and they thought it would break the old ninny's heart. I moved into a room here, and eat the bloody awful food here. I run a clapped-out old Morris which I pay for by correcting the papers of Pakistanis cramming for their Membership."

He poked his toe at a foot-high column of foolscap on the desk.

"Screw them," he said. "I've done with that. I gave up smoking, Jimmy. I blew a fifth of my income on one pint of Guinness and a tot of whiskey a day. For five months you've been swilling your horrible horse piss in the company of a saint, and never once have you stood him a double of the good stuff without expecting to be stood your pint in return."

"I'll put that right, your holiness."

"You'll have to hurry, or you won't catch me before the name of Reuben Kelly is blazoned in neon along the top of the BMA building, and I'm rolling along to Buck House for my KCVO."

"Let's make it tomorrow, before you're famous. Famous men make me sweat. What do you mean by results?"

"Results?"

"You told the Pharmacoid man it would be a year before you got results."

"Oh, that. Paper proving the existence of the two hormones with accounts of the experiments involved; one cathypnic child half cured by injections of the missing hormone; another ditto with a drug to suppress the kinky hormone and injections of the straight one; a third fully cured by both treatments together. Three mongol kids with their disease unaffected by similar treatment. Outline of Kelly's Theory—which is basically a very fancy bit of math—with predictions about the existence of other hormones."

"That's the theory about all possible hormones, is it? It sounds a bit like the periodic table of atoms."

"Yeah, they've something in common—about as much as a Maserati has with a wheelbarrow."

"You did say 'cured'?"

"Yup. Einstein would have got nowhere if he'd had doctors to assess his papers. They'd have wanted to be shown a bit of light bending. Doctors are too stupid to believe anything they can't actually see. Kelly's Theory works. It accounts for all known phenomena in the field in a pure and elegant series of rational steps. But nobody will believe a word of it until I show them a cathypnic child with a normal temperature and sleeping normal hours."

"And no more McNair?"

Kelly had been describing his achievements with jaunty satisfaction, letting all that bottled-up triumph flood out, unstoppable once the first dam of reserve was broken. But now he twitched his feet off the table and looked coldly at Pibble.

"What the hell are you getting at?" he said.

"I only meant it looks as if one result of your work will be the disappearance of cathypny."

Rue continued to look at him. Pibble thought it an odd example of his friend's arrogance that he should take so amiss a mild misunderstanding of his exposition, even if it was the first time Kelly's Theory had been revealed to the wondering world.

"You haven't been listening," said Rue at last. "You think I'm going to come up with a pill which will turn all the kids here into bright, normal, healthy boys and girls, hey presto!"

"No. I don't imagine you can do much for the existing ones, except make them stay awake longer and live longer. But if you can get at them while they are still babies . . ."

"And have two lots of hormones fighting it out in their teeny bloodstreams? Or keep them hopped on the suppressor drug, and the hell with side effects? Institute nationwide scanning system to check all newborn babies for cathypny—i.e., train several thousand more technicians to use electron microscopes to distinguish between almost indistinguishable molecules in blood samples? Lot of money to spend on finding forty kids a year. This is a rare disease, mister, and we get every single one who survives, because even the most boneheaded GP is bound to spot the cathypnic ring in the end. Quite a few must die before that, of course, because they're erratic at producing antibodies and phagocytes and all the other little beasts that keep you from dying every time you catch cold."

"But still . . ."

"Oh, you make me sick! All of you. The kids here are sitting pretty. There's a lot of other diseases for you to worry about—babies born that even their own mothers can hardly bear to look at but which our sloppy society insists on keeping alive though they're only not vegetables because they're dirtier than vegetables. But cathypnics are happy. They're warm. They're not lonely. They're loved and coddled. If they *do* get hurt, they've a very high pain threshold, so they hardly notice. No old age, no neglect, not a care in the world. And then they die as easy as falling asleep. But even if that weren't true, you're not seriously going to argue that sorting out their troubles is one millionth as important as learning how the machinery of the average, useful citizen turns over."

"Do you know, I was set that very equation, in slightly different terms, just before lunch. I can't answer it. Will you be able to tidy up your theory with your pencil and paper and scintillation counter and a bit of looking into children's eyes?"

"Looking *what?*"

"When I came in this morning you were looking into the eyes of one of your patients, and then you told us that another one, Mickey something, had six days to live."

"If you tried to catch burglars by that kind of reasoning, no wonder they gave you the boot. You know about the cathypnic ring, so you think I can use it to see how fast the kids are dying. Ho-ho. That ring is a genetic marker, a side effect of their heredity. *Any* doctor, shown a patient in a coma, looks into the eyes because the coma might be caused by a cerebral tumor, whose effect you can see in the fundus. I check my ward now and then to make sure none of the brats are dozing there for the wrong reasons. That's all. These are shallow waters, Jimmy, but you're out of your depth."

"Sorry. You said something this morning about . . . was it biopsies still to do? What does that mean?"

"Oh, Christ!" said Kelly wearily. "The ecstasy of educating you is not as great as you imagine, Jimmy, my old mate. I've work to do."

Ostentatiously he took the top paper from the pile of foolscap, made a neat note in green ball-point in the margin, and started to read.

"I'll be off in a moment," said Pibble, gawky with the sudden rebuff. "I got a message from Doll that you wanted to see me."

Rue looked at him, put the paper back onto the pile, and took a flimsy green memorandum sheet from the tray beside it.

"Hell, yes, I do," he said. "I'd forgotten in that orgy of popular science. What on God's earth is this about?"

"STAFF ORGANIZATION," said the paper. "On Mr. Thanatos' instructions Mr. James Pibble is authorized to inquire into and report on all aspects of staff organization at the McNair Foundation. I have every confidence that heads of departments will cooperate. PDJ."

"How did Posey take that?" said Rue, sharply genial now.

"Not very well, I'm afraid."

"I thought not. She's signed it with her initials. That means she's furious. You'd better look out, Jimmy."

"It's a misunderstanding. It doesn't mean anything. I'm not going to do it. I told her."

"You'd still better look out. You don't know our Posey. She's a barely suppressed paranoid, and she goes berserk when she thinks anyone is trespassing onto her empire. Six months ago that dismal little switchboard in her room went dis, and superscientist Kelly was called in. I found a hairpin which she'd dropped across the terminals. I teased her, I admit, but if she'd had a knife in her hand she'd have gone for me, simply for showing that her control of the establishment was marginally less than total. Cross her in something important and there's nothing she wouldn't do. Nothing."

"Except hurt the children."

Rue shook his head.

"She's mad," he said. "Mad people don't think like that. You'd have said the same about fathers who suddenly smash their family up with the coal hammer before they hang themselves. They wouldn't have done anything to hurt the children either. And then they do."

"Doctor Silver thinks she's a very good woman."

"Are you clever about people, Jimmy? I know you got the sack and all that, but earlier you must have met men who'd done their own horrible thing, and then been collared. You saw them under pressure. You took them apart, as far as you could, and looked at the bits. But supposing you'd known one of them fairly well *before* he went off the rails—could you have guessed he was going to? Or that he might—that the potentiality was there?"

"Now *you* are making a layman's mistake," said Pibble. "The people who do what you call their horrible thing are practically all deprived, mentally subnormal, and oppressed by life. The typical murder is messy, sad, simple: a mother who's been deserted, gets her maintenance erratically, lives in a rotten basement with three kids, youngest won't pot train—for obvious psychological reasons which the poor girl is too deprived to have heard about. She gets so exasperated and beaten down that one day she starts to hit the kid after its just dirtied its last clean pants, and she can't stop and she kills it. Certainly, if you know the family at all you can spot that that sort of thing *might* happen, but—"

"I know, I know," said Kelly impatiently. "But you must have met a few cases where the villain was neither a moron nor a pauper. What about *them?*"

"I think there's nearly always an element of obsession, and if you can spot that . . . But I've been married to Mary for twenty-eight years now, and though I can guess how she'll probably react to something, I can't be sure. I don't know what it's like to *be* her. People are like weather forecasting. Observation of past patterns can—"

"Ram Silver, for instance," interrupted Rue. "You're going to be involved with him. Do you trust him?"

"Completely/largely/partly/a little/not at all. Tick the adverb of your choice. Then, in not more than twelve words . . ."

Pibble's attempt to joke the conversation out of this awkward area was a mistake. Rue swore at him in chilly Erse. Pibble couldn't understand the words but he caught the meaning.

"I seem to spend my day infuriating the staff," he said.

"Who else?"

"Mrs. Dixon-Jones."

"You told me about that."

"This was the second time. There's an off-chance that this chap, Gorton"—he scuffed the fallen paper with his toe—" might come down here to look for Marilyn. I've been talking to the Yard about it, and they want us to take precautions. I told Mrs. Dixon-Jones about it, and she was very angry indeed."

"D'you mean you've invited a horde of your old mates down here?"

"I don't think they'll come. It's a very long shot. Something Marilyn said to me suggested that Gorton regarded her as a sort of mascot, or oracle."

"Oh, don't come that with me. The kids are too stupid to know what's going on, and if they did their vocabulary is too small for them to be able to formulate sentences that you can interpret."

"You're probably right. But when I came up a lot of them seemed to be drifting down into the hall, without being told. It'll make it far easier to keep an eye on them."

"You'll get used to that, if you stay here. They often gather together for no known reason."

"I expect so. One curious thing is that Mrs. Dixon-Jones is exactly Gorton's type."

"Yes," said Rue in a mildly surprised voice. "Yes, I suppose she is. You want to keep out of her way, Jimmy—not just for your sake but for all of ours. Some days I breathe a sigh of relief when she goes home to that little flat of hers."

"I thought she lived on the premises."

"She's just sane enough to know she'd be stark staring if she did. I'm sorry I lost my cool with you, Jimmy. It's just that sometimes you're too bloody fastidious to be human."

"Oh, I thought it was because I was quoting. If you can't take Shelley from Doll then I shouldn't expect you to take Kellogg from me."

"Great!" cried Rue. "I have bechewed those flakes!" Either he hadn't practiced his mimicry of Silver enough, or his return to good humor was less spontaneous than it seemed.

"Time I went," said Pibble. "I wouldn't like to come between a Pakistani and his Membership."

"Work," sighed Rue, ostentatiously putting his feet back on the desk in such a way that he toppled the pile of Membership papers across the floor. Pibble bent to pick them up while Rue stared at the ceiling and sighed the syllable again.

"Let 'em lie," he snarled as he noticed what Pibble was doing. "Screw them all—I've done with them. Watch your step, Jimmy. See you."

Pibble felt worse than ever as he picked his way through the tools and splinters on the laboratory floor. His fear of Gorton's coming flooded over him. He recognized that this was a superstitious fear—doubly superstitious, because he nearly certainly wouldn't come, and if he did he was still only a man. An aberrant man, but human.

Still the fear remained, mixed with the deep depression of his talk with Rue, which for all its spurts of jokiness had been tense and strained, so that he wondered whether it would ever be possible to resume the Black Boot relationship again. Having seen him on his own ground, having felt his passion for his work—as narrow and obsessed in its own way as Mrs. Dixon-Jones's possessiveness with the children—it would no longer seem quite real to loll and chat about nothing much over their beer. He stopped at the door into the ward, wondering whether Rue had valued their meetings as an island of calm from his obsession, whether he'd chosen Pibble as a man remote from the striving world. If so, all that was spoiled. It might recover, but . . .

The atmosphere in the ward was not much better, because the nurses were quarreling.

"But we've only done two," said the tall one, Angela, a little hysterically. "At that rate we won't get round in a week, and they'll get so sore . . ."

"It's what the man said," snapped the shorter one. "You can cross him if you fancy it."

"I'll go and ask him," sniffed Angela.

She walked off toward the laboratory door as the plump one bent to insinuate a fine tube into one of the children's nostrils. Her buttocks were her most animated feature—no wonder that Kelly's fingers had strayed to the very brink of infamous conduct. Her lively flesh, surrounded by the chill swathed shapes of children who would never reach even to her small tally of years, struck Pibble as a nasty incongruity; he wondered whether the effect was deliberate, engineered by Kelly in his choice of nurses. It was like one of those weird orgies in churchyards to which the adherents of austere medieval heresies suddenly became prone. Or supine, as the case might be. All the bourgeois hairs on Pibble's nape rose at this fanciful tableau of bad taste. He scurried out of the ward.

The hall was worse, though. From the gallery it looked like the aftermath of a massacre—a bomb in the airport lounge. Bodies sprawled patternless; between them figures mooned, as if stunned with shock.

"Satisfied?" said a harsh whisper, and Mrs. Dixon-Jones ghosted out from behind the pillar at the top of the stairs.

"Are they all here?" said Pibble. "Where's Marilyn?"

A shapely finger pointed, and he recognized the dull green sweater amid a jigsaw of chubby torsos and limbs. A head beside it stirred restlessly, as if the sleeper were in the middle of a nightmare.

"I thought the others kept away from her," said Pibble.

"You'll see, if you go down there. Oh, God, I'm not sure how long I can stand this! If you've done it for nothing I shall never forgive you."

I shall never forgive myself, thought Pibble, and went slowly down the stairs. A delegation of three mooned over to meet him as he reached the last step.

"Mister," said one.

"Frightened," said another.

"Please," said the third.

Their high drawl, a voice with the tone of death in it, seemed to make the fear a material substance, a heavy gas lying in a layer above the jaunty carpet. He felt that if he had stooped he would have breathed fear.

"It's all right," he said. "He can't get in. There are coppers coming to look after you."

"Come," said one of the children, and the three of them turned away from him as starving villagers might turn away from a lorry which they thought brought rice but in fact carried a cargo of birth control leaflets. He could ring up the local station, or the Yard, for news. Instead he decided to look outside first. Ivan was in the porch, wearing a First World War trench coat, reading the same edition of the *Evening Standard* that Kelly had had. Mrs. Dixon-Jones must have posted him there—once committed to a course of action, however much she disapproved of it, she would carry it through as efficiently as she could manage.

"Don't they give you the creeps, eh?" said Ivan. "They've never been like this before, not since I've been here. Think it's something to do with this joker?"

He flicked the dismal photograph with his fingernails; Pibble pretended to read the news for the first time.

"Why should it have?" he said. "The man might go anywhere."

"We've got one of the kids here, and that's in the Stop Press, so they must think it matters."

And it was. Pibble wondered whether Callow had held a press conference ("Had to give the bastards something, Jimmy, and there wasn't another crumb") or whether it was an old-fashioned leak from a subordinate, worth about a tenner in these inflationary days.

"They're bound to catch him soon," said Pibble. "A chauffeur's uniform is pretty conspicuous."

"A chauffeur?"

"I thought it said that," said Pibble lamely.

Ivan's brown eyes looked at him, and the little beard shook sideways.

"I hope to God he doesn't come," he said. "Poor sod! No wonder they're scared."

Pibble longed to get away. He was more and more conscious that the whole horror might be the product of his own mind—*his* subconscious revolt against the watery monotony of retirement bodying itself, through the children, into this melodrama. That's what Mrs. Dixon-Jones thought, and would never forgive him. Quite right, too. If he took himself off, perhaps he'd remove the central cause of all the fear; but he couldn't go right away until the local police took over.

"I'm going for a stroll," he said. "I'll be back in ten minutes."

"You know what you're doing," said Ivan, shaking his head again. "I won't come and look for you if you yell, mind."

Pibble grunted and strode away up the gravel. It was not yet dusk but it was cold, and the sun must be low behind the banked layers of cloud to the west. He walked fast, partly to keep warm but partly to get away from the house; the shrublined path to the terrace bent back on itself and became a short flight of steps, at the top of which he turned and looked down the hill. From here you could see that the roof line was just as crankily exotic as the walls, with spires at the farther corners as well as the two he had seen from outside the porch; and at the center of the quincunx rose a glass onion, which must be the dome that gave light to both sets of stairs. And height seemed to confirm his fantasy of the children's fear being like a heavy gas: now he could see what a storm in a teacup the whole preparation was. Gorton, now, would be miles away, skulking in a builder's yard or (if he was lucky and the rest of us not) exercising his electric dominance over some dim-witted tart, who would conceal him and keep him while he built up a base, honed his knife, and then began to stalk the suburb for the woman (fortyish, blond, A/B readership, snappish but confident in her fur-trimmed suede coat) who would be his next slow-dying prey. The odds against his coming to the McNair were so great as to be not worth thinking about, let alone acting on.

Beside his elbow the rhododendrons rustled.

6

His heart bounced once, then settled into a quick, loud thud. He could feel his palms slippery, and his cheeks chill with withdrawn blood. But he did not run—the inertia of civilization kept him still while he waited for the thudding to quiet and for his mind to persuade his muscles that the noise was no more than the rootling of some clumsy bird.

"Don't turn round, Jimmy," said an officer-type mutter.

"Oh, it's you."

"Who the hell did you think it was?"

"I don't know. You found something in the notes, Ned?"

"He kept saying, 'She knows. None of you know.' "

"That might mean anything."

"Yeah. They were turning a Bakerloo tube round at Elephant and Castle when they found an unconscious man in his shirtsleeves. You don't knife a blighter if you want his coat."

"How long ago?"

"Couple of hours. They got on to me just after I'd finished with you, so I came myself instead of ringing the local boys. He'll have tried buses from there, and he won't know his way. I reckon we've got an hour before he comes."

"You haven't found the chauffeur's cap and jacket?"

"We're looking. I want you to clear off now, Jimmy. Nothing personal."

"I'll be glad to go, as a matter of fact. The waking children are all in the main hall, including Marilyn Goddard. Mrs. Dixon-Jones, the secretary, is keeping an eye on them. The sleeping ones are in a ward, with Doctor Kelly in charge—he's head of the medical research side. There's also a Doctor Silver who runs other branches of research."

"What the hell do you mean by sleeping and waking?"

Pibble explained.

"All the waking children are very frightened," he added. "They get it from each other."

"Don't bother me with that kind of rubbish."

"The *Standard* has a piece about the girl in the Stop Press."

"We had to give them something, Jimmy. There wasn't another bloody crumb."

"I know. They've got the builders here. I told the secretary to see that all the ladders were locked up, but there's scaffolding all down one side. You'd better go and see the secretary —she thinks I'm making the whole thing up."

"Heaven help you if you are. So long, Jimmy."

"Shall I take you down and introduce you?"

"Might as well."

With a crash Callow burst from the concealing evergreen. Twigs clung to his tweedy suit and his hair, but his military stance made it look as though he were deliberately wearing them as light camouflage.

"I was doing a bit of a recce," he said. "Last thing we want to do is scare the blighter off—I want him inside the ring, and then I've got him. I've tucked the cars out of sight already. Next thing is to tuck my bods away all round, and then I'll give the building a quick once-over. But even if he *has* got here, he'll lie doggo till dark, and break in then."

"I'd have thought a northerner might fail to find his way here at all," said Pibble. "South London can be very tricky, and he won't feel like showing his face to ask people."

"I rang the prison again. His woman came to visit him before she went to Australia, and he asked her a lot about it then. They forgot to tell me. Bastards!"

"It looks as though he'll at least try to get here, then?"

"That's my thinking. Jesus, what a pile!"

Pibble was interested to find that Callow's sensibilities were not so hardened that the building failed to impress him.

"It grows on you," he said.

"I'd like a place like this, Jimmy. Out in the country, of course—couple of lakes, pheasant shooting, home farm . . ."

"You should meet my friend Mr. Thanatos. If he liked you, he might stand you one."

"Your friend?"

"Only since lunchtime."

"Jesus!"

They came to the porch, where Ivan looked relieved to see a recruit of Callow's meaty bulk.

"This is Superintendent Callow," said Pibble. "Is Mrs. Dixon-Jones still on the landing?"

"Hope he's brought a few of his mates," said Ivan.

"Now listen to me, my man," said Callow. "This is a very serious affair. You are to keep your mouth shut or I'll make mincemeat of you."

"Mince away," said Ivan, cocky, with relaxed tension.

Callow took a half pace forward and swung his arm in a practiced curve. Pibble couldn't see whether his fist was open or shut, but he heard a fleshy crack as Ivan reeled against the wall of the porch and then stood shaking his head. Callow opened the door and walked in as though the place were already his.

"Wonder when *he* last had his ears boxed," he said loudly. "Too long ago, anyway. Hello, here's a cheery lot of little beggars!"

He stood and stared at the stodgy throng. Several of the recumbent ones stirred and sat slowly up, and one child came toward him with a gradualness that again reminded Pibble of the bored explorations of aquarium specimens.

"Copper," she said.

"Officer," said Callow. "And keep a civil tongue in your head, my lass."

"They only know about three hundred words," said Pibble.

"Then they'd better be the right ones."

"Help us," said the child.

Pibble decided that it was only the removal of responsibility that made him sense a faint change in the tinge of terror in the hall.

"Copper come," said a child by his elbow—Fancy Phillips. She smiled. Mrs. Dixon-Jones was coming down the stairs with the pace of a party-giving marchioness about to obliterate two gate crashers.

"And who is this, Mr. Pibble?" she said.

"Superintendent Callow of Scotland Yard," said Pibble. The difficulty of keeping a note of self-justification out of his voice made him sound nervous. "He's in charge of the search for—for the man we've been talking about."

"Indeed?"

"I have a dozen men with me, ma'am," said Callow. "There's nothing to be afraid of."

His tone was manly, reassuring, but somehow subservient, as though he could recognize a superior officer even in the mufti of femininity.

"Do you seriously believe this creature will come here?" said Mrs. Dixon-Jones.

"I am in charge of the case, ma'am. I wouldn't be here if I thought he was more likely to go somewhere else."

"I hope you have better evidence than Mr. Pibble's imagination."

"A couple more pointers, ma'am. Pibble could be wrong, but they seem to bear him out."

(In the eyes of the Yard, Pibble was a sort of ghost; but his shoulders were evidently substantial enough to carry the can once more.) Mrs. Dixon-Jones sighed—as though the presumed gate crashers had turned out to be the bailiffs.

"What do you want me to do?" she said.

"Show me round, then carry on as normal. Who else did you tell, Jimmy?"

"I told Doctor Kelly. Ivan, the man in the porch, worked it out for himself, and I'll be surprised if no one else has."

"Right. But we won't tell anyone we needn't—I don't want a lot of hysterical nurses rushing about. *They* seem to know something's up, I'd say."

He gestured at the children.

"Oh, yes," said Mrs. Dixon-Jones. Callow blinked.

"I'll be off, then," said Pibble, and started up the stairs.

"Hang on if you want to, Jimmy," said Callow with some urgency. Was he wanting an ally, however irregular, for the skirmish with Mrs. Dixon-Jones? More likely he felt that any friend of Mr. Thanatos had better be a friend of his.

"Thanks, but I've got an appointment," said Pibble, and ran the two flights to the gallery. Only when he was there did he release his breath into whispered curses; he knew that Callow had hit Ivan partly for the fun of it, but partly as a deliberate demonstration in front of Pibble of his own power and authority. Even if Ivan made a complaint, even if Pibble supported his statements, the accusation wouldn't stick. A wispily bearded youth, a sacked, jealous, unreliable ex-colleague—what weight would they carry against the bluff, open, Sandhurst manner backed by testimonials from several senior officers who would know perfectly well which side was likely to be telling the truth? But Callow had always been an "effective" officer. Pibble now less than ever. He turned the corner.

The honorable Doll, swinging along in an emerald max-icoat, was coming toward him down the corridor. He stopped cursing and waited for her.

"I've seen my man and now I'm free," he said. "Is the offer of tea still open?"

"Super," she said.

"Is there another way out? The hall is full of people I've said good-bye to, and the stairs just behind are covered with paint pots."

"There are stairs in all the towers, but Posey keeps them locked in case the dormice fall down. My father used to practice climbing the drainpipes during the vacations—it was all he did at Oxford as far as I could make out—and he said they were quite easy."

"Too athletic for me."

"We could get onto the roof through the trapdoor in the linen room and climb down the cedar tree. That's as easy as a staircase, but it's frightfully dirty. You know what cedars are."

"I've never grown one. Don't let's get dirty."

"Thank heavens. This is a new coat. That leaves the fire escape."

Even the fire escape involved an eight-foot drop from the final stair.

"Yippee!" cried Doll, and leaped. The green coat para-chuted round her so that the builders' night watchman, who was feeding a brazier by the arch into the stableyard, must have had a ravishing view of plump legs. She tottered and nearly fell, but backed against the wall laughing.

"If I can, you can," she called.

"Old bones are brittle," grumbled Pibble, and lowered himself until he hung by his hands, then dropped. At once she slipped her arm through his.

"All my life I've been cheated out of uncles," she said. "I don't mind about the aunts. We can get out at the bottom of the melon ground."

"I hope you have a warm night," said Pibble to the night watchman in a jaunty attempt to show that this wasn't a case of breaking out and exiting.

"And the same to you, cock," said the night watchman. It was Alfred.

Doll took him out through the arch, loosing another "Yippee" as they passed beneath it. The stone work yippeed back.

"I always do that," she said. "My father showed me. He always did it, too."

Behind the house lay a square of blue-purple brick paving, tilted toward a central drain hole, for washing coaches on, and later limousines; and beyond that rose a high wall of pitted brick with one wide door in it. This led to a long but narrow walled garden, sloping along the ridge, with greenhouses along two walls and well-drilled fruit trees on the others. The center space was dug to a level perfection that pleased the would-be-peasant segment of Pibble's soul, but nothing grew in it; only careful stacks of cloches showed that it had ever grown one blade of green.

"It's a change from the rest of the garden," he said.

"It's all let to a gentleman called Mr. Sideburn. We don't have anything to do with him, except if he's growing freesias he always sends us a bunch for the funerals. Bad taste is more touching than good taste, sometimes."

"What does he grow in the greenhouses?" asked Pibble, already concerned about the day when his body would have retired as much as his mind. He'd be past digging then, past hoeing, perhaps up to a little pruning on balmy afternoons; but he might still eke a few years' pleasure out of tending alpines on shelves that he didn't have to stoop to.

"Cucumbers," said Doll. "He keeps them beautifully hot. Before Ram came they were the only place where you could keep warm if you didn't want to be with the dormice."

She rubbed her ear purringly against his shoulder and led him down past a long bed of globe artichokes, their last leaves gray as a ghost in the dusk, to a little door in the bottom wall. The key hung by it on a nail; she unlocked it, hung the key back, and let the door click locked behind them.

They were out in the public road, where the violet lamps of evening were on and the traffic hustled; a streetcleaner, busily chivvying nonexistent leaves along an already speckless gutter, leaned for a moment on his broom to peer at them.

"Hello, Mr. Pibble," he said. "How are you doing?"

"Not too bad, Leventhorp. You seem to have come down in the world, though."

"Makes a change from hauling high-minded hooligans off cricket pitches. Good night, sir."

"What on earth was that about?" whispered Doll when they were across the road. Pibble told her. She shivered and snuggled close in against his side as they turned up a long, bleak side road of stuccoed and bow-windowed villas, with the last disheartened blooms of Peace and Queen Elizabeth poking ungainly above the privet hedges.

"Don't let's talk about that," she said. "Do you realize that all this used to be our park? With deer in it? Posey's room was called the Justice Room, because that's where great-grandfather sentenced poachers. Granny's house is still called the Dower House, and we're walking along the private path between the two. It's 'The Way Through the Woods' inside out—you know, steadily cantering through."

"But there is no road through the woods," said Pibble. "Why does Rue make such a fuss about quotations? He was furious when I compared his work to Michael Ventris'."

"Was he? That's nice, because it means it isn't only a way of getting at me. He was brought up bilingual, Erse and English, and made to wear clothes of hand-woven Connemara cloth, and little old pansies who'd once known the big guns—Yeats and people like that—were always in and out of the house. He hated them all, he says. Last winter he made up a blue version of *Dierdre of the Sorrows*, which he spouts for hours when his work's going badly. He hates *me* talking about my family and the McNair, too, and you can't steal that from me because I'm the only one. I expect wife beaters' wives feel jealous when their man bashes other women."

"Yes, they do, usually—sometimes it's the only thing that will make them give evidence. Rue doesn't just dislike the building because it's old and nonfunctional?"

"That's what he *says*, but . . . Uncle Pibble, you're a beast. Why do you want to meet Granny? She's an acquired taste, you realize?"

"Well, I *am* interested in what it was like here fifty years ago, but really I just want to see what she's *like*. Idle curiosity. I wouldn't have had the nerve to ask if I hadn't still been a bit tight on Mr. Thanatos' champagne."

"What's *he* like?"

Pibble tried to give a brief geography of that vast, intricate, and largely unexplored continent, all on the strength of his own brief visit.

"I liked him," he concluded. "You must have had a big park."

"Here we are, you poor old man."

She swung him into a drive. The Dower House had only one spire, but there was still enough light for Pibble to see that the rest of it could serve for a sample of the main building. The gawky intransigence of its convoluted bulls-blood brick gave it an unlikely dignity in the context of the trivial repetitions of the rest of the street.

The hall reeked of damp, hairy dogs. A radio was blaring a dialect account of a shepherd's life in the thirties, with the volume turned up so far that the cheap loudspeaker jarred on every other syllable. Doll put her palms to her ears and ran at the noise as though it were milk boiling over on the stove. It stopped, and a sharp old voice said, "I wasn't asleep, darling."

As Pibble hesitated into the room terriers foamed snarling round his ankles until Doll took them by the collars, tossed them out, and slammed the door. Then she bent over an armchair and kissed the fungus-colored cheek. The old lady dragged a tapestrywork reticule from under the rugs on her knees, fumbled in it with impatient fingers, and fished out a pair of gold-rimmed spectacles, which she held up to her eyes without bothering to open the ear pieces. Through crannies of lens she peered briefly at Pibble, then prodded the spectacles back into her bag.

"He won't last you long, darling," she said.

"He doesn't have to, darling," said Doll as she drew the curtains and switched on more lights. "I brought him for you. He knows all about murder and rape and things like that, so I thought you could have a nice bloodthirsty talk together. His name is James Pibble."

Lady Sospice cocked her head.

"Wife dresses in pink?" she said.

"Usually," said Pibble.

"Got you now," said Lady Sospice. "I told Posey Jones to have you in to find out why that Armenian was flooding the place with money."

"Doctor Silver, you mean?"

"My dear man! He's not got a penny, and whatever he is he isn't an Armenian."

"Oh, Mr. Thanatos. I had lunch with him today. I got the impression that he is genuinely interested in the children's, er, mental powers. He isn't spending a lot by his standards."

Lady Sospice threw her head sideways and up, like one of her own terriers, and sniffed. Doll had left the room through another door and was making kitcheny noises beyond.

"He's up to something," said the old lady. "No Armenian ever gave a penny away without a reason. You do your duty and find out what, Mr. Pobble."

"I gather he now, well, almost owns the place."

"It's a scandal! But he's not been as clever as he thinks. He can't touch the house, because it's a condition of the trust that the children live there, and he can't touch the children because Posey Jones is their legal guardian."

"I didn't realize that," said Pibble. "It's not a common arrangement."

"My husband insisted on it. Do you think, Mr. Pobble, that we gave away that *beautiful* house—simply gave it away— in order that this Armenian should steal it?"

Pibble thought of the capital that must have been realized on the thousand villas that now obliterated the deer park.

"I wonder what he wants it for," he said.

"He wants it because it is beautiful," said Lady Sospice with a definitive nod. "That type of person has never known what real beauty is. Naturally he is envious."

"It must have been, er, even more beautiful before all this building was done."

Rings sparkled as Lady Sospice threw up her mottled hands.

"My dear man, it was a dream. These lovely hills, all spoilt now. I could look out of my bedroom window and not see a tree my husband didn't own. But it was a responsibility, a dreadful responsibility. So close to London, you know. People were always breaking in and wandering wherever they wanted, as if the land didn't belong to anyone. It was not so bad when I was a gel—I married my cousin, you know, so I knew the house then. The village youths could be a nuisance, but they were all our tenants so we knew what to do with the tiresome families. But when this ghastly disease— it is like a disease, don't you agree? a friend of mine used to write me long letters from the leper colony where she worked, poor silly thing—when this disease spread over the fields and there were *people* all round us, people we didn't know and couldn't control, though my husband was a magistrate until he died—well, they used to walk right into the garden, to say nothing of letting their mongrels chase the deer, and they could be most rude when one went to turn them off."

Pibble nodded sympathetically, like a priest hearing a penitent confess to a sin which he didn't know existed. He thought it curious that the smaller but similar pretensions of Mrs. Dixon-Jones, that good woman, were still almost unbearable, while the Napoleonic snobbery of this old bag had become an acceptable aberration. It didn't matter any more, it was make-believe, an exercise in the historical imagination. But Posey Jones could still hurt "dear Mary."

"Why did you choose cathypnics?" he asked.

Again the rings flashed in a gesture of amused amazement.

"Oh, dear, *I* didn't choose that or anything else while my husband was alive. His favorite gamekeeper, a man called McNair, had a child with the disease."

"Shall I tell him, or will you?" said Doll, walking in with a three-tier cake stand populated with little iced fancy cakes.

"I don't know what you mean, darling," said Lady Sospice, and effectively gagged herself by snatching a pink cake and stuffing half of it between her gums.

"Mrs. McNair had her baby in 1901," said Doll. "Grandfather had sent McNair away to fight the Boer War two years before, and he was still away. Grandfather took a particular interest in the child, and brought specialists down when it became obvious that there was something wrong with its health. One of them discovered cathypny, as he'd seen another child with it, and so grandfather started a home for cathypnics as a sort of hobby; at first I think he only wanted to be guardian of the McNair boy, so he made himself secretary and put that in as a condition of the trust, but as the others began to arrive he took just as much interest in them. Anyway, that's why Posey is their guardian now, and that's —"

"I expect Mr. Pobble would prefer *Indian* tea," said Lady Sospice through crumbs. "Is there any in the cupboard?"

"No. Will you have Granny's dishwash or my Nescafé, Uncle Pibble?"

"Tea, please."

It came in a silver teapot, as of yore; but alas no spirit lamp burned blue under a silver kettle on bowed legs. Lady Sospice poured thick cream into hers, added five spoons of sugar, stirred, and at last sucked at the brew with hissing pleasure.

"I've seen Granny take sugar with all five courses of a meal," said Doll.

"Nonsense!" snapped the old lady.

"Soup, peas, pudding, cream cheese, and coffee."

"Coffee's not a course, darling. I don't think I've ever taken sugar with fish. I don't count kedgeree, because that would be breakfast."

She was obviously flattered by talk about her sweet tooth, as though it were the last remaining vestige of many prowesses. Pibble looked out of the corner of his eyes at Doll, who was sitting with her legs twisted under her at the back of a large, lopsided armchair. The half-curled position, her plump smile, and the way her whole body seemed tense with the pleasure of its own existence, made her look as if she were about to purr aloud. Her eyes were brown and bright—not green, and no trace of a ring. But she wore another kind of ring on her ring finger; Rue Kelly could never have afforded that, but the old lady wore several of the same caliber. Doll's father had evidently been a sad ass, a tragic Wooster; the original illegitimate McNair must have received the cathypnic gene from both his parents— Hey! Doll's grandfather and Lady Sospice were first cousins! No, that didn't mean anything—cousins only share one set of grandparents, so he could have got it from the other side, and been one of the males in whom it hadn't surfaced. But there was a fifty-fifty chance that Doll herself carrried the Lord Almighty's idea of a good joke. So Rue would never marry her, not though she supplied herself with fifty engagement rings. He saw the emeralds blaze as she reached down to finger a little scar on the taut knee, and then sensed the silence in the room. Was it his turn to say something new already?

"I met Mr. Costain this morning," he said. "He was photographing the mausoleum in the wood. He was very enthusiastic about its brickwork."

"I don't think I've met the gentleman," said Lady Sospice.

"He's secretary of the South London Preservation Society.

He's been helping the local preservation people—the ones who you said could look through the Sospice papers."

"Ah, *those* little people. I meant to tell you, Dorothy darling, that I do not wish to see them any more. They are becoming a nuisance."

She gnawed at a green cake with some emphasis, but Doll leaned forward in her chair and plucked it from the old hand and held it just out of her reach. It was a game. Pibble watched with fascination over the rim of his piping cup. Lady Sospice was a wicked troublemaker—trouble being excitement, the last sea wall against the rising boredoms of great age—and Doll was expert at playing her around so that she did no harm. The relationship was strangely like marriage; in fact Pibble wondered whether the one had been, or the other would be, so happily mated ever.

"You're stuck with them now, darling," said Doll, "and you know it. You brought them in to tease poor Posey, and —"

"I cannot understand why they refused to make *you* secretary," said Lady Sospice, driving suddenly crosscourt.

"Because I was eight when the job was last vacant."

"They ought to have kept it for you."

Doll handed the cake back.

"No, thanks," she said. "I have more to do with my life than becoming obsessed with dormice."

"Your grandfather wouldn't have liked to hear you call them that, darling."

"It suits them so well—don't you think so, Uncle Pibble?"

"In a way. But it's a symbol for not having to think of them as people, individuals. I'd have thought that might be dangerous."

"Just what my husband used to say," said Lady Sospice. " 'They are not pets,' he was always saying. But then he was always much too clever for me, and much, much too good."

She lifted a tiny lace handkerchief as if to wipe away a tear that had quivered into her eye at the memory of the dead baron's brains and virtue, but used it to brush a large blob of green icing from the corner of her chin. The blob fell to the carpet, and Pibble bent for it.

"Don't bother," said Doll. She bounced up and opened the door through which they had first come, and the terriers streamed in. The blob vanished on a thin pink tongue, and Lady Sospice began to cut three more cakes into smaller cubes, her old, blotched, mauve-veined hand quivering wildly before each stroke and then forcing the knife down with sudden precision. Pibble was surprised to find, when the dogs had lined up for their sugary orgy, that there were only three of them. Lady Sospice fed them in turn, brusquely, as if she were giving them medicine.

It was a soothing scene, a break from the scurryings of the day. Pibble sipped carefully at his sherry-colored smoke-and-hay brew and thought how elusive even the immediate past could be. It had been a day like a battle scene in a low-budget film whose director has tried to conceal the smallness of his armies and the paperiness of his stockades behind billowing cannon smoke and close-ups of horses' hoofs. Gorton was no more than a loom of darkness in the mist, if he was there at all. Mr. Thanatos was a huge figure, certainly, but if you could see him from the side perhaps you would find that he was an inch thick, flat, propped by rough balks. And the most impressive experience of all, the bush telegraph between the children's minds, was also the most airy-fairy. Again, he found, he was half sure that he must have kidded himself into showing Marilyn coin and knife, button and nut, before she had made her choice. And if Thanassi was insubstantial, Ram Silver was more so. The *real* ones were the ones like Mrs.

Dixon-Jones, and Rue Kelly, and this titled harridan. You couldn't imagine a flicker of thought passing between mind and mind in *this* room, not though Gorton himself stalked in.

"Tell us about something nasty," said Doll. "Not you-know-who, but something that happened ages ago, with all the characters dead."

"High life or low life?" said Pibble.

"Gran?"

"High life, please," said Lady Sospice primly, as if she were asking for another plate of cakes. "And I hope you will speak charitably of anybody I might know. I remember the dear archdeacon once . . ."

She launched into an uncappable story about the dear archdeacon's sister and the precentor, which, she claimed, had caused a considerable rearrangement of the promotion ladder to the see of Canterbury "because, of course, that's why he went out to Sumatra and that other man became archbishop. And I believe that he would have been considerably more understanding of that poor weak boy's difficulties than Archbishop Thing was, and then there would have been no abdication and this tiresome war would not have happened at all."

"The war's over now, darling."

"Nonsense, darling. You know quite well that none of the butchers has started delivering again, so that you have to traipse all over the town to buy my doggies' offal. That's what I mean by war."

"Isn't she marvelous?" said Doll. "You ought to be in a museum, darling."

"Yes, I should. There's no such thing as civilized values left in the world today."

"What happened to the precentor?" said Pibble.

"He shot himself. He had *some* decent instincts."

The telephone rang. The dogs yelled at it and went on yelling as Doll ran into the hall.

"You lost your job, they tell me," shouted Lady Sospice.

"Yes, there was a reorganization, and I was almost due for retirement anyway."

She sniffed and gagged herself with another cake. Pibble, left hanging in his defensive posture, drank the last chill dregs of tea. Doll rushed into the room, stumbling among terriers.

"The house is on fire!" she said.

"Then summon the fire brigade, darling."

"Not this house. *Our* house. The McNair. The telephone was out of order, but they found a police car in Montagu Norman Close, and sent a message over the radio. That was Mr. Costain from the phone box by the pond. He said you ought to know. He said it's burning like a torch. There was an explosion. He's just seen two fire engines go past."

"What about the children?" said Pibble.

"He didn't say."

"Fetch my chair, darling," said Lady Sospice. "I would prefer to see it go."

"I'll run ahead and see if there's anything I can do," said Pibble.

"Fiddle-de-dee!" said Lady Sospice. "They've two fire engines there, and I need you to push my chair. It's far too heavy for a slip of a girl. Help me up."

She held out two loose-skinned hands; their touch was as cold as the cathypnics'.

"Now pull," she said. "Not too hard. I'm very light. That's right. Now my sticks. Good. Now I can get myself out into the hall."

"I'm doing a hottie for you, darling," called Doll from the kitchen.

Lady Sospice grunted. She needed all her energy and concentration for inching herself over the carpet. When a terrier tried to fawn on her she stopped and thwacked it with one of the sticks, then inched on again. For the first time Pibble realized that she must live in continual pain, like many of the old. Doll was already in the hall with a wheelchair; neat and quick with practice, she eased her grandmother into a shapeless squirrel overcoat, lowered her into the chair, settled a hot water bottle into her lap, swathed her in shawls and scarves, and finally skewered a black straw hat, such as charladies wore in the George Belcher cartoons of the thirties, to her spindly hair. Pibble took the bar at the back of the chair and wheeled her out, over the doorstep, with a bump into the night.

The sky to the west was an unnatural orange. The villa gardens were full of people, watching and pointing. Some were already drifting along the road to where a fire engine brayed up the hill.

"Quick," said Lady Sospice. "We don't want to miss anything."

"Move over," said Doll.

Together they shoved their senile cargo up the slight slope at a good five miles an hour.

"Come on, Uncle," said Doll. "I don't want to miss anything either. I adore fireworks. We'll go up the road. The paths in the melon ground are a bit bumpy for Gran."

The pavement in the main road already looked as though a procession of major royalty was expected next morning, with loyal citizens already staking out their cheering points, but there was room to push the chair up the steeper slope behind the rows of gawpers. A small crowd was bothering the uniformed constable at the main gate, but Doll ruthlessly nudged the backs of their knees till they let her through.

"Can't come in, ma'am," said the constable. "Move along, please."

"Nonsense, my man," snapped Lady Sospice. "This is *my* house."

"Is Superintendent Callow still here?" asked Pibble.

"Oh, it's Mr. Pibble, isn't it?" said the man. "You don't know me, sir, but I know you—I'm local. I daresay that's all right, sir."

"Has anything been seen of your chappie?"

"No, sir. P'raps he started this fire as a diversion, though."

"Where are the children?"

"The little ones were all outside when it started. They're swaying the big ones out through a window—there's hoists and scaffolding there. Lucky break, sir."

Another fire engine was clanging up the road. Pibble whisked the chair into a nook of rhododendron and let the thing through—it was an old-fashioned one, gleaming like a regiment. They followed it down the gravel to the front of the house.

Doll had been right about fireworks. An oily cloud hung over the roof, its underside lit orange, and into this huge sparks curved and whirled from what seemed a roaring chimney of flame at roughly the back of the hall—yes, those inner stairs, all covered with paint rags and paint and containers of spirit. *That* would go up like a bomb, if a cigarette end had been left smoldering there when the workmen knocked off. Pibble remembered an arson case out Acton way in which two brothers had so soaked their cousin's house in gasoline that they were blown clean into the street when they lit it. Two fire engines were ranged at the near corners of the house, and the latest arrival was already jolting up onto the lawn and disappearing round the far wing. A conference of firemen was taking place in the middle of the gravel, their chin straps seeming absurdly thick and heavy compared to those on police helmets, and their holstered hatchets wagging at their buttocks like docked tails. The whole front of the house was lit, as if for *son et lumière*, by the searchlights on the engines; the house itself supplied part of the *son*—loud crackles and a steady, windy roaring—but most of it came from the deep, intolerable drumming of the diesels that drove the pumps.

"The fire hasn't got very far, has it?" shouted Doll.

"They'll try to get at the base of it," shouted Pibble. "From either side. But remember all that wood, and how dry the heating must have made it. And the smoke will heat it more."

"You seem to know a lot about it."

"I've taken a course."

He looked round the gravel sweep to where the cathypnics stood all together, their moon faces faintly reflecting the orange glare. Higher up was a group of men, among whom he recognized the parade-ground stance of Ned Callow. He didn't feel like another encounter now, so he walked over to the children. Ivan was in charge.

"Won't they get cold?" said Pibble.

"I'm just waiting till Doctor Kelly's finished wheeling his lot into the greenhouses, and then I'll take them down. It's heated there."

"Has he got them all out?"

"Like magic. I ran up to give him a hand as soon as I'd counted the dormice, and he'd got a window out of the ward already—he had some tools up there, see. And we slung them out onto the scaffolding and down on a couple of hoists. We'd done half of them before the firemen came. And he even had a key to the greenhouses. Trust him!"

"Where's—" started Pibble.

"Hi! What's that sod up to again?" said Ivan.

Pibble followed his glance. A pinioned figure was struggling in front of Callow, screened from them by the detective's ominous bulk. Excited stirrings tickled the edges of the group. Pibble looked quickly away. It is difficult to judge the force necessary to arrest and restrain a homicidal maniac; it is also foolish to be a witness of the amount Callow and his team might judge necessary. Suddenly the fire seemed to have lost its drama; it was like some tedious diseuse trying to recapture her audience after the real star's face has shown itself tactlessly in the wings. The night was cold, the fire hot —but not enough to account for the way in which it now felt colder behind him than in front. His neck muscles ached with the strain of not looking round. Ivan had copied him and was also staring purposefully at the orange gouts from the roof and the thickening smoke. Two firemen in breathing apparatus climbed out of the downstairs window at the bottom right-hand corner, and began to report to a superior. He could see from their attitudes that they had been driven out —the fire was still winning.

"Mr. Pibble, sir?"

His taut muscles tried to jump and cringe at the same moment. Callow's sergeant blinked at the convulsion.

"You all right, sir?"

"Yes, thanks—I swallowed a sneeze. Courcy, isn't it?"

"Yes, sir. We've collared a character up there—not our villain, but sneaking in the bushes. He says you can vouch for him."

"All right."

It was Vivian Costain, undamaged. Some instinct must have restrained Callow from hitting a citizen who had the necessary skill and persistence to make trouble for him afterward. Costain had been refused reentry at the gate after his telephoning, so had climbed the wall by the wood and come down through the shrubbery. Pibble explained who he was, and Callow looked disgusted, as if it were intolerable for a military man to have to meet an aesthete without ordering his hair to be forcibly cut and giving him a good kick in the pants.

"I'd prefer to have him officially Ok'd," he rapped. "No offense, Jimmy. Where's that Jones woman?"

"She goes home in the evening," said Pibble. "I'll ask Ivan."

Ivan hadn't seen her.

"But I told the firemen she'd gone home," he said. "They wanted to know whether to search the building. The dormice say she's gone, and they'd know, because she always says good night to them last thing. She was just going off to do her rounds when I last saw her; that's what she always does, too. Posey's gone, hasn't she, Dickie?"

"Posey gone," whined a child.

"Poor Posey," said another.

The fire changed its note, and Pibble looked round. Upward-streaming beards of flame rose now from three windows of the upper floor, to the right of the porch.

" 'ot." said a child.

"They're not themselves, you know," said Ivan. "They haven't been all afternoon. I suppose it's only natch. One thing—it's the first time anyone's seen them all awake together."

Pibble went back to Callow. Mr. Costain was running a finger round inside his collar as if trying to preen out the creases made by the arresting fists. Callow snarled at the news.

"There's that Indian gentleman I talked to this morning," suggested Mr. Costain. "He has status here, I think."

Pibble searched again. More orange flared from the rooms leading toward Kelly's Kingdom.

"They won't save that wing," said Callow judiciously. "Not against the wind."

By the sudden light Pibble saw Silver's white hair shine against the rhododendrons; he had taken off his dustcoat and his dark skin made him otherwise invisible against that background. Pibble crossed to him.

"Could you come with me, Doctor Silver? Just for a moment."

"A pleasure. This is sad, sad, eh? That beautiful house."

"You've been very lucky about casualties."

"Yes indeed. I have seen hospital fires where . . . Aha! It is Mr. Costard!"

"This is Doctor Silver, Ned," said Pibble. "Doctor, Superintendent Callow wants to know—"

"One moment," said Dr. Silver. He turned casually but firmly away, like a monarch who has dispatches to read before returning to gossip with his courtiers; he strolled down across the gravel toward the still unburned east wing, and disappeared behind the thudding fire engine. The group round Callow had watched him, astonished but unstirring. His back was as authoritative as his front. Pibble somehow still felt that the uncompleted introduction was his responsibility and had drifted a few dithering steps toward the building, but when Silver disappeared he began to run. Someone else was moving quickly in the same direction from farther over to his left. He rounded the bellowing pump, whose hoses snaked in to the window of the corridor, and made for the corner of the building. A hand gripped his shoulder.

"He went in there," shouted a voice. It was Alfred, pointing at the open window of Mrs. Dixon-Jones's room; the top center pane of the bottom sash was smashed, but no one would have noticed that slight tinkle amid the uproar.

"Shall I go first, sir?" yelled Alfred. It was an order. Pibble followed him clumsily over the sill. The room was tangy with smoke but not intolerable, and ghastlily illuminated by the searchlight outside. Alfred slipped a pencil flashlight from his pocket and without looking round nipped through the door;

Pibble was half across the room when he stopped. Something caught his consciousness as being different—yes, he had seen without noticing as he was climbing in that the door into the tower staircase was now open. Odds were that Silver had taken the key from the board over the mantelpiece and gone up.

After the glare of the searchlights the stairway was like black felt; the air might be breathable, but it looked stifling. He nipped back into the room—even Mrs. Dixon-Jones's erratic lighter would be preferable to total dark. But it was gone. Nothing for it. He climbed slowly on hands and knees, remembering that it is fatal to work yourself into the frenzy of action when you begin to pant. The bedroom at the top was only permeated by a faint, far smell of burning, though the searchlight glared into it and the pumps and the flames roared together. But the corridor was black, and swirling.

He shut the door, thankful for the dead, misguided craftsmen who had fitted it so well to its jamb that no trickle seeped through; till their work actually burned it was almost an airlock. He counted doors in his mind and decided that the laboratory, Silver's room, and Doll's were the third, fourth, and fifth down the long corridor to the back of the building. He took one more good breath and walked firmly out into the smoke, moving easily to the corner, feeling his way round, crossing the corridor and counting doors. It was difficult not to feel that the smoke was chasing him, as the smoke from a bonfire sometimes seems to. His nerve was already failing him as he reached the fourth door, groped for the handle, found it on the other side, opened the door, and staggered through. Involuntarily he took an eager gulp of air and began to choke; it was breathable, but not good.

And the room was Doll's. It was nice to be able to see, though the light here was not the blue-gray glare of the floodlights but the bloody light from where half the windows on the far side of the courtyard were fountains of murky orange. Tassels of flame dotted the southwest spire below the copper sheathing, and the weathercock was hidden in the upward-flowing smoke. While the wind held, this side was probably safe from the flames, but he felt he had already taken risks enough. He hurried into Silver's den.

It was empty.

Furious with himself at his mad pursuit of a hunch, a belief that for consistency's sake Silver would rescue what he could of his research papers, Pibble stood and swore at the empty leather chair. Its black shadow wavered slightly with the orange light from the burning wing, so that though (perhaps) he sensed another slight movement behind him, he didn't connect it with anything in the room.

The crash of agony at the back of his skull was the first, and last, he knew.

7

Perhaps he was never really unconscious. There was blackness and in it he was being shoved about while his arms threshed weakly at an enemy as vague as smoke. And then there was the orange light and he was lolling on softness, but with a searing head. He tried to jerk himself up, into a posture to meet another attack, but an iron bar across his chest held him back.

"You try to get out, fuzz, and I'll hit you again."

The slow, sad voice was Silver's, not Gorton's. Pibble lolled again.

"The smoke's getting very bad in the corridor," said Pibble. "If these doors didn't fit so well we'd be asphyxiated."

Silver said nothing. He was working through his filing cabinet, carrying folders to the window to peer at the name on the label, dropping some to the floor, and putting others into a big briefcase. Pibble discerned that he was tied to the leather chair with the cord of the desk lamp; he would be able to wriggle out, downward, in a few seconds the minute he was left alone. If he was left alone. Between the diminishing pulses of pain from the back of his skull he tried to decide what to say to Silver—who, to judge by the attack and that single sentence, had assumed that Pibble knew all. No time, with the chomping flames working along the far wing so fast, to try to coax him into believing that Pibble knew nothing after all.

"I thought you'd be here," he said. "I'm glad you weren't simply making a run for it."

Silver hesitated with a file above the briefcase, then tossed it angrily across the room so that it sprayed a trail of papers to the wall; if the firemen didn't manage to save this wing the flames would have a good snack to start with when they got here. From the furnace beyond the courtyard rose a sudden snorting explosion. The blast of it whuffled against the panes and Silver peered out at a part of the far wing Pibble couldn't see.

"Rue Kelly's lab," he said.

"Were you ever a fire chief?" said Pibble.

Silver tore the file he was holding clean across and threw it on the floor.

"You think I'm playacting, don't you, fuzz?" he said. "Just one big game, and if the other side scores against me I do my five years like a sportsman. D'you know how old I am? Sixty-three. And nine years eight months of that time I've spent in prison, sent down by judges who knew less law than I do. 'Prisoner at the bar, you have abused your natural advantages. The court psychiatrist has attempted to help you, but you have been deliberately uncooperative. I have no alternative, in view of your record, but to sentence you to five years' penal servitude, and may the Lord have mercy on the one-fourteenth of your soul which that represents.' I am a man of peace. I do not enjoy hitting even fuzz on the head. But will you give me peace? Four times—*four* times I have had my teeth into my life's work, I have gotten started on a career

173

which would have satisfied me; four times your kind have come shouldering in and picked me out from behind my desk and thrown me into the street. What law am I breaking now? Even my passport is straight—or straight enough. I am using my own name. I have a work permit. I'm not reckoning to lift any of Thanassi's dough, and you try to prove I am. Nah, you won't so much as try. You'll just say, 'This villain has a record. We've pinched him before for conning rich layabouts, and now he's at it again.' And then you, or one of the ones like you, come and lean on my shoulder and breathe down my neck until I slink back into the gutter where I *have* to make my bread out of stupid oafs with money they never earned."

"I didn't mean that," said Pibble. "I meant do you know anything about fires? I've been taught about them, and I've seen quite a few. We're not as safe as we look. You can hurt yourself pretty badly jumping from an ordinary first-floor window, and these are higher than most."

"Ten seconds to the fire escape. I can hold my breath that long."

"In any case, I think you are being a bit precipitate. Mr. Thanatos told me he didn't care how valid your credentials were. You could tell him the whole story, and I think he'd let you carry on."

"You told Thanassi about me?" Silver sounded too sad to be angry.

"Not on purpose. I remembered who you were when I was in the car going up to London this morning, so I used the car telephone to ring a friend in the Records Department, just to check. I told him I wanted the details for a lecture. I didn't tell Mr. Thanatos anything, but I tried to find out how much he knew. I wanted to talk to you. I wanted time to make up my mind. I didn't know that my conversation with the Yard was automatically put on tape, and that Mr. Thanatos would learn about it that way."

"The lays I've had spoiled by crooked little men wanting their cut," said Silver. "Cops, bellhops, clerks, ponces."

"I don't want a cut. I had no reason to tell anyone about you, at least until I'd made sure that you were working a lay. I had the idea that you weren't. When you skipped off just now, Superintendent Callow only wanted you to identify Mr. Costain—they'd caught him in the shrubbery while they were looking for Sam Gorton. Callow's in charge of the hunt, you know. There was a theory that he might be coming here to look for Marilyn."

"That bastard Callow," said Silver. "I know *him*. And I know you, too, though I've never had dealings with you. You're not a crooked little cop, you're a fastidious little runt. You'd tell. You'd argue about being a responsible citizen, yeah, but in your soul, in your soul you'd know you were telling because you were afraid they'd find out without you, and find out, too, that you'd known before them."

"You must have been hell in the confessional."

"Never tried it. I'm *low* church, by habit and conviction."

Silver, who had conducted the previous tirade with heat and vehemence, now spoke in tones of chilly rebuke. Astounded, Pibble realized that he was being snubbed for talking so freely about the privacies of a man's beliefs on the strength of a single day's acquaintance. Some subjects are taboo, even in a burning building. . . . Suddenly he was reminded of the oddity of Kelly's brush-off when he had asked a similarly harmless question. Perhaps it would boost Silver's self-regard, nudge the pair of them back onto the safe and complacent relationship of doctor and layman, if Pibble asked Silver the same question now.

"What's a biopsy?" he said.

The nudge was a disaster, setting off a mine. Silver strode across the room and stood over Pibble, black in the orange light, huge with nearness.

"You want to make it worth my hitting you again when I go, and leaving you here—with the door open?"

He spun round and returned to his papers. The light from the fire was now so strong that he could read them at the cabinet without carrying them to the window. Pibble began to think about burning, about those incredible martyrs who had stood smiling on the faggots while their skins became crackling. He tried to cheer himself by arguing that he'd be very unlucky not to fall unconscious with the fumes, and then stifle, before ever a flame licked him; but that knowledge could not quench the imagination of fire. If he spoke, he'd remind Silver of the enemy who had aborted four careers, stolen one-fourteenth of a soul, walked into this strange pitfall with an idle question about a technical medical term; but silence meant smoke in his nostrils, orange light in the room, fire in his mind. " 'ot," the tape had said. "Frightened," it had added. It had been right.

"I hadn't realized that biopsies were important," he said. "I was just being inquisitive."

Silver snarled quietly.

"The trouble is that now I'm more inquisitive than ever," said Pibble. "If you'll tell me, I'll swap the information for something you'd really like to know."

Silver stood for a moment, weighing a file in his hand.

"You first," he said.

"How do I know that you'll tell me anything afterward?"

"You don't. It's always like that. You want me to let you hold my wallet to show how much I trust you?"

"If you'll let me walk out of the room with it."

Silver laughed shortly.

"Give," he said.

"OK. The man I rang up in Records—his name's Bradshaw, and he gets things right—he says you're dead. You died in the Congo. Your body was found. Your file is closed."

Silver let out a long sigh.

"Dead, am I?" he said. "Hallelujah! Dead! Man, that's great, great!"

"Callow didn't recognize you—"

"Who told you he knew me?" said Silver, instantly suspicious.

"You did. You said that you hadn't had any dealings with me, in a way which implied you had with him."

"Yeah. He tried to pinch me once, and couldn't get the evidence. He worked me over a bit then, and wasn't happy when I stuck it out. I reckoned you told him, so I decided to cut my losses. You learn to ride at a loose mooring if you lead my kind of life."

"Anyway, he didn't recognize you with the moustache and your skin that color. How did you manage that? Injections?"

"In Crete, man? Nah, my skin is that color. My mother was a tart in Dublin. Dockyard area. My father must have been some kind of wog. I good as grew up under an umbrella, to keep the sun off me. The poor old bag would throw a fit if she knew how long I spend under the sunlamp these days, just to keep my color up. But give me three weeks of English winter and I'm white, clear white outside."

"It must have been hard to keep it up in the Southward Islands."

Silver, who was now sorting through his files in a totally different manner, as though he were almost drunk with pleasure at the news of his own demise, laughed again.

"I wore a topee, day in, day out. Best time of my life, you know? First thing I did when I got there was give the jail a raking over. My duke was hot on prison reform, in a la-di-da way, so I could give those jailers hell. Best lock-up in the colonies, by the time I left. Next thing was to screw the police chief's missus, but she turned out so eager that I let her fall flat. There are disadvantages in being a duke, and that's one of them. Then I got all worked up about trying to sort out those poor sods of savages, who'd been left dangling halfway between cave men and factory hands; it was that got me up against my colleagues in the liberation movement—*they* didn't want a happy proletariat, or who'd there be to liberate? They turned out to be a different kind of fuzz, with beards. Fuzz in blue are happy once they've arrested a guy, no matter who, and got him sentenced; that's one more crime statistic on the right side of the ledger. Fuzz in beards are happy once they've shot a guy, again no matter who. Once he's dead he's one less lackey of capitalist imperialism. Y'know they spent three years hunting for me? They got no sense of proportion. That's when I started going out in the sun and wearing Arab clobber."

The light from the window suddenly died. Silver cursed in the new dark and Pibble saw his shape against the faint rectangles of the window.

"Bloody smoke," said Silver. "I should've brought a torch."

"Smoke coming this way?" asked Pibble.

"Yeah. Can't see a thing. You see films of fires on TV, and they're lovely flames, like fireworks. I didn't reckon it'd be like this."

"The wind's changed," said Pibble. "We'd better be going. You can tell me about biopsies later, or I'll look them up in a medical dictionary."

"Fuzz," said Silver explosively, "you're a bloody fool!"

Pibble could just perceive him stalking across the room to

stand above the chair. Then a rift in the smoke let in a second of light, by which he could see that Silver was weighing in his hand, much as he had weighed the file ten minutes before, the Brancusi-like paperweight from the desk.

"All I got to do is lay you out, sling you in the linen room, and go. They'd reckon you'd blundered in there looking for a window to jump from, and there ain't one, so you'd been asphyxiated. If I hit you right, and you got burnt a bit, I don't reckon they'd notice a bit of bruising."

Silver spoke in a peculiar grumbling tone, as though he had been landed with an unwelcome moral responsibility which he would have to see through. The dark returned. It would work, Pibble knew, provided the actual flames got that far. Forensic pathologists hate burned bodies because there is so little chance of discovering the processes that preceded the roasting.

Suddenly an indistinguishable shout—not of panic, but of somebody giving an order—rang down the passage. Pibble almost shouted back, but realized that this might topple Silver over the edge into reluctant violence.

"It wouldn't work," he said, dry-throated. "They've got a lot of firemen here, and engines. The less of the building there is left to save, the more chance they've got of saving it."

Silver dropped the paperweight with a thud.

"Maybe you're right," he said. "I couldn't have done it anyway, I guess. I wouldn't like you to think I'm that kind."

"Let's go," said Pibble. "If we stay here much longer we'll get poisoned, and besides, I don't fancy being rescued. I'd rather get myself out, unnoticed if possible."

"Me, too. And if the wind's changed they'll have men at both ends of this wing. Oh, sod it! I'm too old for jumping."

"Where's the linen room?" said Pibble.

"Over the way."

"Doll told me that you could get up onto the roof through it and then climb down a cedar tree. She said it was easy—easier than the fire escape."

"That Doll," said Silver, still in his grumbling tone. "We'll give it a try. Last thing I want is a lot of goddam publicity, now that I'm safely dead."

As he stooped to untie Pibble's cord they heard another shout, followed by a long, groaning crash. The noise seemed to come not from across the courtyard but from somewhere near the archway at the back—almost in their own wing.

"We'll need your matches," said Pibble. "We'll have to see."

"Right. Grab the back of my jacket. Ready?"

The room, which had seemed so dark when first the smoke rolled over it, was now just discernible. Pibble took a deep breath of the rancid air as he saw Silver reach for the door handle. The door swung open, and the real dark shouldered through, shaped for the instant and solid, an opaque mass. He felt Silver hesitate, then lurch into the smoke. The corridor was a horizontal chimney, a roasting draft, but they were only in it for three seconds before he was crowding after Silver through another door on the opposite side and helping to slam the good mahogany behind him. It was ominously warm to the touch. Cautiously he breathed out a little, then in, and at once all his precious lungful exploded into coughs. While he gasped and stumbled the dark became light, and through his tears he saw Silver standing picturesque, holding a little globule of pale flame, barely bigger than a raindrop, at his fingertips. Pibble's choking subsided; he found that the air was in fact breathable, just.

"See that," said Silver. "Not much oxygen in here. We got to hurry. There's your hatch."

He raised his head toward a square recess in the ceiling,

above a slatted shelf of neatly stacked sheets. Then he dropped the match. It went out before it reached the floor.

Pibble was already climbing up the shelves before the next match flared. Silver handed up his briefcase and the matchbox and then climbed himself. When they were sitting side by side, heads bowed under the ceiling, Pibble struck a match and lifted one side of the hatch about an inch. White smoke poured down as though it had been a liquid.

"Better get to a window and be rescued after all," he said.

"Not me," said Silver. "There'll be cameras out there by now. My friends with beards have a lot of pals in London, pretending to be Chinese waiters. It'd be just my luck if one of 'em recognized me, the very day I learn I'm dead. There'll be a skylight somewhere near, and this roof's only slates. We can shove them off the battens."

"I don't like it," said Pibble.

"OK, I'll tell you what. You wait here while I give it a try. Shut the hatch when I'm gone, to keep the smoke out of here. Count thirty, light another match, and open the hatch again. If I'm in trouble I'll be able to come back to the light. OK?"

"No," said Pibble.

"Screw you," said Silver as Pibble struck a match. In one astonishing spasm of effort, lumbering but rapid, he had risen from the shelves and thrust himself up into the hatch. The match went out with the flurry of movement, but Pibble heard the hatch slap back into place. He began to count. Madman, he thought. And going so fast, using all that energy. He'll be wanting to gasp before he gets anywhere at all. At twenty Pibble had the matchbox out, with a match head poised against the scraping surface. The blundering noises above his head had ceased. He thought he heard another noise, which was not the sound of deliberate action, nor yet any of the clicks and grunts of the woodwork changing shape under the steady heating of the smoke. It might have been anything, even a big half-Arab gasping his life out. Pibble struck the match at twenty-six, worked his feet onto the shelf, and rose slowly until his scalp touched the painted wood of the hatch. This was even warmer than the door. He took a last breath and stood carefully up, hingeing the lid back as he went.

A desert wind smote him from the right and the match went out.

Still quite slowly he climbed through, stood, and walked forward with outstretched arms. The floor was planks, not joists. At the same moment as his fingers touched rough timber his shin knocked into hardness. He pawed at the obstacle, then stood on it. It was about eight inches high and as soon as he moved forward again his shin hit another; he was on a set of steps. He reached in front of him and his fingers found glass, the skylight. With an effort he opened his eyes and saw it, too, white but opaque. He could find no catch at either edge, and was about to kick the glass out when something about the shape of the frame timbers told him what to do. He felt down and found a handle on the bottom frame; a single jerk shot the whole sash back and up, over his head—glory to Doll's great-grandfather and the unwarpable cedar. The direction of the desert wind changed, streaming out and up; he clambered with it and rolled himself sideways onto the tiles.

As he gasped for real air and found it, he was slithering down. Instantly a fresh panic whelmed him: perhaps the parapet only ran across the monstrous façade, and here he would shoot straight over the gutter and fall two stories. He scrabbled uselessly at the slate until his shoulder thudded into stone.

He stood up, shivering, in the lead gutter, and peered over the knee-high wall. The cedar was there, sharp black against the floodlights, a thick branch swooping across the parapet and brushing the slates with its needles. Through the other gawky batwings of branches he could see a cluster of bustle down at the corner of the wing to his right, and another up to his left on the edge of the gravel. An ambulance honked out into the lane. It'd take him minutes to attract anyone's attention, and more minutes for them to get a ladder and professionals up here. He decided to have one go at finding Silver himself. As he turned back toward the hatch, smoke poured in an avalanche down the tiles and drowned him.

He came out of it, weeping and coughing, and saw that iron steps led up from the gutter to the hatch. He climbed them, breathed carefully in and out and in, and felt his way down against the warm rush of air, eyes shut. He fancied that the last sounds of Silver's movements, if that's what they'd been, had come from the northern corner of the linen room ceiling, so the moment he was off the steps he started to crawl to his left, counting as he went, vowing to turn back when he reached twenty. His left hand felt the slanting beams, so that he didn't lose direction, and his right swept in wide groping arcs across the splintery planks. It touched cloth at twelve, barely six feet from the steps.

Pibble felt his way round the inert shape. As he put his arms under the shoulders the whole figure threshed, once, in a galvanic spasm, and he lost his grip. He stood, verified the slope of the beams, bent again, and began to heave the body back toward the steps. No nonsense now about not wasting oxygen. In thudding dizziness he felt the steps nudge against his calves; he dropped the shoulders and plunged for the open air, where he lay for a full half minute, gasping and watching the ridge for the next rolling wave of smoke. Next time in he got Silver's head and shoulders onto the steps, but lacked breath and strength to heave him straight out. Third time, with three tearing bursts of heaving he got the head out onto the rim of the skylight, went down to the bottom of the steps and bundled the loose limbs upward, out, working his own shoulder under the heavy buttocks and shoving at the inert flesh.

Then he had to wriggle past the hateful mess of unbudgeable looseness and breathe again.

This time when he felt his way back from the saving air Pibble found that he had in fact forced the body out as far as the waist. It was only when he was rolling it sideways onto the tiles that he realized it might not be Silver at all—it might be Gorton, come, hidden, and then trapped in the smoke. He groaned with relief as the body slithered into clearness and he could see the noble profile of the confidence trickster.

Pibble was giving him the kiss of life, with none of the squeamishness he'd experienced while practicing the technique during first-aid courses, when Silver suddenly shook his head.

"Get out of my mouth," he muttered as Pibble withdrew; at once he turned convulsively away and vomited onto the lead.

Pibble wriggled his arm under his shoulders and lifted him slightly up. Silver's eyes opened.

"Je-sus!" he said. "Je-sus!"

"I'll get the firemen in a moment," said Pibble. "I haven't had time. How do you feel?"

"So-so. You got me out of there?"

"Yes."

"Thanks. Leave the firemen out of it, for the mo. I've half killed both of us to get me out on the quiet, and it's a shame to waste it, yeah?"

"All right. We'll give you a few minutes to see how you feel. I don't think we're in immediate danger. The wind's shifted again. Take it easy."

Silver smiled and shut his eyes. Pibble coaxed him a few

feet along the gutter out of the mess of sickness and let him lie back.

A quarter of an hour later, when the smoke was beginning to pick out the pattern of the tiles as it seeped between them, he was sitting sideways on the cedar branch and working his way down the slope toward the trunk, his hands sticky and foul with a coating of resin and bark dust.

"In my circus days I coulda walked down here," said Silver from below him.

"I'd rather you didn't try. I'm damned shaky and I expect you're worse. Hold it."

They both sat quite still and let a party of five firemen pass below them. It was ludicrous—two old men, the two oldest people on the premises apart from Lady Sospice, lurking like kids in the bushes while the adults fussed about in the open. Pibble suddenly thought of something which made their adventure more purposeless still.

"We've left your briefcase in the attic," he said. "I'm sorry."

"Forget it," said Silver. "You comfortable?"

"Fair."

"Let's rest a bit, then. I live a nervy kinda life, and the worst of it is I got to seem calm all the time. Yeah, I've had enough practice, so it's almost second nature, but a sort of pressure builds up inside, so when something breaks I over-react, like just now. I don't know what I thought I would do with those files. It's only a few months' work lost, and most of that scratching around. If Thanassi'll have me back I can get it all together again—better, in fact—in six weeks. It's a clean slate, and now I've got you to work with—"

"I'm afraid you'll have to leave me out of it," said Pibble.

"Oh, hell, man. I'll make it worth your while."

"It isn't the money. I could do with that, as a matter of fact.

Did you have any background material on the families from which the children came?"

"A bit, but very patchy. I'd hardly begun. I went and talked to a couple of families in the London area, and I was planning to hire an assistant to cover the rest, all the ones I could find. Why? Want that job? It's yours, but you'd be wasted."

His voice had been becoming steadily fainter, the gasping pauses between the phrases longer and more painful.

"No," said Pibble. "I've been thinking about the people who work here, and Gorton, and myself. Almost all of us are obsessional about something or other, or in danger of becoming so. And even old Lord Sospice seems to have been the same. I've been trying to remember whether Gorton had been in any sort of trouble before he went to live at Paperham, that's to say before he met Marilyn. I don't think he had."

"Uh-huh," said Silver. "One of the families I went to, out Dagenham way, had a thing about newspapers—they bought about six a day and kept them all. They used to keep them in the front bedroom, but a couple of years back the weight had brought the floor down and killed the grandfather, who slept in the parlor. They'd built a shack in the garden after that. They were damned proud of it. They called it the library. They showed it to me. That the sort of thing you're after? Something to do with the kids, you reckon?"

"I don't know," said Pibble. "But I think it's possible that one of the reasons why the cathypnics survive at all is that they're capable of arousing an obsessive protectiveness in ordinary people like Mrs. Dixon-Jones. I can feel it in myself, and I don't like it. Anyway, I was wondering, supposing I'm right, whether their effect on people who already suffered from latent obsessions wasn't to bring them out and reinforce them—I mean whether Gorton wouldn't have gone on being a comparatively harmless bully if he hadn't met Marilyn. And your family with the newspapers: that could be either a substitute for the protectiveness which they'd felt when they'd had their cathypnic with them, and which had now been deprived of its object, or it could be something that the child had brought out. And even somebody as clever and sophisticated as Rue Kelly—"

"Yeah," interrupted Silver. "It's a nasty thought; I'll look into it, statistics-wise. I was going to tell you what a biopsy is."

"Don't bother," said Pibble. "I was only trying to change the subject in your room. I can look it up."

"No. I'd better tell you. Uh. Laymen always get our jargon wrong. A biopsy is a sample of living tissue, taken from a particular part of the body for study purposes."

"That sounds simple enough."

"Hold it. I haven't finished. There's all sorts of biopsies. For instance, you can do a peripheral nerve biopsy, take your sample from somewhere there's a nerve just below skin level, like the knee. No trouble, only a local anaesthetic. Or you can go in for the big time and do a brain biopsy, and that's a serious op and needs lots of special kit."

"You'd have to open up the skull?" said Pibble.

"Depends. For some purposes you could do a transsphenoidal, where you run in a special hollow needle just above the eye and draw out a plug of tissue, which you can either mash up and do counts of or slice off thin and look at through a microscope."

"Like the core they bring up to study when they're drilling for oil," said Pibble, thinking of Mr. Thanatos' favorite sport.

"Yeah, I guess so. A transsphenoidal is a trickier thing, though. You've got to know exactly where you're going, guide the needle on an X-ray screen. You need a proper operating room, germ-free. All that. Yeah."

Silver paused and seemed to go off into a sort of trance.

"I suppose a full-scale, er, craniotomy—isn't it?—is an even more demanding job," said Pibble.

"Sure. Sure. Let's get going."

"There may be a policeman near the bottom of the tree, but if so you can leave him to me. Superintendent Callow may have spotted this way in."

Silver only grunted, and Pibble felt the big bough sway slightly as he began to wriggle along it again. He seemed to be going very slowly, gasping a little as he went. At one point his face passed through a diamond of light where the searchlight of an engine just beyond the corner of the wing pierced between two layers of the black branches. His face was hideous with effort and concentration and far grayer than the unnatural glare could account for.

"Are you all right?" said Pibble, but got no answer. Only when they reached the trunk, already considerably lower than the parapet they'd come from because of the slope of the branch, did he let out a long sigh.

"Jesus!" he said. "I thought I'd never make that."

Pibble managed to work his way past him where he leaned against the trunk and climbed to a lower branch. As Doll had said, it was almost as easy as going downstairs, the branches coming exactly where they were needed. He let Silver rest again and then helped him down as if he'd been a child, placing his feet for him at each descent and talking all the time with an idiotic voice of cooing comfort. If there *were* one of Callow's minions at the foot of the tree, he'd have something to gossip about in the canteen tomorrow.

There was not. Silver fell the last four feet, and Pibble only half caught him. He lowered him to the wet grass and walked down the slope to where an ambulance stood apparently idle behind the busy and still thundering engines. Now that the wind had shifted once again most of the smoke was moving in slow masses toward the south. There seemed to be very little glow from the fire—all the illumination came from the harsh searchlights.

At the ambulance he bellowed and pointed, then clung to the door as they jolted and slithered out of the center of din. Silver was sitting up under the tree, but allowed himself to be eased onto a stretcher and lifted into the body of the ambulance.

"He's had a bad time," said Pibble. "But I don't think he's actually injured—it's mostly shock and strain."

He watched while the men parceled Silver into blankets. Now that he was almost unconscious his face, though still noble, had an oddly nondescript quality, as though the guises of healer and guru and even Arab had been largely maintained by a continuing effort of will.

"How come?" said one of the men, straightening up. "You OK, mate?"

"I think so," said Pibble. "We got stuck in this wing. We were trying to rescue some important papers, but in the end we had to give up and climb down the tree."

"Me Princess Margaret, you Tarzan," said the other ambulance man.

"Have you been busy?" said Pibble.

"Nothing much. Couple of firemen slightly singed, and one of the local kids got knocked over when the cops left."

"Left!" said Pibble, startled.

"Should have seen them. Six cars at least, sirens going, all lights on, blasting up the lane. Cor!"

"Was the child who was hurt one of the inmates?" said Pibble.

"Nah. Just come to watch the fireworks. Only a bit of gravel rash."

"We've been pretty lucky, then," said Pibble. "No real casualties in a fire this size."

"Ah, wait a bit, though—there's one deader."

"Dead—who?" Not steel-hearted Alfred, surely.

"A woman. They fetched her out twenty minutes back."

"I never saw Posey."

It was Silver, speaking from the bed, his eyes still shut.

"The children said she'd gone home," said Pibble. "No, they just said she'd gone."

"I would like to know," said Silver. He opened his eyes and began to lever himself up.

"Hey, take it easy," said the voluble ambulance man. "You're suffering from shock."

"Sure," said Silver. "I'm a doctor. I know what I'm doing. Where's my shoes?"

All his authority flooded back as he pulled rank over the ambulance man, who muttered something, helped him to sit, then knelt and laced his shoes for him.

"Where is she?" said Silver.

"They took her away, sir," said the ambulance man. "But the bod in charge of the firemen up at the front knows about her. Take a couple of blankets, sir. You better keep warm. Sure you wouldn't like us to drive you up? No trouble."

"No. I'm OK."

"My mates are ferrying the kids down to the hospital from up there. You could hitch a lift with one of them, sir."

"Thanks."

Silver stepped out onto the turf. The drapes of the blankets flowing down from his shoulders made him look magnificent in the sharp-shadowed glare, the last of his tribe, never to be bound or tamed by the polymer chains of the cities.

"It could be Doll," he said, as they began to walk up, stumbling where forgotten rose beds made hidden curbs amid the coarse grass.

"Not unless she followed us in," said Pibble. "She came back to the fire with me."

"Rue had his nurses out. I checked the ground-floor staff. It'll be Posey, for sure."

Lady Sospice still sat where he'd last seen her, poised on the slope down to the house as though she were waiting her turn to trundle down into the furnace. A group of cathypnic children, watched by Ivan and a fat woman Pibble hadn't seen before, waited farther along the gravel. Only one policeman was visible, the local man who had let them in through the gate an hour ago. He stood up by the entrance and watched the firemen bustling about round their engines. From two ladders jets of water were being squirted through upper windows into the murk of the hall; but everybody's posture or movement had lost the nervous urgency which had been so apparent when the fire began; they seemed settled, almost relaxed, and gave the scene a codalike quality, telling of a drama that was almost over. A fireman in a white helmet, with three pips on his shoulder—an ADO, Pibble thought that meant—came up.

"Doctor Silver, is it?" he said, unamazed by the blanket.

"That's me."

"I understand that you are the senior official, sir."

"Myself or Doctor Kelly or Mrs. Dixon-Jones, the secretary."

"Doctor Kelly went down to the hospital with his patients. I'm sorry to say that Mrs. Dixon-Jones is dead."

"Ah," said Silver, a perfect portrayal of detached, professional regret.

"We have the fire well under control now, but we've still a lot of damping down to do. We don't want sparks still live under the charred wood, do we? We've saved all that east wing. I thought it was going when we had that shift of wind, but it didn't last. I've never seen a building burn like this, not a domestic building. More like a timber yard. We had to make pumps twelve in the end."

"That means they've got twelve fire engines here," explained Pibble. "Of course the house *is* mostly timber, and they've been keeping it very warm for the inmates, so it would all have been dry."

"I must thank you for your efforts," said Silver.

"All in the day's work, sir."

"Did you find where it started?" said Pibble.

"It seems that the workmen left all their paint and stores on the back stairs. That went up like a bomb. I gather Mrs. Dixon-Jones was a heavy smoker, and she may have dropped a fag end there. I'm afraid the whole thing was caused by the carelessness of several parties. Unfortunately we've no real control over the fire precautions of a private institution like this—we can only advise. There'll be a proper inquiry, of course, to establish the exact cause of the outbreak."

"Oh," said Pibble. He longed to let sleeping dogs lie, but training—habit—forced him to ask another question. "Did you find why the telephone was out of action? It's all well clear of where the fire started."

"Yes, I've looked into that. A hairpin seems to have fallen across the terminals."

The man now spoke with a certain chilliness, as though his former polite formality had been a face for turning to the unofficial public. Pibble plowed on.

"The other thing is a silver cigarette lighter, about the size of a billiard ball, made like the globe of the world. You might find that somewhere near the start of the fire. It's worth looking for."

The fireman stared at him for a moment with real dislike.

"This is Superintendent Pibble of Scotland Yard," said Silver, telling the necessary half-truth.

The fireman relaxed, and looked relieved.

"Mrs. Dixon-Jones gave me the impression of being an extremely fastidious smoker," said Pibble.

"That's right," said Silver. "She was nuts about fag ends."

"I see," said the fireman judiciously. "This will all have to be gone into at the proper time."

"Of course," said Pibble. "I hear that my, er, colleagues have left."

The fire officer grinned suddenly.

"You hear right," he said. "Like the movies, it was. I gather they got their man up in Watford—it was on the seven o'-clock news. That big guy with the moustache blew his top."

"Thanks," said Pibble gloomily. "We'd better not bother you any more. I'm not really here in an official capacity, incidentally."

"That's OK, sir," said the fireman, and turned back to his chores. Silver stood watching the action and shaking his big head.

"It's not like her," he muttered. "Not like her."

A hand touched Pibble's elbow. He turned and saw Alfred, still in mufti. The blond eyebrows rose and the blue glance darted over Pibble's shoulder to where Silver stood. Pibble ignored the question.

"Mr. Thanatos would like to see you," said Alfred. "I'll take you now, if you're ready."

"I can't come now."

"He won't like that, sir."

"Well, he'll have to lump it."

The killer look flicked across Alfred's face. Pibble sighed.

"If Mr. Thanatos wants me to tell him what's been happening," he said, "he'll have to wait. I've got to ask around a bit. I can ring him tomorrow, if you like."

"Will you make it tonight, please, sir? Between half past eight and half past nine. This is the number."

Pibble took the scrap of paper.

"I'll try," he said.

Alfred nodded and walked off. Pibble went dully up the

gravel toward the wheelchair. When he was a couple of yards away Doll dashed from behind her grandmother and threw her arms round his neck.

"You're a mad old thing," she cried, shaking him to and fro. "I saw you and Ram go in, and I didn't know what to do. You looked so furtive I thought you didn't want me to tell anyone, but I've never been so frightened. I know mad uncles are best, but they aren't much good to you fried alive."

Pibble wriggled out of her grip, ready to grab at the trundling chair, but it was still where she had left it, its wheels chocked with big flints from the gravel edging.

"Rue put them there," said Doll. "Isn't it awful about poor Posey?"

Pibble bent over the chair.

"This must be a very sad day for you," he said, politeness merging into obsequiousness.

"Fiddlededee," said Lady Sospice. "I'd much rather see it burnt than live to endure that Armenian turning it into one of his hotels, where *anyone* can come and stay. And with Posey Jones gone there's nothing to stop Doll from becoming secretary. Think of that! Take me home now, darling. You can help us up the drive, young man. It's downhill after that."

"Poor Posey," said Doll, kicking the chocks away and turning the chair toward the gate. Pibble took the bar beside her and shoved, struck by the dismal echo. Never again would Mrs. Dixon-Jones dear-Mary Mary. Posey was gone.

Poor Posey.

8

The soft springs of the old ambulance swayed the coachwork lullingly on the curves. Silver lay supine on the stretcher, hair and face and blanket a progression of gray tones. Pibble sat opposite, and against his left side the last two cathypnics lolled asleep; he was the bookend and they the slovenly books. He had to brace himself at each sway against the chill weight, which would otherwise have toppled him sideways, inch by inch. Their presence, against his will, gave the functional dreariness of the ambulance interior a curious warmth and coziness, made the place into a sort of psychic greenhouse; an involuntary picture floated into his mind of Doll and Rue Kelly necking amid the phallic cucumbers. The two children stirred and blinked.

"Soppy," complained the further one.

"Not me—'im," whined the nearer.

"Sorry," said Pibble. "What's Doctor Silver dreaming about?"

"Dunno," said the further.

"Shove off," said the nearer, and flopped once more against his shoulder.

He wondered how strong the imperative was. In a vocabulary as restricted as the cathypnics' there was unlikely to be more than one word to express the whole range of meaning from a mild distaste for one's company to a terrified loathing; and the unaccented voices gave no help. With all his soul he longed to shove off, fade far away, dissolve and quite forget Posey Dixon-Jones, Thanassi, the cathypnics, Rue Kelly, Silver, and the rest. If Ivan hadn't needed somebody to take charge of this couple, now that Silver had collapsed again . . . No. That wasn't quite fair. The ambulance man would have done as well; but if he'd simply mooched off home, after having begun so much, caused in particular the whole vile Gorton imbroglio . . .

"Your fault," said one of the children without opening its eyes.

Yes, and not only that. If Posey Dixon-Jones had committed suicide it was because of the pressures on her—Thanatos, Costain, and finally Pibble with his mad babble of lurking murderers. She could herself have been meditating arson, and thus triggered off the word or two he had heard on that first tape. No . . . that was too early. . . . Suppose she wanted to burn the building down, to keep it out of Costain's hands, and had laid herself out when the incendiary material exploded. He remembered again that pair of arsonists in Acton who'd overdone the gasoline and blown themselves clean into the street. Possible. She'd have been expecting to give the alarm, and get her adored fat charges safely out. Pibble, in fact, had helped her by making them congregate in the hall. And Kelly's Kingdom? She couldn't have reckoned on Rue having all the equipment he needed for instant rescue. . . .

No, he didn't believe it. Earlier he'd talked to Rue about how far it was possible to know someone—to know Posey in particular. He'd overstated his case: it was possible to know *some* things. She might kill herself; she might fire the McNair; but she would not risk burning a cathypnic child, even the ones lost in the long dream of "upstairs." Silver thought so, too.

Alfred, then? For the insurance? Thanassi short of pocket money? Huh!

An irritation like a forgotten itch tickled his mind. An itch which you remember only when you happen to touch the spot. In his mind's eye he saw the chisels and hammer lying amid the splintered shelving on the floor of Kelly's laboratory.

"Sharp," complained one of the children, edging him at once into the easier speculation about the limits of their strange abilities. They hadn't commented at all on his thought processes about Posey, which had been coherent and largely abstract. But an aimless picture stirred them to react. He looked sideways and saw that they were both now smiling—because he was thinking about them, paying attention to them? Bloody little showoffs. Just like any other kids. The smiles didn't change.

With an effort he forced himself to think again about Silver's extraordinary little lesson in medical practice, perched amid the sticky cedar boughs. That meant something—something important enough for Silver, man of peace, to meditate murder over. Murder not for money, but to cover up something dangerous, something that *bad* happened. A biopsy had been performed, as a result of which . . . yes, a child had got meningitis and died, the only one they'd lost in Ivan's time at the McNair. It had happened in Kelly's Kingdom, which meant that Rue . . .

The final swing of the ambulance in through the hospital gates threw the children against Pibble. He was bundling them back into place, propping them floppily against each other like sheaves in a stook, when he realized that the machine had stopped and would sway no more. As the ambulance men ducked in to pick up Silver's stretcher Pibble found that his mind had once more slid away from its hateful task to wondering about the cathypnics. How did the waking children react to the idea that their mates in the haven "upstairs" were being probed and sliced? Perhaps their minds were not capable of receiving the idea, or perhaps they didn't get any message from upstairs except the communal dream. The two children in the ambulance were still smiling as other hospital attendants came in, lifted them deftly onto stretchers, and whisked them away, grumbling about the weight. Pibble followed them out. He decided to call Mr. Thanatos.

The vestibule of the hospital was like that of a hotel, with carpet, bright lights, flower stall, and bookstall (both shut), and contextless people sitting in small groups. Pibble had a tedious wait for an empty telephone booth until a heavy, slab-faced woman, dressed in black like an Italian peasant, emerged from one. As he edged forward she glared haughtily at him and nipped back in, only to stride out again carrying an expensive pigskin briefcase with what looked like a coronet embossed above the clasp. Pibble found that he was gaping as he let the door shut behind him. The ringing tone had given only half a purr before the receiver at the far end was snatched up and the dismal bleeps began; he pressed his sixpence home.

"That you, Jim?" said the voice, more metallic than ever.

"How many Jims do you know?" said Pibble.

"Only one that's got this number, Jim. Alfred says you're playing hard to get all of a sudden."

"No. He said you wanted to see me and I told him I couldn't come tonight. So he gave me this number."

"Right. What happened at the McNair, Jim?"

"It burned down. All the children were rescued and are safe in Saint Ursula's hospital. Mrs. Dixon-Jones died."

"Yeah, I got all that. Theory seems to be that she burnt it down to stop Viv Costain getting his hands on it, and killed herself by mistake. You go along with that?"

"*Viv* Costain?" said Pibble.

"Yeah, that's the guy."

"He saw the Rolls," said Pibble.

"I don't get it."

"When I met him this morning I told him the Foundation had acquired a rich benefactor. He didn't know about you then, but now you're on Christian-name terms."

"Doesn't mean a thing, Jim. I'm on the same terms with everyone."

"You broke your agreement with Mrs. Dixon-Jones when you sent the car for me. You'd promised her that you wouldn't advertise your connection with the McNair, but somebody was bound to recognize a machine like that, and Mr. Costain did. I don't know what sort of bargain he arranged with you, but I know he's got a lot of behind-the-scenes influence about planning permission and so on, and I also know he thinks the McNair should be a public garden and park. He could have offered you some sort of deal—not opposing your South Bank plans, for instance. It's got to be something fairly urgent and important, for you to be sitting over the telephone like that, and Alfred said tomorrow would be too late. You want to know whether I've noticed anything which might upset your deal."

Thanatos' cackling laugh rattled the receiver.

"Jim"—he chortled—"I know why they fired you now. Well, did you?"

"I don't see why I should tell you."

"That's my Jim! You played your cards pretty damn close to your chest about Ram Silver this morning. I thought we were friends. I liked you."

"I warned you three times. You said so yourself. It was no business of mine, either."

"Hoity-toity."

"As a matter of fact I think he's going straight now."

"Ah. Great. So you don't think he rubbed out this Jones woman?"

"No. He had a motive, I suppose, if he was setting up a fraud and all the money was channeled through her hands. But he wasn't expecting the fire—at least he dashed back into the building to try and rescue his research papers. And at one point he had quite a good motive to kill me, and a first-class opportunity, and he couldn't bring himself to do it. He loved her, I think."

"So you go along with this theory she did it herself?"

Pibble hesitated too long.

"So you don't?"

"I don't know."

"Tell me."

"I can't. I don't *know* anything."

"I'll buy your guesses."

"No."

"Jim, Tony's been talking to the Yard."

"Yes?"

"Theory there is you've done your nut. You're trying to prove you can outdetect the organization. They don't like you very much."

"I'm not surprised. If they're right, you mean, I may be making a mystery over this other thing where none exists?"

"That's about it."

"It could be true. I've thought of it."

"So've I. But then you nail me about this Viv feller, and I have to reckon maybe you're not so screwy at all."

"Thanks."

"Jim, you aren't going to take the next step, are you? You don't figure I sent Alf down there to rub her out, so I could deal with Viv? Let me tell you one thing. I've always known my enemies couldn't outwit me, but maybe they could out-shoot me, so it's been against my interests to start any kind of a shooting match. You watch Westerns? I'm the cardsharp sitting over in the corner of the saloon. My skills go for nothing when the gun slingers start up."

"Yes. Besides, Alfred wouldn't have known about the hair-pin."

"I've lost you."

"Never mind. What do you plan to do about the cathypnic children, Thanassi?"

"Why?"

"From what you said just now it sounded as if you ex-pected Silver to carry on with his research—and Doctor Kelly, too. That means you'd have to find a home for them, and so on. I wondered if you'd thought it out."

"You're talking to one of the world's great thinkers, Jim. Yeah, I've thought it out. You've read about this disposable-hotel project of mine? I need a demonstration place, show agents over, ambassadors, that kind of trash. I'll find a nice site, edge of some country town, larks, blackbirds, put the kids in there."

"It'll be useful for you to have your show hotel inhabited by children who make visitors feel happy, won't it?"

"Don't you get sharp with *me*, Jim—not if you want a job on the payroll."

"No, thanks."

"Oh. I figured you were after some sort of deal."

"I am."

"Every bloody little man in this bloody little island thinks he can screw Thanassi."

"Hard luck. Damn. I'll put another sixpence in. You still there?"

"Yeah."

"Look, if I'm right about what I think—that's to say if I find it all fits together, because I don't think I'll ever be able to prove anything—I'll tell you. Your side of the bargain is that you put in somebody of Mrs. Dixon-Jones's caliber to keep an eye on the children's interests."

"I'll think about it. This guess of yours, Jim. Will it play hell with my other, er, you know what I mean. . . ."

"No. You can go ahead with that. But I hope the inquiry turns you down."

Thanassi cackled again.

"Attaboy!" he said. "Don't you worry for me, Jim—I've got that all fixed. This Viv feller couldn't shake it a scrap. What I need him for is to make guys like you think it's a good thing. I want it accepted. Who's gonna stay in a hotel which the natives think is an outrage? Cultural roughnecks, that's who. I don't want that kinda custom. Jim, mate, I'll think about this deal of yours. You do right by me, and I'll name one of the honeymoon suites after you. So long."

Pibble sighed as he replaced the purring receiver. All that roaring confidence and gusto. He didn't envy the money so much. For a moment he wondered whether to ask Thanassi to make Mary secretary. She had the drive, now thirty years frustrated. No, it was a pipe dream.

He had to lie quite freely to persuade the receptionist to tell him which ward the cathypnics were in. As he walked down the wide and bustling corridors he found that he was moving more and more slowly. Wards P and Q were at the very end of the maze, opening left and right off a stem of corridor, and separated by four or five small rooms in which he saw furniture shrouded in dust sheets. He chose the wrong ward and found the smaller cathypnics being coaxed into bed by Ivan and the fat woman he'd noticed at the McNair and two little colored nurses in the natty uniform of Saint Ursula's. He backed out and crossed to the other ward, where he found the two nurses he'd seen before, and Rue Kelly. All three looked very tired, but Kelly glanced up from where he was taking the pulse of one of the sleeping children and grinned. When he'd made the necessary note on the chart at the foot of the bed he strolled over.

"Hello, my old pal," he said. "What brings you here?"

"I wanted to see how you were getting on. You were lucky to find a place where they could fit you all in together."

"Lucky, nothing. The Deputy House Governor's the only person here I'm still on speaking terms with. I knew they'd had to close a couple of wards because of staff shortage, so as I had my own staff I got her to open them up for me. We're all right, mate. Some of the kids chilled off a bit in the ambulance, but they're picking up nicely now. You nip home and sleep easy. I'll see you in the Black Boot."

"No," said Pibble.

Kelly's whole stance seemed to change, though the only muscles that moved were the little ones by the side of his nose as he sniffed the hot stale air of the ward as if it had been Wolf Wood. Then his hand came up to stroke his long chin.

"Something biting you?" he said compassionately. "I'm not surprised. But it wasn't your fault, Jimmy. I mean you may have triggered the old bag off by bringing a crowd of your mates down to prowl among the evergreens—and boy, is your name mud with that lot! I heard them saying a few words about you before they tootled off—but Posey was going to blow her top any moment. If she hadn't done it today she'd have done it tomorrow, about something quite as trivial."

"She couldn't make that lighter work," said Pibble.

"What lighter?"

"A silver one which she kept on her desk to tap with her pen when she was angry. You must have seen it. It wasn't on her desk when I went in there after the fire had started. I think they'll find it somewhere near where they found the body."

"She musta took it along because of the symbolism. Me ould friend Father O'Freud would have the words for a woman that was forivver banging a sphere with a rod."

"You think they'll find it there, too?" said Pibble.

"Jesus, I don't know. I'm just trying to follow you into your fantasy world. What else have you got on your conscience?"

"Ram Silver told me what a biopsy was."

"Ram!" said Kelly scornfully, "He—"

"At one moment he was thinking of killing me—the first time I asked him. In the end he told me. He didn't tell me why it mattered. I had to work that out."

Kelly felt for the bed behind him and sat slowly down, looking at Pibble all the time. He settled himself carefully against the hidden form of the patient and slapped the fat buttocks affectionately, like a farmer with a favorite pig.

"You're in a tangle, mate," he said. "You bring down a horde of cops because you have a fantasy about an escaped homicidal maniac. You've evidently got another fantasy about somebody doing for old Posey. And now you've got another about Ram Silver trying to do for you. I'm not going to sympathize with you—I don't hold with mollycoddling nut cases. . . . Yes, nurse?"

"Mortimer's breathing a bit funny," whispered plump, pinchable Molly.

"What rate?"

"Same as before, but wheezy like."

"Temperature?"

"Same as before. And the pulse."

"OK, I'll come and see. You hang on here, Jimmy. I'll be back."

Pibble waited dismally at the foot of the bed and watched his friend bend over a motionless shape at the further end of the ward. He looked wholly confident and competent as he listened briefly with a stethoscope, took the pulse, raised the child's eyelid, and then stood considering. Age him thirty years, gray the hair and recede it over the scalp, wither the skin a little, and you could see him, the great Sir Reuben Kelly going round the wards, harbingered by frowning nurses, attended by tiptoeing students, ushered out by the awed whispers of patients well enough to gossip. By then those fingers would have prodded royal torsos. Into his bank balance would flow the dollars of oil-rich sheikhs, come to London to be healed of their twitches. He would have saved innumerable lives, prolonged innumerable dotages. . . . A useful man, yes. The whole human race would be better for his existence. It would turn out to have been a privilege to have known him, let alone to have drunk beer with him day after day.

Suddenly Kelly laughed, said something sufficiently indecorous to make Molly flush, and came striding back. He walked straight past Pibble with a follow-me jerk of the head and led the way into one of the little rooms between the wards. Briskly he flicked the dust sheets into a corner and revealed a Spartan office.

"You sit there," he said, settling into the chair behind the desk and lolling back. "Begin at the beginning. Have it all out. Christ, Jimmy, if I didn't like you so much I'd kick you out. I think I can see what you're getting at."

"I expect so," said Pibble. "I was talking to Silver this morning about the problem of getting even scientists to acknowledge the force of statistical probability if they don't like the conclusions. And here you can't even quantify the odds."

"What odds?"

"Well, for instance, when did you last rearrange the work schedule in your ward?"

"Yesterday."

"And before that?"

"Oh, not for a couple of months. It's not really rearranging; the girls like rubbing the children's backs—it's for bedsores, but it's also the only way of loving them—so every few months you find that they're spending more time on the massage than anything else, and you have to crack down. They hate it."

"Say every two months—roughly ten to one against your having done it in the last week. How many departments are there at Saint Ursula's? Twenty? How many people on the staff of the McNair? A dozen?"

"Fourteen."

"And how many of those would have a key to the greenhouses?"

"How the hell should I know?"

"How many wards have scaffolding and hoists outside the window? Not one in a hundred. How many small labs contain carpenter's tools strong enough to take a window out? Say one in ten. Ten times twenty times fourteen times a hundred times ten makes odds of nearly three million to one that somebody knew it was going to be necessary to evacuate your ward in a hurry, without using the main stairs; then to keep them warm on the spot; and finally to get them into a hospital. The fire would not have been started unless somebody had known that all that was possible."

Kelly had been listening with a kind of joking attention, like somebody playing a radio panel game, anxious to show the audience that he knows it *is* only a game, but equally anxious to score every conceivable half-point.

"Where do you get your twenty from?" he said.

"The only department in Saint Ursula's you hadn't quarreled with."

"You couldn't quarrel with Monica. Her life's work is to atone for all those eleven thousand virgins."

"Yes. Some of the odds are coincidence, if you look at it that way. Look at it the other way, and they are opportunities which can be taken advantage of if you arrange a few further coincidences."

"I told you about my cousin from County Clare?"

"You did. You also told me that Mrs. Dixon-Jones only signed her initials when she was angry, but I'd seen her do it when she had every reason to be pleased."

"You're clutching at straws."

"The straws are in the wind. You can also see the wind by the straws in it."

"Old Mongolian proverb. Do you wish to show the good doctor any more symptoms of this mild but not very pleasing mania?"

"You sent a message for me to come and see you. You wanted to tell me about the hairpin and the telephone, and to make sure I thought Mrs. Dixon-Jones was unbalanced, and to find out whether you could do business with Mr. Thanatos, and whether I knew that Silver was a professional con man. But you didn't want to plunge straight in with all that, so you broke the rule about not talking to laymen about your work, just to keep the party going. Once you'd started you found it difficult to stop, until I said something about there being no more McNair. That pulled you up because you thought I knew what you had in mind. I'd already told you about Mr. Thanatos, but unfortunately I also told you that Mrs. Dixon-Jones was in a near-hysterical state about me and Gorton, and that all the children were in one place. You realized you mighn't get a better chance. You could say that I pushed you over the edge."

"Aha!" said Kelly.

"Wait. One other thing. You always put on a show of being lackadaisical, but you're fanatically tidy and conscientious about your work. You went on correcting Membership papers when you could afford not to, for instance. But this afternoon you knocked a pile of them over and let them lie. You knew the flames would get them. That was just as I left. You'd already decided, and were thinking out the details."

"Spur-of-the-moment stuff, is it?"

"You'd thought out the main outlines before. At least I'm convinced that somebody was thinking about fire, and about killing Mrs. Dixon-Jones, some time before that."

"Balls. My serve, I think. I won't even answer your telepathic maunderings, but tell me if I leave anything else out. I'll go backward. I was worrying about you when you left, because I could see you were going round the bend. I picked the papers up as soon as you were gone. Anybody would be curious about Mr. T. Anybody would warn a pal about Posey. Anybody with a grain of sense would have spotted that Ram was a fraud—I was inquisitive to know how quickly an ex-copper would get on to him."

"You hadn't been all that quick. I'm told you were bloody to him at first—that must have been until you realized he wasn't a qualified doctor."

"Correct. I don't like doctors. Criminal, is it? But *you*, Jimmy—did you tell your pals about him?"

"No."

"Oho! We'll come back to that. Let's get on. I told you about the telephone because it was a striking example of Posey's mania. The fact that she used a hairpin to fix the phones today shows how struck she was by it. Now I'll cut down your odds for you. You can't have more than evens on the nurses' work schedule—I only crack down *when* it gets out of hand. That means that most of the time it's *in* hand."

"This was a new arrangement. They hadn't done it like that before."

"I'd got tired of the old system always slipping out of gear, so I fixed something they couldn't muck around with. The tools—I've always kept some, rather than hang round waiting for idiot carpenters when I want to change some little thing. I could have broken into the greenhouse with them if I hadn't known where the key was, and so could anyone else on the staff. I could have kept the children there all night if necessary—they'd have been OK, though the air's on the steamy side—and we'd have found a ward for them by morning. The scaffolding was luck, but listen, mister: the rule is you're allowed one piece of luck before you start counting coincidences. Anyway, I could have slung the bedding out of the window and carried the kids down the tower stairs at the back."

"They'd have been in the cold much longer—and if one of them chilled off in the ambulance just now . . ."

"Like I said, it was luck. I'm not going to do your idiot sums about what that adds up to, but I'll offer you six to one the lot. Nothing like the odds against you and Costain and the cops all coming the same day to stir old Posey into blowing a gasket."

"No. Those aren't odds. You were waiting for a day when she'd been seen by somebody on what looked like the edge of sanity. You were in a hurry. It had to be soon. But you knew that any interference with her domain could produce a dramatic scene, and if we hadn't come you'd have arranged for something. You'd been thinking about it for some time, but during our talk you realized that you might not get a better chance."

"I was in no hurry, mate. Research takes years and years. I didn't want some demon in the States to pip me, but I knew I was way ahead of the field."

"It wasn't that. It wasn't even the convenience of having a fire bomb on the pantry stairs. It was Silver. You thought he was setting up a fraud, and when he'd brought it off he'd just vanish. You needed him to stay because he brought in the money for your equipment, and also because you needed him. He was the perfect assistant for you, medically competent but medically unqualified, and so unable to claim any of the credit for your discoveries. You would have had to fall back on sharing your research with a real doctor somewhere, or perhaps a team of doctors. Earlier on, before you quarreled with the endocrinology department down here, you had been prepared to put up with that. But by now you weren't. I think it's something to do with the cathypnics themselves—they bring out people's obsessions. I was talking to Silver about it just now. Anyway, you yourself—"

"Balls," said Kelly in a harsh voice. "I am what I am."

"Yes, of course, at any given moment. So'm I. So's everyone. But we're also what we have become. But forget about that side of the children—I shouldn't have dragged it in. One of them said several things which made me believe that somebody was planning to kill Mrs. Dixon-Jones—I thought it was Gorton, in fact—but you can't argue from that kind of premise. . . ."

"I should bloody well think not," said Kelly, pouncing into geniality. "But I can. Talk about obsessions. You fell in love with those kids, Jimmy—I could see it in your watery old eyes. One of them says about three syllables which imply that there are dirty deeds afoot and off you rush like a retired bloodhound which is suddenly allowed to snuffle around again."

"That's what Mrs. Dixon-Jones said."

"Oho! Posey had a lucid interval, but you take no notice because in your heart you know she's loopy. Come on, let's have it all out. You haven't told me why I bumped the poor girl off. She was a nut case, but she was a damned good administrator. We were lucky to have her."

"She was the children's guardian. You needed her consent before you could take the children to a proper hospital and have a major operation, a brain biopsy, performed. She wouldn't give it. But if she were dead, the odds were that Doll would be made secretary, and you thought she'd do anything you wanted. You'd already done as much as you could on your own. I think that when the Pharmacoid money was withdrawn and you quarreled with the professor here, you had nothing to do but sit down and think. You made up a blue version of *Deirdre of the Sorrows*, but you also came up with Kelly's Theory. Doll has a funny little scar on her knee, which looks as though you might have done a peripheral nerve biopsy there, and I wouldn't be at all surprised to find similar marks on some of the children in your ward. But apart from that you were stuck. Then Silver turned up, with money to buy the instruments you needed, and sufficient ability to act, for instance, as an anaesthetist with simple equipment. So you tried another step and did a trans some-thing . . . dammit . . ."

He paused. Kelly had turned his head and was staring not at the ceiling but at Pibble. The word suddenly came.

" . . . transsphenoidal operation. I think it probably produced the evidence you wanted, but the child died of meningitis. I don't think you would have minded about that, though it's heavily on Silver's conscience. Anyway, you have now got to the stage where everything you do must be aboveboard. Or else you think you will soon get there. The operations must be performed by a proper surgeon, so that no questions are asked about how you got your evidence when you finally publish your results. The surgeon wouldn't steal any of your glory—he'd simply be a technician, as far as you were concerned. I suspect you'd have liked to do a bit more checking up, so as to be sure you would get the exact results you wanted from the final operations, but that Silver dug his heels in. I don't know—"

"You don't know anything, mister."

"I know a few things, but not enough to prove you killed Mrs. Dixon-Jones. On the other hand—"

"You know why I'm in such a hurry and still mucked around burning down the McNair? Six months that'll put me back."

"Not so much, I suspect. I'd be surprised if all your relevant papers, or duplicates of them, weren't safe somewhere for some perfectly good reason. But you hated the McNair, and you probably knew that a body brought out of a fire is the pathologist's nightmare. What can show up, provided you lay your victim out without killing him, and then see that the flames really get at him? And then there's a good chance that after a thorough shake-up you could go to Thanatos direct, tell him how close you were to results on the physical side, point out that this was an essential element in approaching the telepathic side, and get yourself set up with everything you want."

Kelly swung himself out of the horizontal and leaned earnestly forward.

"Jimmy," he said, "I can explain everything."

Tone and cliché were equally unexpected.

"You're nuts," he said. "Occam's razor slices through. One single hypothesis accounts for the whole Heath Robinson structure: J. Pibble is bonkers. Even Scotland Yard have realized this, though they are politely covering up for their ex-chum; but when they learn that the said Pibble has been larking around with a professional confidence trickster without letting on to anyone, they'll be sending a squad of psychiatrists down here at the double. You try telling them that I've done Posey in, and what'll they say? Seriously, Jimmy, you'd better go and see a mind bender. None of the ones here —they're useless. Leave it to me and I'll get in touch with a guy. But for God's sake keep your trap shut in the meanwhile, because if you go spouting like this you can get yourself into all kinds of trouble. Me, too. My horrible profession is like a whispering gallery—mutter a rumor one end of it and you find it's being bellowed about at the other."

"I don't think I can tell the police," said Pibble. "As you say, they wouldn't believe me. If something were to show up in the autopsy which set them asking questions, I'd—"

"She was very roast, poor bitch. Medium rare, at least."

"Yes."

Kelly was relaxing. He looked strangely content, a man who has had a tiring and difficult day but has dealt with it all to his satisfaction.

"I've never believed in retributive justice," said Pibble. "But I believe in deterrence."

"Oho! All over London there are brilliant young medicos on the verge of major breakthroughs, blocked by the silly superstitions of one female?"

"No. I think you are dangerous. I expect you always were, but that working with these children has brought it out."

"First I'm a cunning assassin, planning my dirty deed in

tiny detail; then I'm the sort of idiot who does a job and finds he has to do it all again, and has to be deterred."

"The risk will seem less. It always does. I'm not talking about Mrs. Dixon-Jones—it's that child who died. Suppose someone were to question Silver and your nurses and perhaps that matron who left? Ivan and Doll, too. Then I think one would have enough evidence to show to the BMA. It doesn't sound to me as though they were sufficiently friendly to you to try to cover up for you."

Kelly's tired face went white. His head jutted forward on his neck and his hands clenched and unclenched.

"You're mad," he said. "You want to smash me because your own life's smashed. Look, Jimmy . . ."

His eyes flashed a couple of times round the room. Pibble wondered whether there was any kind of a weapon in this bleak nonspace. A doctor in the familiar maze of his hospital ought to be able to find ten thousand several doors for men to take their exits. A pill, a needle . . .

"Suppose it were true," Kelly burst out. "It's not, but suppose it were. What good would you do by mucking around with the way things have come out? The kids would be without a proper doctor, anyone who knew how to cope with them, so you'd probably lose a few while the new idiots were learning. All my work would go for nothing, and it's *important* work; it might be years before anyone stumbles on the clues I found; nobody's going to pick up where I left off, because everything I've done would be discredited. And you'd be in a jam, too, Jimmy. You've been keeping quiet about Ram because if you let on you'd lose your whack of the lovely lolly Mr. T. doles out—and now everybody would know if you start raking about. . . ."

"I'm not going to take the job," said Pibble. Kelly sat silent, his hands still unconsciously strangling emptiness.

"I'm not going to go raking about, either."

"Glad to hear it."

"Perhaps I ought to. As you say, I've fixed myself over Ram Silver. And, again as you say, more harm than good might come of it. So I've got to try and fix things so that you don't start treating your patients like laboratory monkeys again, and also (I suppose) so that you don't take it into your head to eliminate the people who might be able to give evidence against you. I can't think of a perfect solution, so the best I can do is this. Mr. Thanatos is prepared to set the children up in a new home somewhere. I think he'll keep Silver on, though he knows all about him, and I think he'll keep you on, too. He very much wants to know the truth about what happened, and I've said I'll tell him provided he puts somebody of Mrs. Dixon-Jones's caliber and integrity into the place as secretary. I am fairly sure he'll keep it to himself. He's the type who likes to know secrets, and keep them. But if you try to pull a fast one on him, *he'll* smash you. I don't think he's God—though he does—but he's quite powerful enough to do that. And if I tell him that he's financing a future Nobel winner, he'll—"

"Jimmy, you won't tell him anything. Or anyone else. It's all in the mind. Your mind."

Pibble shook his head.

"Most of it can no longer be proved, but they aren't imaginings. Things like the way you shut up when I asked you about biopsies, and your reaction when I said, 'No more McNair.' And your acceptance that Mrs. Dixon-Jones probably did take that lighter with her. Then there's everything Silver told me in the cedar tree, and the way he told me. Do you seriously want me to press him any further? Or the nurses? But even if I were still in the police force, and in charge of this case, I don't think I could *prove* that you killed

215

Mrs. Dixon-Jones. But if something shows up to persuade the police that it was murder and not suicide, then I'll have to tell them what I think. After all, they might latch onto someone else—Silver's got a motive, with all Mr. Thanatos' money being channeled through her hands—but if they are satisfied, and if I can come to an agreement with Mr. Thanatos, then I'm going to keep quiet."

Kelly looked at him, opened his mouth, and shut it again.

"I hope Kelly's Theory is valid," said Pibble. "That would be something saved. I hope you manage to prove it by decent means. But I think you should give yourself a definite deadline, and if you haven't finished by then you should pack it in and get out of this atmosphere. Get away from the cathypnics. I'll try to explain to Mr. Thanatos about—"

"Screw him. Screw you. You think you're God, too, don't you, Jimmy? Well, if you are, so'm I."

He whisked himself upright and started for the door.

"See you," he said.

"No."

The door slammed.

Drearily Pibble got to his feet and rubbed the stiffness out of his hams, wondering what else he could have done. He saw now how deeply he had fallen into the trap of the oracles; by believing them, he had brought all their prophecies to pass. Like Oedipus. Rue, no doubt, had toyed with the idea of fire, but it had needed Pibble's news to make the flames real. And Pibble's news was not news, for Gorton had never come—was not coming—and so there was no cause for Mrs. Dixon-Jones's fury. Even the corporate terror of the cathypnics had been Pibble's own, unnecessary terror, caught and amplified. And how had he, hardened to years of horrors, been suddenly so Gothically afraid? Was it, perhaps, an outwelling from his subconscious, a desire for terror, because that would mean that he was caught up in his own world once more, active and useful and respected by men doing the same job? Your fault, the child had whined in the ambulance.

As if the guilt squatted in the room, and he could get away from it, he ran to the door, only to pause again in the corridor outside. If that was true, then Rue could be right, and he was imagining murder for much the same reasons. For a moment he was tempted to go to one of his old friends with the whole story; if it could be proved, the guilt would be less. But they, too, every one of them, had cases in the shadow of their conscience—some old woman found dead in her kitchen, a child who had "wandered" to the flooded gravel pits—where they were helpless. And they were still active coppers.

As he turned toward the stem of corridor which would eventually bring him back to the bustling hospital he saw a round shape mooning toward him, a girl with her eyes so heavy that they were almost shut, and even at her slow pace she wavered from side to side until she brushed against the wall and began to waver back in the opposite direction. Still, she was making progress—away from the ward of waking children and toward that of the still ones. Her feet were bare; she wore striped pajamas, the top half covered with a hairy sweater.

"Hello, Marilyn," said Pibble. "Where are you going?"

"Wanna go there," she whined. "Lovely in there."

"No," said Pibble. "Come back to your friends. You aren't ready to go in there."

"Lovely in there."

But she allowed herself to be turned round when he took her doughy hand, and led back into Ward P. Ivan was talking to the fat woman just inside the door.

"Hiya!" he said. "What's up?"

"I found Marilyn wandering outside," said Pibble. "Didn't I, Marilyn?"

"Shove off." she said.

Pibble used his free hand to gesture toward Ward Q, and at the same time made a grimace of disapproval.

"Shove off," said Marilyn again.

He saw that Ivan was looking at him coldly, and the fat woman with real enmity.

"You heard what the lady said," said Ivan, taking the child's other hand. "Beat it."

"OK," said Pibble. "Good night."

The last thing he saw as he turned away was the child beginning to smile.

Other mysteries you'll enjoy from the Pantheon International Crime series:

Peter Dickinson

"Sets new standards in the mystery field that will be hard to live up to."
— Ruth Rendell

Death of a Unicorn	74100	$3.50
Hindsight	72603	$2.95
The Last Houseparty	71601	$2.95
King and Joker	71600	$2.95
The Lively Dead	73317	$2.95
The Old English Peep Show	72602	$2.95
The Poison Oracle	71023	$2.95
Sleep and His Brother	74452	$3.95
Walking Dead	74173	$3.95

Reginald Hill

A Killing Kindness   71060 $2.95

"A cause for rejoicing....Sparkles with a distinct mixture of the bawdy and the compassionate." — Robin W. Winks, *New Republic*

Who Guards the Prince?   71337 $2.95

Cornelius Hirschberg

Florentine Finish   72837 $2.95

"A crackerjack murder tale, swift, well-handled, well-written."
— *Saturday Review*

Dan Kavanagh

Duffy   74442 $3.95

"Exciting, funny, and refreshingly nasty." — Martin Amis

Fiddle City   74441 $3.95

"The snap and crackle of Raymond Chandler." — *Book Choice*

Hans Hellmut Kirst

The Night of the Generals   72752 $2.95

"One of the finest detective novels from any source in many years."
— *New York Times Book Review*

Hans Koning

Dewitt's War   72278 $2.95

"I recognize in this book all the subtlety of my fellow writer Koning."
— Georges Simenon

Norman Lewis

Cuban Passage   71420 $2.95

Flight from a Dark Equator   72294 $2.95

"A beautifully staged safari into the nature of evil in faraway places."
— *New York Times Book Review*

Peter Lovesey
The False Inspector Dew   71338 $2.95

"Irresistible...delightfully off-beat...wickedly clever."

        —Washington Post Book World

Keystone   72604 $2.95

James McClure
"A distinguished crime novelist who has created in his Africaner Tromp Kramer and Bantu Sergeant Zondi two detectives who are as far from stereotypes as any in the genre."   —P.D. James, *New York Times Book Review*

The Artful Egg	72126	$3.95
The Blood of an Englishman	71019	$2.95
The Caterpillar Cop	71058	$2.95
The Gooseberry Fool	71059	$2.95
Snake	72304	$2.95
The Sunday Hangman	72992	$2.95
The Steam Pig	71021	$2.95

William McIlvanney
Laidlaw   73338 $2.95

"I have seldom been so taken by a character as I was by the angry and compassionate Glasgow detective, Laidlaw. McIlvanney is to be congratulated."   —Ross MacDonald

The Papers of Tony Veitch   73486 $2.95

Poul Ørum
Scapegoat   71335 $2.95

"Not only a very good mystery, but also a highly literate novel."

        —Maj Sjöwall

Martin Page
The Man Who Stole the Mona Lisa   74098 $3.50

"Full of life and good humor....His novel is a delight."   *—New Yorker*

Julian Rathbone
"Right up there with Le Carré and company."   *—Publishers Weekly*

A Spy of the Old School	72276	$2.95
The Euro-Killers	71061	$2.95

Vassilis Vassilikos
Z   72990 $3.95

"A fascinating novel."   *—Atlantic*

Per Wahlöö
Murder on the Thirty-First Floor   70840 $2.95

"Something quite special and fascinating." *—New York Times Book Review*

Elliot West
The Night Is a Time for Listening   74099 $3.95

"The major spy novel of the year."   *—New York Times*